THE
LIE-CATCHER
IN THE
PRIMATE HOUSE

A NOVEL BY LINDSAY CRANE

Print and Pixel Books

Lafayette, California

Published by Print and Pixel Books
Lafayette, California

Crane, Lindsay. *The Lie-Catcher in the Primate House.*

ISBN-13: 978-0983305194

The Lie-Catcher in the Primate House may be ordered from Amazon.com, Barnesandnoble.com, and Printandpixelbooks. com. Also available electronically.

Printed and bound in the United States of America.

Cover photograph by In Cherl Kim

All of the author's profits from this book go to the non-profit organizations mentioned at the end of the book.

———————————————

Library of Congress Cataloging-in-Publication Data

Crane, Lindsay

The Lie-Catcher in the Primate House Lindsay Crane

THE
LIE-CATCHER
IN THE
PRIMATE HOUSE

A NOVEL BY LINDSAY CRANE

⁓? Prologue ?⁓

I sat huddled at the back of the walkway, trying not to shiver. We'd been up here only two minutes, but it seemed a lifetime since the gun went off.

I'd never been shot at before. What made me think it was gunfire? One short popping sound in the room where Desta had been working. Maybe it was just Desta slamming a locker door, or dropping a box of supplies. We'd laugh about it later. I should just climb down right now and…

My body didn't believe me. I stayed put, leaning against Kijana, holding my breath because my body told me to. Please, Kijana, be still. Now is not the time to play the alpha male.

Scattered bits of the last three minutes replayed in my head…the voices, that popping sound, the weird sliding noise that came afterward, the flight to this hiding place.

And now the ominous silence. Footsteps, slow at first, then faster.

Kijana began to fidget. I had to make him stop or they would hear us. Don't look him in the eye – he didn't like that. Gingerly I put my hand on his hairy arm and gave a little shake. It worked. He settled back against the wall next to me.

What was happening down there? Desta had been in the next room doing routine chores, nothing exotic; no visitors were expected. I tried to remember what she had been saying just before the sound. "Kijana is here. We're ready for you to give him his inoculation." A perfectly normal morning's phone conversation.

Then something broke the routine. Desta's voice became sharper. "I'm sorry, sir. This area is off limits." Then came words I couldn't understand in a deep man's voice. "What do you want?" she had said. "I can't understand you." More baritone rumbling. Then Desta again: "No, really, I can't show you. I'm working now. Perhaps one of the docents..." There had been a clatter like a person being shoved against metal lockers. Then the popping sound, a scrambling falling noise, and silence.

Remembering all this cleared my head a little. I leaned against the wall and tried to be small. Found you can survive on almost no air.

A second voice spoke, higher than the first. "Kwa nini wewe tenda?"

The cadence was familiar. I could almost recognize what the words meant. Deep voice replied.

"Niache."

Somehow I'd gotten my arms around Kijana. He hugged me back. He trusted me. I was thankful and surprised, since I hadn't known him long and understood his language only enough to convey basic words like "friend" and "good."

He squirmed again, making me slide toward the railing. "Kijana," I used his language. "Stay here. With me."

Voices in Desta's room again. "Wapi a?"

"Labda kule." High voice became more insistent. "Wapi a?"

Deep voice replied. "Sijui." A door opened and slammed. A third voice spoke.

"Quit your babbling, you two. Where is she?" Footsteps stopped. "Oh, shit, what have you done? Who is this?" Pause. The bullying voice went on, "You fools. *You* can't do *anything* right. You got the wrong one. I *told* you she had blond hair."

Oh, god. They knew I was in the building. The third voice brayed on, interrupting deep voice's excuses, "You *imbecile*, you weren't supposed to *shoot*. We'll have everyone within miles on top of us in a minute. Can't you get it through your thick heads that we want her alive?"

Please don't play the hero, Kijana, I begged silently. He could jump down from this catwalk in one bound and tear the man apart. For a moment I indulged this fantasy. But no – even Kijana, robust and made of pure muscle, was no match for a man with a gun, a man who had already used it. Let alone three men. "Stay here," I repeated.

Suddenly I had an awful thought. Suppose the men were looking for him, too? By now I'd recognized the language the men were speaking. Maybe I could catch the next words. I strained to hear them. The braying man spoke in Swahili this time, angrily emphasizing each word.

"Na nilete sokwe mtu. Yeye azizi." I'm pretty sure that meant: "And bring the chimpanzee, too. He's valuable."

So they wanted both of us. They would search the human offices, and then the chimpanzee quarters. I hoped they didn't know about the overhead walkways that linked the separate animal enclosures. We were only six feet above the floor. All the attackers had to do was look up and they would see us. I shrank back against the wall, praying the walkway wouldn't creak. It was inconspicuous, near the ceiling. Anyone unfamiliar with this strange building wouldn't think to look up.

Except these guys. They were hunting. For me.

I didn't set out to hobnob with hairy apes. Well, maybe some of my past boyfriends might qualify. I just set out to help a colleague. Given what I do for a living, that happens a lot, but it's usually more tame and civilized. Take the time my friend Hallie roped me into helping her expose a dishonest schemer. She pulled me aside in the hall outside the faculty lounge, looking troubled. "Julie, could you help us out again? We have to make a decision this week and I'm worried."

"Did the hiring committee send you?" I asked, remembering the last time they'd asked for my advice.

"No, I'm alone on this one. Everyone else thinks he's a Nobel prize waiting to happen. Especially the department chair. But something is fishy about him. I can just feel it." Hallie is a biologist who pursues microbes and frankly admits she has hunches. She went on, "He looked promising during the first round of interviews. He can talk about his research in excruciating detail. He has plans for attracting new graduate students, not that we need any more, but it's a nice touch."

"Does it seem rehearsed? Maybe he's just done too many job interviews."

"No, it's not that."

Hallie and I were standing in the hallway outside my office. This was obviously going to take a while, so I invited her in. She tossed her purse to the floor and sank into the comfy armchair I offer my visitors.

"It's about one of his publications."

"Uh oh. Plagiarized?"

"No, not unless he dug up some source unknown to our anti-plagiarism software. He is pretty young to have such an impressive resume." She sighed. "I wish it were as black and white as stealing someone else's work."

"What is it, then?" I pulled some cookies from my treat drawer and handed her one.

"I double-checked his publication list. Everything was fine, except for a paper in the *Journal of Consulting Toxicology*."

"What was wrong with it? Retracted later? Copied from a professional newsletter in an obscure language?"

Hallie gazed at me with that wait-till-you-year-this-one look. "There's no such journal."

Oh, geez. You'd think a fake artist wouldn't do something so obvious. But people do, from songwriters to executives. Some resumes should really be filed in the fiction department. Hallie went on.

"At first I thought it was one I hadn't heard of. After all, new journals are popping up every year or so. But I searched every single database we have. Reread some recent trade papers for announcements. No dice." She shook her head. "I suspect he just wanted to pad his resume, to seem even more impressive, and figured no one would notice."

"Or maybe the journal is a 'zine' he edits in his basement."

"Julie, this is not a joking matter," she said reproachfully. "He almost got away with it. No one else checked. And my department chairman is drooling to have him, thinks he's a grant magnet. Of course I could tell the others about the suspicious publication. Maybe it really exists and they could find it." She paused. "But I think there's something else, something he's hiding. I just can't put my finger on it. That's when I thought of you. You can see what we can't. So will you do it?"

Of course I said yes. I love actually nailing the liars, not to mention helping a friend. I'm a psychologist on the faculty at Berkeley. I research people and how they deceive – and how to catch them at it. I conduct studies on deception, the various cues that indicate someone is holding back information, or stalling, or outright lying. Mostly I do pure research, setting up controlled conditions for observing facial muscles, eye movements, body language, vocalization, gestures, and so on. My findings are used by police departments, employers who are hiring, and government agencies deciding whether to give higher clearance to one of their own employees.

"Count me in," I said, so Hallie got me invited to the suspicious character's next interview. There were four of us in the room with him. The man was tall and rangy, in his early forties. The department chair kept asking easy questions and giving hearty, admiring responses. The other committee member asked more pointed questions, which gave me more data. Without too much difficulty I reached my conclusion.

The man was lying.

Oh, he looked convincing enough. I could see why the hiring committee had fallen for him. He was intelligent, smooth, and full of cutting-edge ideas about endocrine disruptors. He also had an indefinable extra ingredient – he just *looked* like someone you wanted in your top-ranked molecular toxicology department: His auburn hair was tousled just enough to capture that look of casual brilliance and he was sitting urbanely at ease as if he had already been hired.

I waited. After the others posed a few more questions and nodded sagely at his answers, I asked him blandly, "What are your plans for future research?"

He swiveled his head to make the civil eye contact such meetings demand.

"Well, Dr…"

"Heidebrecht."

"Dr. Heidebrecht, at present I'm continuing the research I started at Cornell," he began. His mouth flickered in a polite smile as he recited his list of projects and how he would expand and complete them at our university over the next two decades. Impressive – if you only listened to the words. But non-verbally this man was giving the subtle warning signals that Hallie had picked up on. Privately I called him Mr. Oily Man.

Fortunately, I know nothing about toxicology. I could tune out the substance of the dialogue and focus on his face and voice. After half an hour, I wrote a short instruction on my note pad and nudged Hallie so she would see it: "Ask him again about his career plans." Sure enough, that question brought out the red flags. Subtle facial micro-expressions, too much detail, and an unexplainable change in the pace of his speech. Dead giveaway.

I pegged Mr. Oily Man as an exploiter, an opportunistic job-hopper who would stay just long enough to gain extra prestige and contacts, learn the department's proprietary discoveries, start up a medical products company on weekends, and bail from the university as soon as he got funding. In my presence, he hadn't lied about his work – but he had lied about his plans.

"You were right," I told Hallie after the man had been thanked and excused. "He's trouble. Take me to dinner and I'll spill all." So she did, and when I explained my findings, she expressed that mixture of relief and regret that you feel when a suspicion has been confirmed.

Hallie took my observations to the hiring committee. They sighed and searched for the missing journal. When they couldn't find it either, they pumped some of the people he had named as references. The hesitations over the telephone, and dark hints about unchecked ambition, were very different from the glowing testimonials they had sent on paper. Even the chair began to have doubts.

They sent the candidate a polite letter declining his services and hired someone else. That exploit was gratifying, one more notch on my belt.

But the adventure that got me in so much trouble started the following day. I was at my office just shutting down my computer when the phone rang. "Is this Dr. Heidebrecht?" said a voice I didn't recognize. Immediately I was wary. My graduate students call me by my first name – at least the ones who have been here more than two weeks – and friends use my home phone. It wasn't the shady character from yesterday's meeting; his vocal characteristics were quite different. But the caller had pronounced my name correctly, so it couldn't be a telemarketer.

"Is this Dr. Heidebrecht?" the caller repeated.

"Who's calling?" I said with cool formality, trying to strike a balance between courtesy and haughtiness. It just might be someone worth talking to. I've never been approached by a headhunter, but I have hopes. My salary at the university isn't enough to pay for all the globe-trotting vacations I have on my list, not to mention the gadgets I could use to upgrade my office. I like my work. The students are bright and curious, though some of them are atrocious writers, but I'm weary of trying to do so much on a tight budget. I have occasional fantasies of being a lady and a scholar with a real research budget, sabbaticals, my own lab… the works.

Meanwhile, the mystery caller was about to answer my question. I decided to pay attention.

"This is Tony Tilbertson," he said. "I met you at the forensics conference in Chicago last year." Hmmm, who could this be? The conference had been crowded. I had given two presentations, one on micro-expressions (ultra-brief facial reactions that can only be caught on videotape) and the other on vocal frequencies that are most commonly heard when people are lying.

"I was interested in your conclusions about vocal frequencies," the caller went on. "Is now a good time to talk?"

"Certainly," I said, and punched my computer's shutdown button.

"I thought your presentation last year was very suggestive," he said. "We use something like it in my work at DeTek Labs. I was going to wait to see where it led – you know, catch your next symposium. But something's come up and anyway, I happen to be in San Francisco now. Could we meet for coffee some time this week?"

"By all means," I said and quickly scanned my schedule. "How's Thursday?" I still didn't know what he wanted, but meeting with colleagues is one of the best parts of being a researcher. At conferences I get to meet the folks who actually use my findings. They tell juicy stories and give me new ideas.

We set the time and place, and rang off. Stuffing my star student's latest dissertation draft in my backpack, I locked my office door and got on my bike. I rode north along Shattuck, past the gourmet ghetto until I reached the beginning of the hilly streets north of campus. By the time I got home, I was comfortably breathless and rid of the day's annoyances.

"Hiya, sweetheart," I said to Scalawag as he jumped all over me and breathed happy doggy breath in my face. Terry had already brought in the mail. I live in a grand old Maybeck house that my parents left me when Mom moved to Orlando after Dad died so she could be closer to my brother Jimmy and his wife and daughter. I would never have been able to afford something like this on my associate professor's salary. It's big enough that I can rent out the basement, which has its own entrance and bathroom. Terry has been here for six years and we get along fine.

Terry is 28 and often changes jobs, despite having a first-class education. I guess that's ok when you're in your 20s. A plaintive note lay on the hall table next to a check for her share of the utilities. "The antepenultimate electric bill bankrupted me, so that's why this is late." What a monstrous exaggeration! The second-to-last bill had been perfectly normal for this time of year.

After dinner, I read my star student's latest draft. He was following up my idea that it is possible for a person's motivation for deceiving to change over time. At the beginning, one could deceive others for the thrill of it, then it can become a convenient way to dodge commitments and deadlines. For other deceivers, it can start out as the solution to a heart-pounding emergency and gradually morph into business as usual. Then there are the people with personality disorders, for whom deceiving is a way of feeling special, exempt from the rules everyone else has to obey.

I'd always been interested in deception, ever since Jimmy set the doghouse on fire and told Mom and Dad with an innocent face that I had done it. He got away with it, too. I couldn't understand how he fooled them. How could they not know Jimmy had set the fire? The shock of discovering they were not all-knowing was worse than the mild punishment they set me. Ever since, I looked at people in a new way, wondering what they were holding back.

In college, this skepticism protected me from a few heartbreaks and made me popular with the more naïve girls in my dorm, since I helped them develop some social radar. When I found out I could major in the study of human beings, I was as happy as a mall rat with two cell phones. I kept thinking I would find the answer to the questions: Do people who are deceiving others have to fool themselves first? How do people decide simply to tell a lie, and when do they go to the trouble of fooling themselves into believing what they're saying?

People who fool themselves are more interesting. True believers are so dogmatic that they don't just *ignore* inconvenient evidence; they twist it around to prove they're right. When cult members have predicted the world is ending on May 10 and quit their jobs and sold their homes to go join the rapture, they have some tall explaining to do on May 11. One cult leader claimed that extraterrestrials were coming to take them away on Tuesday night. Her followers assembled and waited eagerly for hours. When nothing happened, she made excuses. After the third non-occurrence of the apocalypse, she declared that the Judgment Day was deferred *because of the virtue of her little group*.

Religious nuts love this kind of defense. I wrote my dissertation on cults and the ways they seal their beliefs against facts. Unfortunately, there's no money in unearthing defensive self-deception, unless you count some aspects of psychotherapy, but I'm not cut out for that, so I took the next available faculty position researching social deception. After 15 years, I'm an associate professor at Berkeley. There are advantages to having my specialization. If my students haven't done their assignments, they don't even try to make excuses, convinced I can instantly detect every lie. I let them think it.

As I snuggled down by the fire for an evening of dissertation reading, I felt a surge of silent appreciation that my star pupil was a good writer. We always have a few good writers among our students, but I spend a quarter of my time teaching the other ones how to put together a decent sentence. As a consolation prize, I collect the funniest examples of their deathless prose:

"Man seems cursed with a half-eyed blurry vision of truth."

"The aftermath of such a psychological storm which is often generational, is an enigma that can be stopped!"

Secretly I'm fond of these prose disasters. They're awful, unaesthetic, and illogical, but they blow your mind, which can be a good thing. A howler is a peek into another person's skull, a fresh look at how people construct the universe. Anthropologists yearn to know how early humans thought about the world. I could tell them. Every generation reinvents it in a million zany variations.

I got up to put more logs on the fire and wondered what my caller of this afternoon wanted. Was Tilbertson the one at the conference who had questioned the use of vocal frequencies in criminal settings? The questioner said that being hauled into the cop shop makes everyone's voices go up half an octave, so any interpretation of vocal frequencies in that setting was bound to be misleading.

I have a lot of odd facts squirreled away but I sometimes forget where I got them. This weakens my capacity for showing off at faculty parties, so I'm used to looking things up to check my memory. My latest rationalization is that this shows how wide my interests are – my memory is *too* good. If only I forgot more tidbits, I wouldn't be wondering where I got them.

This matters because I also have a passion for precision. The two selves constantly struggle within me – the undisciplined curious magpie, and the scholar who respects logic and evidence. I drill students about this, insisting that they must use real evidence, not rumors or what they read in the paper. Sometimes I tell them about Mark Twain. When he was still a young newspaper reporter, his editor demanded that he write nothing he could not personally verify. Twain (or Sam Clemens, as he was then called) obediently produced the following account of a high-society fete: "A woman giving the name of Mrs. James Jones, who is reported to be one of the society leaders of the city, is said to have given what purported to be a party yesterday to a number of alleged ladies. The hostess claims to be the wife of a reputed attorney."

~.? || ?.~

The Ariel Café is across town. Unlike my local fave, which is fashionably grungy and harbors clusters of students with navel rings, uncut hair, cell phones, and laptops, it boasts stuffed armchairs and skylights, and caters to sober homeowners and brightly elegant socialites who have taken coffee connoisseurship to new heights. Here you can specify what country, even what region, your coffee beans come from. Tony had said I'd recognize him by his copy of *The Economist* laid out on the table.

"May I call you Julie?" he asked courteously, half rising from his chair. He was a huge guy who would have taken half an hour to unfold to his full height. He looked like a former linebacker who had forgotten his body. Slightly receding hair gave him a distinguished but lived-in look.

"Of course." We gave our orders and engaged in the usual pleasantries. I'm usually reluctant to make small talk about my work. People cringe and say, "Oh, you'll know what I'm thinking." Sure, I can spot outright lies a mile off, but I do not use my x-ray vision in personal life. Besides, we can't read people's exact thoughts, only their emotions, such as anxiety when lying. Over the years I've learned to say, "I study human communication skills." I have a series of more and more precise explanations. Anyone who gets the full job description has won my trust. Tony, of course, already knew. He told me about his work designing anti-crime software, arriving at the point in perfectly gauged timing before I became impatient.

"Look, Julie, I've been approached by a government agency. If you're interested in the assignment, I'll tell you more about them. This is way outside my area of expertise." Reading my silence as assent, he took a breath, as if putting unfamiliar thoughts together. "It seems that all kinds of things are being smuggled into this country – well, we know that. Besides drugs, of course. Turns out that other things are just as valuable. Did you know coffee is the second most traded commodity after oil?" His eyes wandered around the room. "Legal, that is. The most profitable commodity behind drugs is also contraband." I wondered what this might be. "Our people can't catch them – the goods are being brought in suitcases, but mostly by crates in trucks coming over the southern border. Someone finally thought of training dogs to smell the pelts, but that program isn't up and running yet. So they figured, let's catch the couriers, not the cargo. But our Customs people, well, they don't know too much about this particular contraband."

I was intrigued. "Expensive scotch that hasn't been taxed? Ancient artifacts from Babylonian archeological digs?"

"No." He paused and screwed his courage to the sticking point. "Birds."

"Contraband *birds*?" I was trying to understand where I fit in this picture. "Trained pigeons that drop messages? I thought telecom made that obsolete.

Unless they're making a comeback because the counter-spy gadgets are so good?"

"Endangered species," he said.

"Oh," I said, trying not to sound too disappointed.

"Don't say 'Oh' like that," he said reproachfully. I smiled. Already we were on bantering terms. A refreshing change from studied politeness. This easy friendliness happens when you go to conferences. People skip the formalities. There's something about studying, learning, and expanding the boundaries of knowledge that cuts through social barriers and speeds up the friendship timetable.

Our drinks arrived. Squeezing a lemon wedge into his tea, he went on, "This is important stuff, I'm discovering. My friend at Customs roped me in. I got a crash course from their website. The smugglers stuff the birds into cardboard tubes, you know, like the ones inside a roll of paper towels, and fill up a suitcase with them."

I was appalled. He went on, "Frankly, I don't care much about extinction, so that's when I thought of shoving the whole thing off my desk, er, that is, referring it to an esteemed colleague. The original request was from a friend of mine, so I'm doing him a favor. That is, if you'll sign on," he added belatedly.

"So where do I come in?" I asked. "I just study facial expressions and vocal characteristics, things like that. My private line of research – no funding, you understand – is distinguishing people who are lying for some kind of payoff from people who are lying to protect their self-image."

"Interesting. But what about sociopaths? They know they're lying, but they give none of the body language. They pass lie detector tests easily."

"Exactly. One research team at UCSF is working on that very thing. I personally want to know about politicians. They lie all the time. They have to." Tony agreed. "I think the voters screen out the candidates who can't lie well." We debated whether brain scanning would ever become a practical tool. Suddenly he remembered his original agenda.

"So, Julie, what about it?" I sighed. If only he lived here in the Bay Area we could have indulged in more free-floating speculation (that's what it's called when you have tenure; when you're an undergraduate, it's called a bull session), but he probably had a plane to catch, and he wanted this task shoved off his desk. I would have to decide.

"Birds, you say?"

"Well, of course, your job is to observe the people. Teach the Customs folks how to grill the couriers, pull suspicious ones out of the line at frontier checkpoints. Tell which ones know English better than they're letting on."

"What countries are they from?"

"I forget. Jungles." Boy, he really did ignore things outside his field. He didn't know that "rainforest" is the word now. Even I know that.

"Do I get to go there?"

"Yes, the regional chief of Customs wants to meet you."

"No, I mean *there*. Jungles. Rainforests."

"Uh, I don't know. Maybe. Talk them into it. Field research. Say you need to do *in situ* studies... cross-cultural studies of squinting..." I could tell he was improvising, and he could tell I could tell. We laughed.

"Randy Carstairs – that's my friend at Customs – college roommate, in fact. Kept in touch. Now he's doing some sort of inter-agency project. They need some outside expertise."

"By the way," I said, "What are bird pelts good for?" He looked at me blankly. "You said scientific dogs who sniff and smell the pelts are en route even as we speak. Why are they smuggling bird pelts?"

"No, no, live birds. Exotics. For pets. Pets, not pelts." He'd forgotten already. It was obvious I'd have to find out for myself.

⁓ ᦉ ᧉ ⁓

Once or twice over the next few days I thought about the strange encounter. I scribbled on my star's dissertation and returned it to him for revisions; lectured to a large class of sophomores; attended a faculty meeting dedicated to workload assignments; and stayed home all one morning to let in the furnace repairman. There were always plenty of student papers to bring home – short essays from the undergraduates, research proposals from the graduates.

Scalawag gazes at me mournfully when he sees me unload a tall stack of papers from my backpack. He knows I'll have less time to take him outside. Gambado never seems to know the difference.

She's clueless that way. Whenever I start packing for a conference or a visit to Mom in Orlando, she clambers happily in and out of the suitcase, kneading the sweaters with her front paws and meowing gently, drawing no deductions whatever from the familiar signs of my imminent departure. Scalawag, however, gives a heavy sigh and gazes at me balefully. Anyone who looked at him then would unpack immediately and cancel the trip, so I carefully keep my eyes on the growing pile of clothing and gear.

Spring break came. I was still curious about this bird smuggling business. What exactly was so enticing about exotic birds that it would trigger this awful trade? I decided to investigate and went to the nearby Oakland Zoo to see the birds. I hadn't been there since taking my niece Vanessa a few times when she visited me during her elementary school years. Most of it looked familiar. There were two new lions, young ones. I read the plaque. "Sandy and Leonard came to us last year," it read. "They were rescued from a ranch in Texas." What were lions doing at a ranch? A person in a zoo uniform noticed my perplexed look. "The ranch's owner collected exotic animals," she said. "He had dozens of zebras, lions, different kinds of deer. Cages and paddocks full of them. Then he went to jail on drug charges…" She paused, gritting her teeth and slowly shaking her head in disgust. "He didn't tell anyone about them. Didn't arrange for anyone to take care of them. They were there for weeks with no food, no water. Finally a neighbor complained of the stench and tipped off the authorities." Another pause. "A lot of them were dead. Sandy and Leonard were pretty thin. They had to be quarantined for two months in our hospital. They're still getting used to their new home."

"Are you a keeper?" I asked.

"No, a volunteer. The birds? They're over there – I'll take you. We're rebuilding the primate house and the paths have been changed." As we walked, she told me more about the lions' recovery. I listened with half an ear. For a volunteer, she was pretty dedicated. I was to learn, over the next few months, that there are thousands of people like her in this country, mostly women.

We walked past an enclosure equipped with a pool and a slide. Lithe furry brown creatures were sliding down into the water. I stopped to watch. The sign identified them as river otters. They were playing, splashing, sliding, swimming around their loop and hauling themselves out on its deck. Sometimes they would chase each other, and sometimes one would lie on the deck and groom itself while the other swam. You couldn't help smiling.

Finally, after many stops (my short attention span again), I reached the African bird enclosures. My volunteer guide waved goodbye and returned to her station while I admired the violet turacos, lilac-breasted rollers, malachite kingfishers, and crowned cranes. They were beautiful, little multi-colored flying jewels. Reluctantly, I could see why people would capture them and put them in a cage to look at them. But then I imagined a flock of brilliantly colored birds flashing through the sky. What did it look like when they were migrating, nesting, or feeding? The kingfishers made a loud scratchy creaky call, but the other birds sat quietly on their perches or flitted from one end of the enclosure to the other. I wondered if they felt confined.

Confined… Confinement is being stuffed into a cardboard tube.

~⁓~

A week after my meeting with Tony, my home phone rang. It was Randy Carstairs, asking to meet me at a café near his domain in San Francisco. I sighed, calculated the distance and traffic time, and agreed. You don't often get to rescue a malachite kingfisher.

This café serves the usual things – doughnuts, soft drinks, national brand coffee. I get spoiled, living and working in a university town where the treats are unique and counter-culture. Holding my mug of tea, I eyed the carbohydrate display. Though I'm in fair shape for 40, one can't be too careful. Just as I was convincing myself that the glistening yellow blueberry muffin was not too degenerate, Randy arrived. He looked about 35, with thinning hair, a slouch, and a harried manner. He plunged right in after giving his name again and ordering his drink.

"We need more expertise in people reading," he began. "I called my friend Tony at DeTek. He said you're the best in the business and we should get you." I smiled, knowing the back story. I am good, though.

"I'm one of the few guys in the department who gets to save animals. Most of 'em are stuck doing drugs and terrorists. I'm part of a multi-agency task force – we have people from Fish and Wildlife Service, Customs, some local district attorneys. Anyway, this whole story started a few years ago when a drug dog alerted on a suitcase that belonged to a guy coming in from Bolivia. There were no drugs in the suitcase – believe me, they tore it apart – so it must have been dust from some previous trip. Anyway, what they did find was birds stuffed into cardboard tubes. Must have been fifty of them in that one suitcase. Our guy almost lost his lunch. Most of them were dead. A few were alive. I was called in. I have a friend at the Oakland Zoo, so I sent the live ones over there. Go see 'em some time."

"I already did."

Randy smiled in pleased surprise. "Anyway, that got me interested so I've kept tabs on the trade. You can make a fortune on exotic pets – birds, snakes, monkeys. Trouble is, most of them die en route. Or they kill the mothers in order to get the kids."

I sat in appalled fascination.

"You mean they take baby birds before they're, what do you call it, fledged?"

"Naw, I meant the monkeys. And chimps. They ride on mom's back or front, sometimes till they're two years old. You want one of them, you shoot the mom. She falls, you scoop up the baby."

He was sounding too casually familiar with this procedure, or too burned out.

"So you track all the species they bring in?"

"Body parts, too. You know that tiger penis is used to make aphrodisiacs? Chinese guys seem to believe it works. Best thing that ever happened for tigers was Viagra. We get pelts, ivory, gallbladder juice from bears…"

I interrupted the flow of information. "What does all this have to do with me? I'm a psychologist. I research people, human behavior, teach, go to conferences. I wouldn't know an ocelot from an octogenarian."

"You study deception, right?"

"Yeah. Body language, pauses in dialogue, vocal frequencies, discrepancies in facial expression…"

Randy said triumphantly, "That's just it! We're having trouble nailing the couriers. They say the crate wasn't theirs, they don't speak English so good, that crate we pulled wasn't theirs, it just *looked* exactly like theirs. They crate is always addressed to some anonymous warehouse so there's no personal name on it. Our men can't hold the guy on suspicion. We want you to train their front line men. Give 'em the latest info on spotting someone who's lying."

Hmmm. This could be interesting. Who were the couriers? How high up in the smugglers' organization were they? How recently recruited? How much did they know, and how much were they pretending not to know? Then I saw a flaw in his logic.

"But don't they search luggage now *before* it gets on the planes? Since 9/11 surely…"

"Yeah, it's actually not suitcases so much any more, not for the big smuggling rings. A few jerks still try it, but when we catch them we haven't made much of a dent in the trade. Besides, a bribe will get some customs guys to look the other way."

"Maybe they should hire me to check out the customs guys, then, instead of the couriers," I suggested.

"Yeah, maybe some day. Political hot potato. Right now my job is to catch the couriers. Anyway, now it's crates in trucks coming over the Mexican border, crates that started in Panama, anywhere south. FedEx boxes, too."

I thought about that for a while, then asked, "You don't want me to do profiling, do you?"

He shook his head. "I think they got someone on that already. Naw, they want the practical stuff." I let that pass. "How to catch someone who's standing right in front of you. Didn't I read somewhere that you can tell if someone's lying because they blink a lot? That kind of thing."

People always remember the blink research. I wish I'd thought of it myself. People do tend to blink more when they're lying or otherwise thinking hard; it's a good tool for gathering initial impressions. Researchers in Australia are doing some neat studies on it. It makes you self-conscious just to think about it. You try not to blink. You're so busy trying not to blink that you can't even count the other person's blinks.

Meanwhile, I was mystified that Randy and his task force would approach an outsider like me. Didn't federal agencies have a stable of experts of all kinds? Weren't they always first in line when Congress wrote the budget? Maybe that's another outdated misconception. Besides, bureaucracies don't always share information. They have turf wars, like competing academic departments on a big scale, or rival companies trying to rush a product to market before competitors steal or copy it. The big intelligence shakeup going on now might help... if the new agency can get past the egos. Back to the task at hand. I asked, "Why me? Surely there must be better people to do this."

"Search me," he said casually. I could tell there was more to it than this. He gave what we call a masking smile – there was an underlying emotion he was trying to suppress.

"Randy – may I call you Randy? I'll be frank. You're asking me to help because I can read faces. Let me prove it. You're doing your best to hide something from me."

He stared down at his drink.

"At a guess, I'd say it's nothing you're ashamed of – you're not giving off the guilt signals. It's more like anger. You want to cut this conversation short. It's not personal – you think I'm ok."

He gave me a rueful smile. "Keep going."

"With all due respect, *you* keep going. What's this about?"

He put down his glass slowly. "I hate this. It happens all the time. We get a case started and have to hand it off to another agency. We don't even get to call it hot pursuit like the cops."

"I can sympathize. Go on."

"And the other agency gets huffy if you follow up. Oh, we're *supposed* to share the credit, blah blah blah."

I knew about that, too. But there was something else he wasn't saying. Getting the credit didn't account for the stiffness in the buccinator muscles in his cheeks. I gave him my best "out with it" stare. He coughed and squirmed.

"The other guys think I'm getting soft. It's just a job, they say. Well, actually there are a few others like me. I'm going to have to move on. This is going to drive me to drink." I read between the lines. He cared. It wasn't just a job to him. "Getting soft" meant that he was upset by what he was seeing. He had seen too much suffering.

How could I not help? "Look, Randy," I said firmly. "I'll come to a formal presentation. Give me the full picture. This is outside my expertise. That's the best I can say right now." He nodded, satisfied with my half-answer, and I left the café with as many questions as I'd had before.

I debated whether to accept this oddball offer. I'd done some consulting before, mostly with local police departments, such as reviewing taped interviews of husbands whose wives had died under suspicious circumstances. The idea of detecting animal smugglers was new.

Then I thought of Scalawag and Gambado. How would I like it if someone kidnapped them? I drove back over the Bay Bridge, barely beating the rush hour that begins at 2 pm after the New York financial markets close and San Francisco traders have finished their paperwork. While merging onto the bridge lanes, I began to imagine the actual face-to-face encounter, always the most intriguing part of any job. I'd make eye contact with the suspected bird smugglers, ask searching questions while watching them carefully…

To prepare for my upcoming meeting with Randy, I pulled together some basic guidelines and dug out a training manual I'd prepared the previous year for the campus security department. They were having trouble identifying non-students who lurked around campus stealing books and bicycles and then reselling them. I could use some of these guidelines for the animal smuggling job. Maybe I could start doing some consulting on animal smuggling and start writing overseas vacations off my income tax. This little job sounded harmless – I'd be just training a few line agents. I reviewed the basics I might include in the course:

> **Eyes**. Extra blinks.
> **Hands**. Extraneous gestures.
> **Movement**. Fidgets. Shifting weight from one foot to the other.
> **Speech**. Pauses before answering questions. Unexpected change of pace.

I'd have to put together a good acronym, a quick checklist the customs inspectors could memorize and run through for every customer picking up crates. MESH, perhaps. Anyway, this was only a stopgap program, since the detector dogs would be coming on duty in a few months to sniff out and alert on live animals. What difference did it make if I wasn't the best person for the job? I could give some information, earn a little, and help a little. It would be better than nothing and it wouldn't be too stressful.

Well, that's what I thought at the time.

—◯ III ◯—

Matt would have urged me to take this job. Matt and I were an item, on and off, for four years. He was a photographer who never tired of trying new things. As a personality, he scored high on the novelty-seeking scale. We went to obscure Caribbean restaurants, floated in samadhi tanks, and traveled to secret scuba diving sites. I drew the line at bungee jumping.

It irritated Matt that I wouldn't go parasailing or even take pictures on vacations. This was heresy to him. But I had no desire to stick a box in front of my face between me and the waterfall or the cathedral. I'd rather look and look and memorize, storing images in my mind. It amuses me to see people whip out their cameras the minute they find a famous or beautiful place. I guess they won't believe they've been there unless they take their own personal snapshot of it with their own personal camera. Well, unlike carving your initials in timeless monuments, at least it's harmless, and even useful. Other people's vacation photos have occasionally cropped up in my criminal cases.

Matt died after we broke up the third time. He had gone sky diving again, one of the things that made me nervous and caused friction between us. His chute tangled with another diver's chute. Neither survived.

I wondered if we would have gotten back together. Even though I hadn't seen him for a month before his death, I was devastated. I took a week off work and went to stay with my brother Jimmy. His daughter Vanessa, who was six at the time, had been told what happened. I overheard her on the phone, breathily telling one of her little friends, "My aunt Julie is visiting. She's sad because her boyfriend went sky dying."

That was five years ago. Now I was listening to Randy's presentation, the one I'd promised to attend. He was saying,

"And this is a diagram of the smuggling routes, showing potential points where we can intervene. We could take the poachers in the act of catching the animals in the wild, or at the point where they transfer them to the middlemen who transport them to the destination country, or as they enter the destination country, or as they reach the local fences or pet shops or whoever sells them to the final buyers."

I was in an office at the customs agency in San Francisco. Randy was reciting information that was obviously well known to him, but he was a good presenter and made it lively. He kept glancing at me to make sure I was following his train of thought, and went on. "The weak point in the chain used to be the ones who actually carried the suitcases. Now that suitcases are searched, it's the peons who pick up the crates from shipping companies." He didn't mention the bribed customs officers who let loaded suitcases in. I wondered why.

We were alone in the room; everyone else in his office had already seen the heart-breaking photos of broken bodies, snares, and claustrophobic crates that he had been showing me for an hour. He ended his talk with earnest bullet points. Catch the smugglers before the birds get put on the plane. More likely to save more of them. Get closer to the head of the pipeline. Make it less profitable for the masterminds.

Randy finished his formal presentation and sat back to see my reaction. I gazed into the middle distance as the kaleidoscope of facts and images spun around in my mind, falling into different combinations. And underneath it all, a sad amazement at the things human beings do. Bank robbers, embezzlers, and philanderers were my bread and butter; I'd become used to them. They were just the ones who obligingly generated all the interesting data I studied. Animal smuggling was fresh. Horrible. A grim trade in little bodies, most of which ended up in the trash, all so an unknowing suburbanite could have a yellow bird in a big cage in the living room.

Sensing my hesitation, Randy casually offered me a chocolate. I could almost read his mind: Let the lady think. Every second she isn't saying no is a second to the good. Buying time in my turn, I asked, "What's it like, doing what you do?" Feigning casual lack of urgency, he pretended to think about this obvious question and told me about the time he had found a pair of shivering monkeys in a refrigerator, obviously stashed there hurriedly when he'd knocked on the suspect's door.

Aghast, I said, "Ever think of another line of work?"

"No. Where else could I catch villains and get paid to sit on the beach?" Hmm, this was another side to Randy. He was not totally burned out. He smiled and told me about the time he had posed as a tourist on Kauai so he could trace people who traded in sea turtles. He went on, "Tony told me what a wizard you are. I was pretty excited, to tell the truth. Hey, your work on micro-expressions is good." Hmm. He had looked up some of my stuff. "I knew about it already, of course – I used it in a paper I did for the proceedings of our association."

"You publish? I thought you were a…"

"Simple cop? Well, yes, but we agency investigators do have our own field, you know."

"Wait." I had just remembered something. "You said it was important to catch the smugglers closer to the *head* of the pipeline. Aren't I going to be working with people here at the *end* of the pipeline?"

"Did I say that? Well, that would be nice. You'll be working here in this country, if that's what you mean." He gave me a mischievous grin. "Don't you like getting inoculations?"

Au contraire, I thought to myself. If you really want to get me to sign on, wave a ticket to Brazil in my face. Still, even the domestic project could be interesting. The pictures, the bullet points, his tales – the whole thing began to seem more real. It all clicked and I said, "I'll do it."

⁓꙳⁓

Since Randy told me he had used my ideas, I went online and looked up the Science Citation Index to see if he had actually cited (mentioned) my paper in the published version of his paper. He had. The SCI is like a popularity measure for ideas. Some books and articles are so important that they are cited by everyone for the next thirty years. Others make a splash for a while and then fade, eclipsed by newer ideas. Some drop like a stone and are never cited by anyone. You can look up your own article, if you like, and see if anyone has mentioned it. I never bother because I'm always busy developing the next great idea. But it was gratifying to know that Randy had used my work.

To learn a bit about smugglers, I watched some videos about drug runners on the university's electronic research database. But those people were very different from the ones I was supposed to look for. I had to avoid the trap I was forever catching my students in – making useless vast generalizations about everyone. What was going on in the public schools these days, anyway? I resignedly drilled into them that no matter what their topic, the real question is always, "Which people, in which circumstances?"

Besides, some people can lie without signaling deceptiveness. That's the bane of our field. They're either psychotic and believe what they're saying about the voices, or they're psychopaths completely untroubled by discrepancies. The third case is false memory. There are masses of field and lab research to show you can implant a memory and people will believe it and defend it, even after the experimenter debriefs them. You can't tell a true memory from a false one by brain scans – the exact same lobes light up. Even memories you concocted yourself begin to seem real, complete with the image, the sounds and smells. I could have sworn that there's a scene in the BBC series *I, Claudius*, where the emperor Augustus stands on a chair in his garden, picking figs straight from the tree to make sure no one has had a chance to poison them. But there is no such scene. It must be in the book, and in my imagination I'd transposed it to the film.

Meanwhile, animal smugglers didn't fall into any of these classes of undetectable liars. Was I about to discover a new one? Hmmmm, maybe this could become my next journal article (cited widely, of course). My department chair would be impressed. Then, in addition to a lab of my own, I would have a full-time secretary to do all the photocopying and run to the post office to send manuscripts to publishers and order the new testing materials and instead of all that laborious administration I could dream up more experiments and publish them. Sigh. This is the real world. I probably wouldn't follow up with further tests, the way you're supposed to. I'm not very good at nurturing my little chicks.

Oh, well, the profile of couriers was probably something obvious. The smuggling masterminds would entice the most starving and desperate people, the way local cocaine distributors do. No personality disorders need apply. *Which people in which circumstances...* Hungry people, or people with hungry relatives over the border. They would tell themselves the cargo wasn't any of their business... that muffled squawking noise was just their imagination... rationalizing like mad and trying not to sweat.

I put together a presentation outlining the main points of lie-catching and gave a run-through to Randy. He listened inscrutably but smiled at the end and set up a date for me to teach the agents.

"By the way," I asked, "Could I see their workplace? There may be features of the location that could help."

"Better than that. I'll let you watch a shift." He reminded me that I'd forgotten to ask for a contract. There was something still guarded about Randy and I almost challenged him then and there. But this gig sounded interesting, so I flagged my question for later review and let it pass for now. As I'd done before on occasion, I would give him enough rope to hang himself.

A few days later, I did the customs equivalent of a ride-along. From my place behind the counter (wearing a borrowed customs uniform) I tried to watch the couriers, but my attention kept getting drawn to the officers instead. One in particular seemed out of the ordinary, never meeting my eyes when I moved around, answering my questions in extra-short sentences, interrogating at great length people I thought were innocent, which was all of them.

During our post-shift wrap up, I told Randy that it was a waste of time to teach officers to detect couriers. He needed to start interrogating his own employees, maybe even his colleagues. With a sigh, he agreed. On Randy's face I read a mix of sorrow and relief, and diagnosed that he had already suspected some of them but was conflicted about turning them in. So he had brought me in to provide the proof. The courier story was just a line to tell the customs agents and get me behind the counter. I was glad his deception was so minimal and so understandable; I liked Randy and wanted to trust him.

"Ok, so here's what we do," I said. "I want you to list five of your people for me to question and set up appointments, all in a row, two days from now. Don't tell them what it's about. It's ok to let them know about each other's meetings. In fact, that would be useful. Up the ante a little."

On receiving the list next day in my email inbox, I found (not entirely to my surprise) that the one I suspected was on the list. The day after, I returned to meet them. So that Randy would have some idea of what the normal benchmarks were, I had put the suspicious guy third. I began the first interview by leaning back in my chair with my arms folded and giving an intimidating stare while Randy asked the man some questions. As instructed, Randy glanced over at me now and then without introducing me, until we had the guy thoroughly confused. But his confusion and his facial characteristics told me he was not lying when he denied taking bribes.

"Send him straight back to work," I told Randy. "I don't want him talking to the others."

We did the same routine with employee number two. My target, number three, gave himself away immediately with his rapid breathing and forced eye contact. After I caught him making another false smile, I knew he was the one who was taking bribes to let wildlife smugglers claim their living cargo – and probably enabling other villains as well. We ran the last two employees through our little gauntlet, just to make sure.

"Wow, Julie, you're good," Randy said at the end of the day. "I hate to find bad guys on our side of the fence, but we had to do it."

"I know," I replied. "Next time don't put yourself through such a moral wringer for so long. Call me in as soon as you suspect someone." He agreed, and the day ended on a friendly note.

I got a nice letter a few weeks later (it arrived before my check) saying they had dismissed the corrupt officer and were expecting to improve their rate of arrests. Good news... but it was too bad the customs checkpoint was so far down the pipeline.

◦⟩ IV ⟨◦

I left a note for Terry. "I took Scalawag to the vet. He could have started an epizootic." This was the latest salvo in our little game. We leave enigmatic messages and feel defeated if we haven't driven each other to the dictionary to figure them out. An epizootic is a plague among animals.

Animals… wouldn't it be fun to follow up on the smuggling adventure? I love my work at the university, but there's nothing like getting out in the field. Most summers, at least when I can't get away for an overseas vacation, I help some police friends of mine with their cases. This animal project could be an interesting new way of getting real-world experience. I decided to spend some time gathering some deep background information on this black market, just in case another animal case came my way. After all, I had a whole summer ahead of me.

The academic year had ended on a pleasant note. I closed this year's file on insane student sentences with a new favorite: "It is a viscous cycle that has no end." The last faculty meeting for our department was a bit more rowdy than usual. We'd settled the most contentious curriculum issue, and people were feeling benevolent and willing to indulge in harmless pranks. My department chair awarded two junior faculty members IgNobel Prizes, copied from the spoof awards that MIT presents every year for ridiculous (but real) research. My favorite was the peace prize given to the authors of a study which concluded that 4,000 trained meditators had lowered the rate of violent crime in Washington, DC. A Japanese agency was (dis)honored for a seven-year study of the impact of catfish tail wiggling on earthquakes. Our own IgNobel prize went to my pal Jiang Li, for determining that erratic copy machines do not perform better after being exorcised. Today we decided that the physics department owed us, big, for the time we helped them settle some intra-departmental conflicts. We debated how they should express their gratitude. I stood up.

"I say we demand as tribute a shipment of liquid nitrogen ice cream." My colleagues clamored for an explanation. I had always wanted to try this delicacy, ever since I'd heard that you could stir liquid nitrogen (stored at minus three hundred degrees) into an ice cream recipe. Supposedly, it freezes the cream so quickly that there's no time for crystals to form. There was some other virtue of this harebrained concoction, but I forgot what it was.

My motion was carried by acclamation. We debated what flavor to demand. I nominated pistachio but was outmaneuvered by the strawberry bloc. The physics department was duly instructed to repay their debt by providing us, at our next department meeting, copious servings of strawberry liquid nitrogen ice cream. After all, they had access to the key ingredient. I made a mental note to attend all future faculty meetings, just in case they complied.

I had lunch with my friend Carl. He's 45, slightly rounded in a comfortable way that should give paunches a good name, and disarmingly unpretentious. I had known him for two years before I found out he had been on the Olympic sailing team in his youth. Once we were seated and served, he talked about his therapy practice. I imagined him dispensing wisdom and strength, being a rock and shelter for the troubled. He also can be a heck of a challenge and not let you get away with things.

I had met Carl a dozen years before while lecturing at a psychology convention on defense mechanisms in cults – the findings from my dissertation, still my area of interest at the time. When I recounted stories of cult members defending the leaders who exploited them, I saw a man in the first row wince and shake his head. I had seen this reaction before, so I wasn't entirely surprised when he sought me out after my talk was over.

"Is there *anything* that can get people out of these cults?" he asked. A sad blend of hope and despair showed in his eyes. He looked like a man who had nerved himself to make one final attempt. Carl had waited to be the last in line for questions (there's always a small huddle of people reluctant to leave after my talks) and I was hungry, so I said, "The next symposium needs this room. Join me for lunch?" While we waited for our food, he explained about his sister.

"She got into this nutty group one summer after her third year at college – that's the age cults go for, as I'm sure you know, late teens, early twenties. She was three years younger than I, sensitive, an idealist. She always seemed ok – I never knew…" His voice trailed off and he shook his head. "Turns out she had so much self-doubt. Why didn't she tell me?" He asked the unanswerable question. I hazarded a guess, a risky move since I didn't know him yet, but he seemed like the kind of person who could face the truth.

"Maybe you were part of the problem."

He sighed. "I've wondered that. What did I do wrong? Mom and Dad wondered, too. Worse for them, of course."

"Is this why you became a therapist?" He didn't answer immediately, but said,

"I found out Mom was giving her money, over $50,000. It all went to the cult."

Sad to say, I wasn't surprised at the amount, but obviously it had been a shock for Carl and his father. I asked, "What happened then?"

"Shelley walked in right in the middle of our powwow. She was actually coming to get more money that very day. Dad was furious and Shelley suddenly showed a side we'd never seen – harsh, critical, bitter. She went on and on about the saved and the damned, all that stuff. She told Dad he was ruining Mom's chance of being saved. I got in the middle – always did. That's what makes a person become a therapist, by the way, being the family go-between. Where was I?"

"Fire and brimstone."

"Oh, yeah. Mom was not exactly surprised where the money was going, or she wouldn't have kept it secret for so long. But still, she was embarrassed.

Giving to Shelley wasn't the problem. I mean, they had paid for my grad school, why shouldn't they help her get an education or a down payment for a house? See what I mean?"

"But not to give to a cult."

"Right. It was called the Brothers of the Heavenly Light."

"And I bet their party line was, when people hate and revile you, it just shows what sinners they are and how blessed you are."

"Exactly. That's why I needed to talk to you." Though I couldn't really help him, by the end of the afternoon, our friendship was firmly established. In the dozen years since then, he has occasionally informed me about the latest developments with his sister.

Today, between bites of pita bread and baba ganoush, he said, "I admire your publications. I keep thinking I'm going to pull my thoughts together on this or that and publish, but I never get around to it. How do you do it? Maybe if we lunch often enough, your writing juice will rub off on me."

"Journal articles? Publishing is fun, but your manuscripts are like ping pong balls, always coming back from the editor for more revisions. Besides, I'm not getting cited enough. I hope my department chair hasn't noticed."

"Well, if you'd only stick with one idea long enough to make it known…"

I shook my head. "Too boring. I can't resist the next brainstorm. I think there's something a bit pathetic about people who plug one idea for twenty years, rewriting the same old article and making the same old conference presentations with minor twists. I just publish things and send them out into the world to find their own way. If people like them, fine." My bravado sounded a bit churlish, after his kindly interest. I sighed and added, "But it is too bad, in a way. My publications are a bunch of orphans." He shrugged and changed the subject.

"It's lonely, being a therapist," he said. "It's an odd thing. People tell me their darkest secrets. I have intimate, profound shared moments all the time. But I have no one who sees what I see, no one to talk it over with. Not like you. You have colleagues, people down the hall. You have someone to commiserate with over the elections, someone to drive you home if your car breaks down. Laboriously scheduled lunches with colleagues just aren't the same."

I understood, remembering the landmark events that had happened over the years in our department. We had our squabbles, but also graduations, parties to celebrate each other's latest books, and spontaneous hallway conversations that led to new discoveries. And some day soon, some liquid nitrogen ice cream.

"And you don't have to say it," Carl added. "I know that a regular workplace isn't all roses. There are plenty of times I'm glad I'm my own boss and work alone. I hear things about management behavior and co-worker warfare that would curl your hair."

I laughed in recognition and said, "I know what you mean." Despite an overall constructive university atmosphere, we have the occasional conflict in my department, like the time a colleague got a feeble dissertation approved over my objections.

Shaking himself out of his ruminations, Carl asked, "So, tell me about your James Bond stint. Did you get to arrest them yourself?" I decided to humor him and described my work with the customs agency. Carl was interested in this adventure, so as we paid our checks and left, I promised to let him know if I found out anything else.

Early in the summer I got another call at home.

"Dr. Heidebrecht?" The voice sounded familiar. "This is Randy Carstairs from Customs. I want to thank you again for your help in training our agents."

"Call me Julie, remember? You're welcome. I got your note." It was a bit odd that he didn't mention the colleague of his that I had caught lying.

"Did your check arrive? Government red tape, you know. I just wanted to make sure."

"Yes, last week."

"Good, good." There was something else in the air. "I hope you enjoyed working with us."

"Yes, yes, I did." I was curious. His vocal frequencies were incongruent with his words – I judged that the real topic hadn't been brought up yet. I waited patiently. Tackling smugglers had been a nice change from reading and writing so much.

"I was just wondering... would you be interested in another project?" Here comes the other agenda. I thought for a minute.

"Well, it depends. I might have some time." I hadn't planned a vacation yet and the "might" was a delaying tactic. But this could be interesting.

"By the way," I added, "You had some nerve feeding me that courier line at first. Did you think I wouldn't find you out?"

Randy laughed and said, "And were you trying to fool *me* that you believed me?"

My turn to laugh. "Just give me the straight story this time. It'll be faster." So I agreed to hear his pitch and walked right into the most hazardous adventure I'd ever experienced. My old flame Matt would have been proud.

This time at Randy's office there were three new people watching me from across the table. They had video equipment set up, and coffee and snacks. Good thing I'd cleared my calendar this morning. This was going to take a while. After the usual pleasantries, Randy cleared his throat and said, "Dr. Heidebrecht…"

"Julie, please."

"Ok, Julie. This is Don Amberg from National Institutes of Health, Gary Brown from Fish and Wildlife Service, and Melissa Tang from the American Zoo and Aquarium Association. We're part of a task force coordinating with the Centers for Disease Control to keep diseases out of the U.S. I don't know if you realized that more and more diseases are crossing the species barrier. AIDS started in monkeys, you know."

"I wondered where your funding was coming from."

"Yeah, human health. So anyway, NIH and Institute of Medicine set us up. Hard to believe any money's going into prevention these days, but go figure. Some congressman probably…"

"Actually, it was Maurice Gordon. The Intext founder. He's given half our budget," interrupted

Melissa, who was skinny but fierce-looking under her severe haircut and bangs. "He likes to travel."

Don chimed in. He looked like a hefty truck driver, with heavy jowls and a mustache. "Yeah, that's actually part of the problem. Germs can get halfway round the world in one day. Just one lousy tourist pesters a monkey at one of those temples in India, presto, microbe's back to California before you can say knife."

I knew all this. I wasn't interested in microbiology or disease vectors. They must have sensed my impatience because Don said hastily, "Can you help us stop the smugglers again? The real problem is primates."

I was puzzled. "Primates? Gorillas and monkeys?"

Melissa added, "Yeah, there are hundreds of chimps and monkeys in labs. They're similar enough to humans that medical researchers use them. Share 99% of our DNA, as I'm sure you know. Psychological researchers use them, too." Her tone was slightly disapproving.

Now I remembered. Tony Tilbertson (the anti-crime software guy who had started me off on this whole escapade) had said "pelts." He must have garbled his briefing, but he got one thing right – mammals were a commodity, too. We were talking about live ones, but I knew there was also a trade in exotic furs and skins. I ignored Melissa's dig at my profession.

Don said, "We're afraid illegally imported primates could spread disease, so we're trying to stop the traffic altogether. Primary prevention, you know. It's pretty difficult."

"Thankless, too, I should think," I said sympathetically, "Taking all these precautions for something that might never happen. You'll never know if you were right."

"Well, England has kept rabies out of the country by quarantining incoming animals," he said with satisfaction. "It worked for a century." This success had fortified his resolve.

I decided to go straight to the point. "Who's doing the smuggling?" This was not a stupid question. They probably had some inkling, some knowledge. They looked at each other. Finally Randy spoke.

"We think they may be part of the zoo community."

"We do not," said Melissa indignantly. "They've *infiltrated*. Real zoo people would never do this. We don't take from the wild any more. We're the ones *saving* endangered species."

Randy said, "Well, it *could* be a zoo person. They know which species are valued and who wants them. They have contacts worldwide, especially the people who manage Species Survival Plans."

Melissa winced. I looked at her inquiringly. She explained, "Species Survival Plans are agreements on saving and breeding endangered species, like Siberian tigers, pandas, you know. Zoos and even countries exchange individual animals for breeding purposes."

"Oh, like an animal dating service."

"You could say so. They keep careful records so they know which stock is inbreeding too much. A stock is a local population of a species."

Randy went on, listing more reasons it could be a zoo person. "The older employees remember the days of collecting expeditions…"

"The *really* old ones," Melissa muttered.

Randy ignored her. "…when it was possible to go into a country and come out with cages full of all sorts of animals, no questions asked."

Melissa was becoming restless, but she didn't interrupt again. I suspected there were a few embarrassing zoo scandals behind her pained silence.

Randy went on. "Some zoo people can be pretty heartless – acquire a baby tiger to boost attendance, then sell it to a circus when it grows up and stops bringing in the crowds."

"The accountants make them do that! The MBAs!" Melissa again.

Gary Brown, the Fish and Wildlife guy who hadn't said anything, was looking sadly at the floor. I wondered if he knew more about animal trafficking than he wanted to know. He didn't want to be here, but he couldn't stay away. I pressed on.

"What would I do? Obviously you can't stuff a primate into a cardboard tube."

They all spoke at once.

"Well, actually you could…"

"Shh, Melissa. We're working on chimps, not marmosets or tamarins."

Randy spoke up. "We have some suspects but we don't want to tip our hand until we know their whole supply chain. We're hoping to bust the whole ring from beginning to end. We'd like you to confirm our suspicions about a few people – maybe even rule out a few. Then we can get started."

I posed the necessary question. "How much of my time are we talking about?"

"We don't know yet. Maybe a few weeks, maybe more. Will you just think it over?" Randy added craftily, "We read some of your papers." That was gratifying. My name was not writ on water after all. "Your idea about the length of a pause after a question. We really liked that one."

Hmm. This could be fun. A non-tenured bull session, with pay.

I asked, "Are these the same people? The same smuggling ring I worked on before? Are they like wholesalers or something?" My metaphor drew a wan smile from Melissa.

Randy said, "No, these guys need larger containers and ready markets. They can't afford a delay after the animal is in this country. Birds die quicker but if you deal in volume it doesn't matter." This made me feel ill. "Each primate represents a big chunk of their expected profit so they like to turn them over quickly. Whole different game."

"Wait, why is NIH here? I thought you guys *wanted* monkeys and chimps, to do your experimenting on."

Don sat up stiffly. "We are developing other forms of research," he said primly in what seemed like a well-rehearsed line. "Most of our animals are captive bred, supplied from here in the U.S." I wondered what internal battles this line represented. "Besides, we want to reduce the variables as much as possible, so we prefer to use known genetic pools. As long as we don't interbreed too much." Melissa nudged him. "I'm on this task force because it's to our interest to stop diseases at the border. It's cheaper than fighting them after they get in."

Each member of the little group had an agenda. Melissa wanted to keep the zoo world's name clean, Randy wanted to stop some leaks, and Don wanted to halt an epidemic. Gary was the wild card.

I brought the discussion back to the action item. "So you'd like me to help you identify people – individuals or groups – in this country who know they are in possession of smuggled exotic animals, right?"

"Exactly. We're starting with primates. They're closest to us genetically."

This had possibilities. I would have a short time with a captive audience to identify the likeliest liars. I would have people to teach and lots of high-tech equipment to play with. It could be fun. I thought a minute and said, "Let me think it over."

⁓ ᏽ ℭ ⁓

I drove home to take Scalawag out for a run at the park. A note from Terry was on the desk in the front hall, next to the mail. "Had to go to the shoe store with my uncle. He's sesquipedalian." Ooh, she was cheating. No one can be sesquipedalian – it means a foot and a half long. Terry is very independent, but she worries about my adventures.

As Scalawag ran around, I pondered the offer. This was going to be a longer project than the first one, and more complicated. Was it a good idea for me to get involved in this? Carl's envy of my publications had triggered a mild urge to revisit and defend some of them. This trip might just drain my time and leave my orphans even more neglected. I needed a second opinion. Surely two handshakes away I could find someone who could give me perspective.

At the back of my mind arose a vague memory… What was that organization my father had talked about in his later years? He had intended to make a donation to save some land in the rural county he'd grown up in. He'd heard a mall was being planned and wanted to help the farmers. Darn, what was that organization? They bought land.

So I called Mom. She might remember. I hadn't talked to her in a week.

"Hi, Mom."

"Why, hello, sweetie. Let me turn off the stove. Okay, I'm back. What are you up to?"

Censoring vigorously, I said, "Oh, student papers, taking Scalawag to the park. Just got the furnace fixed again. Fortunately it was still under warranty."

"Jimmy wants you to call. He says, what's the use of having a lie-catcher for a sister if she won't help you weed out dishonest employees?"

"Not again," we sighed in unison. Jimmy had grown into a hard-working but soft-hearted store owner specializing in electronic gadgets. He was regularly bilked by his own employees and no matter how often he fired one, the next turned out to be dishonest, too. Maybe the slackers scrawled cryptic signs on his door, like the hobos of old who scribbled in code, "Good lunches here." Only now they would write, "Full benefits, no supervision."

After we'd caught up on family news, Mom gave me a perfect opening by asking me to help with her investments. Dad had left her enough for a comfortable retirement, and she was careful to manage what she had. I promised to check out a bond fund she was considering. The university had a good investment advice program to help faculty members stretch their dollars.

"Mom, speaking about money, do you remember that charity Dad was talking about…" I didn't want to say, "the year he died," so I said, "right after I got tenure?"

"Which one, dear? He had so many."

"The one about the land. To save Blendon Woods."

"Wouldn't it be in his will?" Rats, his death had come up anyway.

"No, I don't think he ever got around to putting it in writing. He just kept saying, 'Now the way to save land is to do what that Nature Conservancy does.' Wait, that's it! The Nature Conservancy. Thanks, Mom. I never could have done it without you." With unseemly haste I hung up the phone, promising to phone Mom later for a real talk.

I looked up The Nature Conservancy and found it is headquartered in Virginia, works mostly in this country, but also has a significant international presence. This was better than I could have hoped for. I prepared my speech by massaging the facts a little, mostly with strategic omissions. I had to strike a balance between knowing enough that they'd bother to talk with me, and actually asking the elementary questions I needed to have answered.

I dialed the Nature Conservancy. "Hello, this is Dr. Heidebrecht. I'm working on a project with NIH and AZA on the primate smuggling problem. Could I speak to your expert on Central Africa?" This didn't sound too dim and got me as far as their director of land acquisitions. This formidable lady was, however, very busy negotiating for land to serve as safe corridors for animals migrating between established wildlife sanctuaries. When she heard I was phoning from the Bay Area, she suggested that I contact Norm Gershenz, who runs a rainforest nonprofit right here in San Francisco. Thanking her, I rang off and called him up before I could get cold feet.

Norm Gershenz's operation is called SaveNature. Org, and it saves whole habitats, not just individual species. We met at his San Francisco headquarters, a three-room, one-secretary outfit in a commercial district south of town. Norm is about my age. His polite expression was superimposed on a background of worry, which showed in the corrugated brow lines.

His t-shirt was emblazoned with wildly colorful insects and the slogan **Amazon.bug: World's Largest Selection**.

His secretary, a woman in her sixties, was talking on the phone and a young volunteer gave me a quick smile during Norm's introduction and went back to entering addresses into a computer. Norm showed me his mini-zoo of amazing insects that he takes around to schools to get kids interested in places like Madagascar and Borneo. I had no idea that walking sticks could be five inches long or that cockroaches as long as your thumb could hiss in self-defense. He offered me some tea and we sat at the large table in the center of the room. I told Norm about the assignment and asked for his opinion.

"I travel a lot," he began. "I used to do more field work before I set up SaveNature. What do you want to know about… monkey body parts in meat markets in Rwanda? Pet stores in Indonesia selling baby orangutans? Mighty hunters bringing back trophy heads?" I shuddered and tried to frame a less gory question.

"Is it true that primates are being smuggled here from other countries?" I asked.

"Sad to say, yes. It isn't my main focus, but one thing we try to do is save and protect land. It doesn't do much good to champion a species if they haven't got a place to live." Uh oh, he was going into his stump speech. He recognized my reaction and pulled himself back. "Anyway, you were saying…"

"Who do you think is doing it?" He sighed.

"Anyone. Everyone. It's just a part of the economy in some places. You might as well ask who's doing clothing and car parts." Seeing my chagrin, he said, "Sorry, this is painful to talk about. Didn't mean to take it out on you. People live in the rainforest. They get hungry, they catch a colobus monkey. Some guy has a little more entrepreneurial spirit than the others, he turns it into a business. Finds the fences and the dealers, starts doing it full time."

I didn't want to irritate him any further, so I skipped ahead and asked, "On the international level, are there likely to be lots of competing smuggling rings?"

He shook his head. "I don't really look for these guys. I could inquire the next time I'm in the field. Try the U.N. website. The United Nations Environment Programme has something called the Convention on International Trade in Endangered Species. CITES for short. That's the key organization for you, I should think. Also the Jane Goodall Institute has links to all those people. But I definitely think you should do the Customs job. Every little bit helps."

I tried one more time. "Can you tell me anything about the profiles of the smugglers?"

"Only that they recruit locals to do the actual poaching. The locals do it because they have no other way of making a living. See, we need to get jobs for them. Half a dozen park rangers have told me they used to be poachers and gave it up the minute there was a job at the park."

"So you don't know who are the buyers at this end?"

"Not really. Sorry I haven't been more helpful." But he had helped. He thought the task force project was worthwhile, and I now had a few more hands to shake and a pile of colorful brochures.

"Could I call you if I have any other questions?" He said yes and invited me to his next event, a fundraiser in honor of an important rainforest expert. So by the end of that meeting, I was still thinking it over.

At home on the sofa with Scalawag and Gambado, I looked over some of the brochures Norm had given me. Breathtaking photographs of red-eyed tree frogs, brilliant blue morpho butterflies, and fan corals filled the pages. Matt would have loved them. Underwater photography was Matt's first love; after he'd developed a reputation as a dependable and creative nature photographer for the dive magazines, he branched out into other outdoor adventures.

Matt was not one of those crazed impulsive risk addicts. He just loved moving and seeing new places from impossible angles. It seemed as natural to him as breathing. I met him while scuba diving – the tamest thing Matt ever did – on a trip organized by my local dive club. On the first day of a two-week trip to Grand Cayman, the divemaster paired us as buddies. A dive buddy is someone who checks to see that your equipment is properly assembled and then goes underwater with you for the dive and checks in with you at the end so no one in a large group gets lost or in trouble. Matt was a good dive buddy – he was quick and skillful with the equipment checks and his pace for exploring underwater reefs and canyons matched mine perfectly. After a few days, the pats and touches needed to check each other's gear became longer and soon crossed the threshold into frank flirting. On the last day of the trip, I wrapped my arms around him and said with a vixenish smile, "Liberate yourself from my vise-like grip." He smiled down at me and said, "Why should I do that?"

Matt traveled so much for his work that it took a while for us to become an item. He'd call and say, "Come with me to Kauai" or "to the Red Sea" or "to the Kalahari." I have my own travel bug, so I was easy to persuade, especially between my first few academic jobs. Later he couldn't understand why I sometimes said, "It's mid-semester" or "I can only come for three days." He was aghast that I didn't take photographs on my trips and shook his head in disbelief when I asked, "Who is Galen Rowell?" In his circle, it's blasphemy not to know the great nature photographers, preferably in person.

His daring showed even when we were in town. He put a new spark arrestor on my chimney and scampered around the second-story roof as if it were as safe as his kitchen. He seemed politely interested in my work. He came to a few lectures I gave and asked one or two intelligent questions, and after that took my work for granted. I think he sensed that in my own way I was pushing frontiers and exploring the unknown, but he didn't understand why there was so much drudgery in learning – reviewing one's findings, checking the method, predicting what the critics would say and responding to them, being one's own critic… the ratio of excitement to labor in my field wasn't high enough to keep him interested.

Friends have asked me if I ever longed to give up my regular life and join his adventurous one. The truth is, no, I didn't. Learning and detecting are catnip to me; time evaporates when I'm in the lab on the trail of a new discovery. I never feel chained to a desk and think I'm lucky to be paid for what I do.

It was the danger that separated us, at last. I crossed an Andes canyon on a rope bridge – he cleverly went over first, knowing I'd always go toward him – and rafted down the Colorado River, but I wouldn't bungee jump or climb the Eiger. He could be very persuasive, but his pained, baffled expression when I said no… I think he got tired of begging me to accept what he *knew* was better than gold.

It wasn't fear. I just didn't have a burning desire, or even a tepid desire, to cling to the mast of a tall ship in a storm. I just didn't *want* to. I think that's when he gave up. As long as he thought it was fear, he was sure he could talk or wheedle or educate or trick or seduce me out of it.

We broke up twice over this, but it didn't take. We couldn't stay away from each other. Within a week, one of us would pick up the phone… After a month apart, my desire for him would become a desire to be wherever he was, and I would jump on a plane and meet him on the pampas or the delta. But eventually I had seen him in enough terrifying situations – dangling from a rope below an overhang, leaning out of a swooping helicopter to take a picture, emerging from a spelunking expedition in the world's deepest cave – that fear did creep in, fear that I would lose him to a crevasse or a faulty piece of equipment or loose piton. I began to dread the days when he would say, with his irrepressible grin, that he had a new idea... why not go heli-skiing in Austria or sledding across Antarctica... My passion for him had lured me to all the places it ever would.

That final night at our favorite restaurant was bittersweet. We respected each other – at the funeral, his climbing buddy surprised me by saying that Matt had often bragged about my academic victories. We drank our wine and watched the ice floes carrying us to different currents and looked fondly at each other across the table.

A month later he was dead.

Did he die happy? As he and the other skydiver spiraled downward, trying to untangle their chutes, to set out the reserve chute, then knowing it was too late – as the earth raced up toward him, did he think, "It was worth it"?

After he died I got Scalawag to keep me company.

⟞ VI ⟝

Gradually I was being drawn into the anti-smuggling project. My desire to follow up on some of my old papers faded away. Before deciding to commit, I went back to the zoo, looking for some real-world animal life to observe. I skipped the birds and big cats and went straight to the primates. The first species I found was the cotton-top tamarin. I peered into the enclosure but couldn't see anything except lush vegetation. A bird with a huge brightly colored bill hopped from one branch to another. Then I discovered how to find a zoo animal: look at the person standing next to you. A man and a small child were gazing raptly at a branch just above eye level. Then I saw it. It was tiny – it seemed to be smaller than its own name. Small bright eyes looked out at me from a face no larger than a walnut. The body was smaller than a squirrel's. I had no idea primates could be this small. It was black, with fluffy knots of white hair standing up on the top and sides of its head. It looked like a troll made of scraps from a skunk factory.

As if offended by my image, the little ragamuffin leaped gymnastically to another branch. How could a creature so young be so agile? I looked around for the adults. Then I realized that it was the adult.

"See there?" said the man to the child. "There's the baby." Incredibly, an even tinier cotton-top was peering out from behind the adult's arm. Its head was the size of a pencil eraser. It stuck like Velcro to the adult, who leaped to another branch. Soon they disappeared overhead.

Reluctantly tearing myself away from the cotton-top tamarins, I promised myself I'd come back to look at them again one day. They score high on the cuteness quotient. They're so tiny they could fit in your pocket. Oh no… or in a cardboard tube.

The half dozen chimpanzees who live here have a quarter acre, complete with climbing structures, cargo nets, logs, a termite mound, and a mess of toys. High above, on one of the exposed steel beams that held up the roof of the enclosure, a big black ball of chimpness sat contemplating the state of the world. I leaned against the railing and watched as another chimp appeared from behind the climbing structure, dragging a blanket. She had an odd teetering gait. Then I saw why. She had stood in the middle of the blanket, grabbed a corner with each hand, and shuffled forward, using the blanket as a kind of moving rug. From the front she looked like a short bowlegged cowboy wearing chaps. This went on for a while. A woman at the other end of the exhibit was watching the chimps and periodically typing earnestly into a small computer. Her t-shirt said, "Please do not disturb. Scientific observation in progress."

Suddenly I heard high-pitched screaming. A chimp I hadn't noticed before came rolling along on three legs, holding a toy in one hand. Behind it chased another chimp, screeching. They ran around the enclosure until the pursuer caught the first one.

More screaming. The toy was dropped and left behind. Children eagerly ran up to see what was going on. Their parents patiently followed, pushing strollers laden with juice and toys and the other impedimenta of parenthood. Finally the uproar quieted and the humans drifted away.

In one corner of the enclosure was a bare dirt hill about two feet high with a round hole on one side. This was an artificial termite mound, the sign said, meant to resemble the real termite mounds in Africa. The plaque explained that chimps "fish" for termites (their favorite snacks) by sticking a branch they'd stripped of leaves into the termite mound entrance. As soon as the defending termites bite the branch to investigate this outrageous intrusion, the chimp pulls it out and munches the termines like a matron nibbling scallops off a shish kebab. I waited almost half an hour to see this enterprising act of animal initiative, but none of the chimps approached the mound.

The volunteer who had led me to the birds a few weeks ago walked over and saw me intently observing the animals. "Are you here again?" she smiled. "You've been watching the chimps a long time this morning. Most people don't stay in front of an exhibit more than twenty seconds. It's been measured."

"I need to brush up on my primates," I said, and suddenly had an idea. "Is there anyone here who can tell me more about endangered species?"

"Oh, you mean the bushmeat trade? or IUCN?" she rattled off a few more bits of jargon. The only term I recognized was "stud book."

"Uh, I guess so. I'm helping stop smuggling…" Pretty soon I would start believing it myself.

"Oh, that would be Anne Wendell," said the friendly volunteer. "She's our director of conservation. Come with me. She'll be so excited. Are you with AZA?"

I had to confess that I knew less about all this than she did. She took it in stride, though with a shade of disappointment.

"Are you a reporter? I thought they already covered our new elephant's arrival. He's doing fine but won't be on exhibit for another month." We had arrived at the building where classes for children took place. "Marie, is Anne here? Oh, good. I have an endangered species expert to meet her." This friendly conduit guided me through a maze of hallways. We passed rooms where children were making collages. A knot of docents in identifying t-shirts huddled over a schedule. We finally reached a private office where a pretty blond woman was working at a large desk. To forestall another of my guide's misplaced role promotions, I hastily introduced myself.

"Hi, I'm Julie Heidebrecht. Your… associate thought you might have some time…"

The woman looked up. My escort beamed and nodded encouragingly, waiting for electricity to strike. Pause. I continued,

"I'm a psychologist at the university and I've been recruited to help stop smuggling." Anne listened intently, though I could see by the state of her desk that she was juggling a dozen tasks. My guide waited around hopefully, but beyond an appreciative nod and smile, Anne didn't include her in our greetings, so eventually she melted away. I sat down in the chair Anne indicated.

"I didn't know there were any new initiatives," she said, with a brow-knitting face.

"I don't know if this is new or not. I'm just coming on board. I'm helping a federal task force recognize the people who…"

"I didn't realize they had psychologists assigned to primates." She was rightly doubtful, but then so was I.

"Well, I've only done this once. Birds, that was." Anne perked up when I described my customs adventure, omitting the bribed officer.

"How many people did you catch?"

"Did the customs guys catch," I corrected. "A few more than before. They're being nice and giving me some credit. I guess they're desperate."

Anne sighed. She picked up the phone, tapped out an extension number, and said, "Larry, can we move our meeting to 2.30? Thanks." Looking back at me, she said, "We are all desperate. We're trying to save habitats, breed animals in captivity, stop smuggling, get food to people in Africa so they don't kill all their wildlife… I can't even let myself think about animals in labs." There was a silence. Anne shook herself, in what looked like a familiar signal to get on with doing the small steps she could do.

Suddenly I had an alarming thought. Melissa, the fierce zoo defender on my task force, had said that smugglers had infiltrated the zoo world. What if Anne was one of them? She was perfectly placed – she knows the animals, the countries, which people wanted which animals. Surreptitiously I looked around at the awards and thank-you letters on the walls, some of them dating back fifteen years. She'd been in this wildlife world a long time. Didn't that argue against her being a turncoat? Who would work so hard doing one mission while secretly undermining it? But it had happened before – think of those cold war Soviet moles, installed in America as dormant spies, living unnoticed for decades until activated by their handlers. Or maybe… Hold it, Julie, I said to myself. This is ridiculous. Anne was speaking, asking, "What can I do for you?"

I regretted that I hadn't planned a request, but who could have known that I would find a person like this at a zoo, let alone be ushered so quickly into her office? I don't enjoy appearing like a bumbling idiot any more than the next person, so I thought fast. "I think it would help if I were more familiar with the characteristics of the most common primates that are smuggled. Like, what makes which ones valuable for which trade? Are pet traders significantly different from research traders or medical body parts traders?"

"The entertainment industry is a big sector, after laboratories. In this country we use over 50,000 living monkeys and chimps in labs."

I was shocked. That's the size of a small town.

"Plus another 40,000 kept for breeding." Anne looked grim. "Then the government has another 1200 or 1500 or 1800, depending on whose figures you read." There was a pause. "Those are the ones we know about."

I thought I'd heard it all, but I was wrong. She added, "Then there's the military. We don't know how many they use to test weapons on." I thought it was time to say something.

"Also, I have to be candid, NIH is concerned about diseases. They…"

"I know. AIDS, Lyme disease, avian flu…" I detected impatience by the way her eyes moved. There was some subplot, I saw. Something that made her want to skip this part of the story. Or maybe she was just tired of seeing animals get blamed. I'd read somewhere that 90% of rattlesnake bites occurred to young men between the ages of 19 and 24… who had been handling the snake.

"Well, you're welcome to observe our chimps, of course. I could arrange for you to stay after exhibit hours, if you need to. We're part of a behavior research project with the Jane Goodall Institute – you may have seen one of our observers at the enclosure collecting data. And the new docent classes start next month. That's every Saturday morning for twelve weeks. Then there's our library." This was more work than I intended to do. I just wanted to pick her brain. I asked,

"How hard is it to restrain and transport a chimp? Would it take a small army?"

"I've never done it. You'd sedate them, of course. Animals are exchanged between zoos all the time for breeding programs. You'd need to talk to our curator about that." She gave me the curator's name. I cast about for another suitable question. "Do the chimps fight you the whole time? Do they ever get sent back to you? You know, rejected by the zoo you traded them to?"

Suddenly Anne made an emphatic gesture. "I know! You should go to Glenn Madison's place in Arizona. Glenn and Carolyn Madison have a chimp sanctuary where they teach chimps to use sign language."

"Like what's-his-name... Silvana? The one that signaled back in the 1970s? I read about it in my undergraduate anthropology course."

"It *is* Silvana."

"Good heavens, is he still alive?"

"She. Why not? Chimps can live to be sixty. Her whole family is there."

"I thought she was an orphan."

"I meant her offspring, the family she created. She had two babies of her own, plus one who died. She also adopted another infant Carolyn and Glenn rescued. You should read about how she bosses the others around. I could loan you some books."

Anne had accepted me and was becoming more animated. Describing the doings, the intelligence, and the crafty tricks of these near relatives brought her to life. For me, this was like a window in time. Decades had passed since that undergraduate course. The paragraph about the signing chimp felt as ancient as a daguerreotype. Yet that chimp was alive, had lived all these years while I was in college, graduate school, post-doc training, with Matt, after Matt…

We were also straying from my immediate mission, but something told me to let this connection grow in its own way. Anne had jumped on my project as if it were her dream come true. I decided she wasn't a mole, pardon the expression. No one could fake this much love and enthusiasm. Finally she sat perfectly still and looked at the wall across from her desk.

"You need to go to Tucson. Let me call to see if they're in the state." Anne picked up her telephone. I presumed that "they" meant the top people, not the ones who kept the place running whenever the directors were traveling to raise money and speak at conferences. Miraculously, she reached them at once. I thought that only happened in movies. She spun her chair around to look out the window as she spoke. I looked around at her office. Every wall was adorned with pictures of animals – big cats, giraffes, small furry creatures whose species I could not even guess. There were certificates of appreciation from organizations ranging from the local scout troop to international wildlife associations. Children's drawings, piles of letters, a box full of two-way radios, colored ribbons that could be given out as prizes, stuffed llamas, framed portraits of individual animals. A sign on the wall gave instructions on how to respond if an animal escaped from its enclosure. "Use your radio to contact Animal Management," it began.

Anne hung up the phone and spun her chair around, beaming. "It's fixed. I'm coming with you." She laughed. "This is probably more than you bargained for when you showed up here today. You *have* to go there."

I took a chance. "Sounds to me as if *you* have to go there. And not a minute too soon." I hoped I hadn't overstepped the bounds of hospitality, but Anne smiled calmly. She looked like someone who had just scratched an itch.

"You said you had the whole summer off, but fortunately we don't have to wait. Pack your bags. Next weekend."

This was pleasantly strange. It was as if I'd known Anne for a long time. Maybe saving wildlife was like academia – bringing people together because of the things they loved.

"I have a meeting now," she said, and stood up to indicate that the encounter was over. I admired how unruffled and businesslike she was, segueing smoothly from excitement back to the tasks of the present. "I'll phone you tonight to make arrangements." Taking my card, she graciously escorted me out of the building and back into the zoo proper. "Stay a while," she offered. "I bet you haven't seen the siamangs."

She was right about one thing. This *was* more than I'd bargained for, in a good way. I'd only gone to the zoo again to check out the primates, and suddenly here I was about to be introduced to some top experts. My deep background research was progressing quickly – in Tucson I could quiz the experts about a commonly smuggled species; this would surely give me some insights. On top of everything else, I would be able to study how our closest living relatives practiced deception. I would write off the expenses as research.

I chuckled at the helpful volunteer's misintroduction and reminded myself to emphasize to Anne and any other people I met that I was no animal expert. Or maybe I should let people be mistaken about who I was. It had worked well this time. A professional question crossed my mind: does passive failure to correct misinformation count as deception?

Since Anne had forgotten to give me the books she'd impulsively promised, I picked up a few at the local bookstore on the way home. It's always easier to buy than borrow. You'd think that as an academic, I would look on libraries as a second home, and I do, but I also can't resist the pleasure of taking books home, knowing they're mine to scribble on, dog-ear, and leave open with a coffee cup holding my place. I just can't concentrate the same way if I have to treat the book as a religious object.

Three days later on the plane, I found out why Anne was so eager to come. She had participated in some of the early research on signing and had once even conversed with Silvana, but when her children were born she needed to earn more money than a research assistant would ever make. Ever since, almost eleven years now, she had had her hands full running the zoo's conservation department. She was helping habitats around the world and inventing ways for the local zoogoers to realize how interconnected our world is, but she missed the direct contact and was eager to venture back into the wild. Standing in front of a fenced chimp enclosure and teaching docents how to do instantaneous behavior sampling didn't even come close.

We landed at the airport and rented a car for the drive to Tucson. Night was falling. Stars came out one by one and I realized how long it had been since I'd seen so many stars.

By bad luck, there was a cheerleader convention in town and every hotel was full. We had to settle for most hideous bed and breakfast inn it was possible to imagine, which had one room we could share. The furniture was painted a garish silver – all of it, beds, nightstands, cupboard. There were tall twisted plastic vases full of artificial flowers, not silk, but a crude heavy cloth that had been sprayed silver, to match the beds, I supposed. Drooping dull gray ostrich feathers had been tastefully arranged among these metallic monstrosities. The throw pillows had covers with designs of bizarre 1950s themes, like fishhooks, guppies, and candy canes. On top of the television there was an ashtray that looked like a potholder imagined by Salvador Dali's fevered brain. Yet somehow this wasn't purely a chaotic nightmare of kitsch. I sensed that it had been lovingly assembled. Someone really sought out this tacky stuff, and hung the homemade oil paintings *just so* above the triangular corner knick-knack shelf.

Throwing her duffle expertly into the corner, Anne tested her bed for springiness. She was not interested in how the room looked. "This is way better than a cot," she remarked. "On nature treks you get all kinds of comfort levels. But you'd be surprised how comfortable a tent can be." I wondered if she was trying to recruit me for something.

"Hey, let's practice some signs," she said. "Here. This is how you say, '**Open**'." She made a simple gesture. "They sign that when they want you to open a door to let them go outside, or open a cupboard for their treats." I copied it. "And here's '**More**'."

I clumsily imitated the gestures. She corrected me. "Gosh, I haven't done this in years," she said happily. Anne was in her element. "Once while I was working with Silvana, one of the volunteers missed work for a week after her six-month-old son died of sudden infant death syndrome. When she came back to work, Silvana snubbed her for days until the volunteer signed to her, '**My baby died**'."

I didn't know chimps understood the concept of death. Then I remembered that Silvana had lost one of her own infants. "How did Silvana respond?"

Anne said softly, "She signed 'cry'." Anne made the sign for me, tracing teardrops down her cheeks. I was silent for a minute. I copied, tracing "**cry**" on my cheek. Then I asked, "How do you sign 'Come here'?"

"Like this," and she showed me the signs. "There's no need to sign the word 'here.' Sign language is pretty telegraphic. Just sign the key words." I wondered if individual signers had idiosyncrasies and whether regions of the country had the equivalent of accents. Could you identify where a signer came from? I began to wander into familiar mental tracks about detecting and interpreting. More important, I wondered if I would inadvertently sign the wrong thing – make a pun or a faux pas, like the gauche American in Paris who insisted on ordering his own restaurant meal. His French acquaintance tried to intervene but was brushed off. "I told you I can order for myself," the American said importantly. "Well, perhaps," his companion sighed, "But I just distinctly heard you order a flight of steps."

To make the sign for "**sorry**," you put your right hand into the shape for the letter A and circle it around your heart. For "**more**" you tap your fingertips together twice. For "**happy**," you place your right palm on your chest and brush upward twice. Anne and I tried to hold conversations, mimicking signs out of an ASL book I had brought.

We stayed up late and giggled. She told me about her husband (who didn't care much about animals and worked as a city planner) and I gave a censored history of my last few boyfriends. While describing sifakas, rare lemurs in Madagascar, she showed me their gait by dancing across the room sideways. This looked improbable to me, but she assured me it was really how they move when they are upright on the ground. Evidently they're more graceful in the trees. This was puzzling. Why would any creature move in that awkward way? Why get on the ground at all? Surely it was inefficient and must have exposed them to predators as they clumsily leaped sideways. Well, they had survived this long. Maybe a hundred generations from now their descendants would be walking smoothly. It was like watching evolution in action. So I showed her my imitation of a chimp loping around the room, the one I'd used to entertain my niece Vanessa when she was sick in bed with mumps. Anne laughed uproariously and demonstrated how to do the chimp's main call, the pant-hoot. It sounds just like the name. Was I going to be using this sound tomorrow with Silvana? By midnight I felt as if I'd known her forever. I hadn't been to a slumber party since I was fifteen.

Next day we arrived at the sanctuary shortly after it opened. After the obligatory tour of the facilities, we went into the visitors' gallery. On the other side of a huge window was the chimps' living space. Six of them lived here. Their living room had ladders, hammocks, tree branches, rubber balls, hats, mirrors, and other toys. A chimp could keep busy here, or sit in a corner and loaf.

Glenn greeted Anne warmly – I guess friendships in the animal world last over time and space and career changes. While they caught up on their doings and their zoo news, I rushed over to the window and started watching the chimps. I could see three of them. One was almost out of sight in a hammock high in the air – I could just spot its hairy head and one arm trailing over the side of the hammock. Two others were huddling close together in the middle of their playroom. Ah, this must be the famous grooming session. One sat perfectly still, looking across the room, while the other appeared to be touching and scratching him. Or her. I couldn't tell. This operation was very absorbing to Chimp B, who patiently inspected each square inch of A's back and shoulders. Occasionally B would look closely at something in its fingers before flicking it away. It reminded me of a roomful of teenage girls practicing blemish removal.

Finally Anne brought Glenn over and introduced me. Glenn is about 60, of middle height and with the fulfilled expression of a man whose work is his true calling. He transferred to me some of the warmth he had bestowed on Anne. After a few pleasantries, he pointed to the chimp in the hammock and said proudly, "That's Silvana." She happened to look our way, and Glenn made a hand sign. "**Come**," he said out loud for my benefit. In a leisurely manner, as befits a matriarch, she majestically swung down from her perch and ambled over to the window in front of us.

"**Silvana, this my friend**," said Glenn as he signed. That was nice. I'd been promoted.

"**Drink**," Silvana signed. "**Bring drink**."

"**Drink all gone?**" he signed.

"**Thirsty**," she signed. "**Hurry**." Glenn chuckled and instructed an assistant to bring some water to pass through the door. Silvana grabbed the bucket and slurped greedily. Another chimp approached, but waited until the matriarch's thirst was satisfied before seizing the bucket. Finally Silvana gave the chimp equivalent of a wave and meandered back to her comfy spot. Wow. I'd just seen a requisition take place. As if nothing special had happened, Glenn said, "That's Patty over there grooming Zanzibar. They're best friends."

"What's the grooming for?" I asked. "Fleas?"

Anne hastily answered. "No, dead skin, dirt. But really for social bonding. It's how they cement relationships and make up after quarrels." I was embarrassed that Anne had to explain this basic fact to me and wished I'd remembered my homework better. We chatted a bit more. Glenn smiled indulgently and said, "Chimps look small, but they're incredibly strong. Any one of them could beat up an adult man or two. Even our youngest chimp, who's only three years old, could hurt you. We don't want to use fear to subdue them, so we don't let visitors in."

We pulled some chairs up to the picture window. Anne got Patty's attention and signed, "**hello**." At first she didn't respond, but Anne kept at it patiently. Finally when she signed "**hello**" for about the tenth time, the chimp signed back. Anne was delighted and I caught the signing bug. Communicating with these black, human-shaped creatures felt somehow magical. In half an hour we had signed to three of them, and one had signed back.

That was an exciting moment. You can't possibly mistake the sign – "**friend**" is made by hooking one index finger over the other, then vice versa. This was not an accidental gesture that eager advocates twisted into a meaning. Anne had told me that the idea of primate-human communication had plenty of critics, all looking for reasons to discount the possibility. The critics said the chimps were just responding to rewards, or making vague movements that overeager observers twisted into meanings. The critics even tried to discount irrefutably meaningful messages – like the time the Silvana, on seeing a tiny doll someone had stuck into her water glass, signed unmistakably, "**baby in my drink**."

I didn't understand why the skeptics would fight it so hard. Why shouldn't animals communicate with us? They communicate with each other – bees with their dances, dogs with their snarls and scents, cats with hisses and fluffed tails. Scalawag is in constant communication with me. He and I read each other well. Go for a walk. Scratch my tummy. Not now. Dinner time. Millions of other humans communicate with their dogs. So why were these pedants disparaging the concept and disbelieving the accumulated evidence? Hadn't they looked at the hours of videos? I know every field needs its critics and skeptics, but not to the point of sheer denial. Well, denial is nothing new. Galileo couldn't get the bishops even to look through his telescope.

I also don't understand why some scientists doubt the intelligence and feelings of animals. Maybe they are the same people who used to say that human infants don't feel pain, so it's ok to circumcise or do minor surgery on newborns without anesthetic. How do they explain away the screams? What motivated the people who kept minimizing the existence of animal minds? My therapist friend Carl would probably say it's to protect the human self-image as the pinnacle of creation, special, superior, inimitable – and conveniently entitled to use animals for our own purposes. If animals are too intelligent, too conscious, we couldn't exploit them so ruthlessly. So the critics kept denying the observations, policing the species border, even if they had to make up new rules and definitions along the way.

Personally, I had never felt so special as when a member of another species looked me in the eye and signed, "**friend**." This was the chimp called Dougou (short for Ouagadougou, an African town near Timbuktu). I was so enchanted I almost forgot to keep signing. Quick, what can I say next? "**Happy meet you**," I signed.

Dougou made another sign. "Quick, what does that mean?" I asked.

Glenn signed and said, "**What say?**" Dougou repeated the sign he had made for me.

"Oh, he's begging for treats," Glenn said with an indulgent smile. "He tries that with every new person."

Just like a four-year-old, I thought.

Glenn explained that Dougou had been in the entertainment industry for years before being sent here. "He's still very reactive. We can't walk by the window carrying a cane, for instance. He freaks out."

"Why does he object to canes?"

"That's what they used to discipline him when they were training him to make commercials."

Hastily Anne added, "But at least he didn't get stuck in a laboratory." I didn't know what went on in laboratories and wasn't sure I wanted to. "Thank god, the worst of those have been shut down." She and Glenn traded comments on this development, mentioning people and places I hadn't heard of. I drifted back to the window and watched the chimps.

Anne had to go back to Oakland Monday morning, but I stayed an extra week. I spent hours in the indoor enclosure, watching Silvana and her friends as they played, napped, and squabbled. Sometimes they went outside into their fenced yard and I watched them through a big picture window. Of course I hoped to see them using sign language every minute, and Silvana actually did about once an hour, sometimes to humans, sometimes to other chimps. It was enough. As a researcher, I'm used to a high dross rate, when nothing appears to be happening.

Monday I watched some videos the researchers had prepared and learned more signs. "**Tickle me**" was apparently a favorite. Chimps are as playful in their way as otters, though they have more conflict. Loud conflict! They scream, chase, fight, and form factions. One of the books I'd brought with me was even called *Chimpanzee Politics*.

Glenn and Carolyn (his wife and co-founder of the sanctuary) were busy dealing with a budget crisis, so a senior technician, Desta, was my main source of information. Desta was young but had already worked here for years. She was about to be transferred to the San Francisco Zoo to start a signing project there, taking with her one of the chimps we had been watching – Kijana, the youngest. Anne had been ecstatic at the news. A signing chimp – she would be able to do some signing again only a half-hour drive from home! Anne had heard rumors about this project, but in the zoo world you never believe anything until it actually happens. There are so many possible disappointments – the other zoo or country changes its mind, war, funding crashes, quarantines, snafus with permits.

Desta was in her mid-20s, tall, with kinky black hair and a preference for t-shirts that had messages on them. Her mother had been in the Peace Corps when she met Desta's father, an Ethiopian working for one of his country's health organizations. Desta (which means "joy" in Ethiopian) spent her first five years with her parents at their various postings in Africa, playing outside in the bush with Ethiopian and later Cameroonian children. Her mother brought her Ethiopian husband and little girl back to the U.S. They had settled in Chicago, where a younger sister and brother were born, siblings whose idea of "outdoors" was "the space between the front door and the car." In America, Desta's love of animals had at first to be satisfied with kittens and parakeets, but when her parents realized she was not going to grow out of it, they gave her their blessing to become a junior docent at the Brookfield Zoo and later paid for a first-class college education in biology and conservation.

"When did you get interested in sign language?" I asked her one day when she was taking a break.

"My brother started dating a deaf girl when I was in college," she answered, "and I just wanted to make her feel at home when she visited. I just learned a few signs, you know, hello, glad to see you, the bathroom is down the hall – stuff you learn in any foreign language. She appreciated it so much! And the signs are fun to make." I agreed with that. It's like dancing with your hands. Desta went on, "I was getting interested in chimp communication. Of course I'd read about Silvana. Then after I graduated and read about this job, I jumped at it."

"And now you're going to San Francisco," I prompted.

"Yeah," she said, her eyes shining. "I'm taking the Madisons' methods with me and I'll teach them to the other keepers. We'll be getting some grad students, too."

"They must trust you a lot."

"Well, you know," she said shyly. "I guess I am the assistant they've had the longest. They hate to see Kijana go, of course. But that's ok, I'll be in touch with them all the time. We're even going to have Kijana-cam, did I tell you?" She steered the conversation away from her own virtues to the wonders of video cameras and the internet. Going to San Francisco was a promotion and an opportunity for her to be in charge of a new program, though of course she'd remain in close touch with Glenn and Carolyn. I warned her about the high cost of living in San Francisco, but nothing dampened her excitement.

That week Desta was spending most of her time getting Kijana ready for his trip, but she took some breaks and taught me some more signs. I enjoyed putting the chimp favorites "**tickle**" and "**chase**" into action, running back and forth in front of the window while Dougou ran alongside me on the other side. Desta was interested in my deception research. Primates can deceive, too, I learned. Two adults can hide from the jealous alpha male the fact that they're having sex. A chimp can pretend that she doesn't know where a treat has been stashed by the experimenters, or look innocent after he's poked someone or stolen a toy. Just like my kid brother.

One afternoon, I told Desta about our anti-smuggling project.

"Really?" she exclaimed with undisguised admiration. "You're going to catch the smugglers?" She was eager to help. "I just love my guys so much. It kills me to think of them in traps or lab cages. What can I do?"

"Hmmm, you could tell me what you remember about Africa."

Desta laughed. "Julie, I was a child then. I didn't know anything about smuggling."

"Still."

"Well," she put down her work and thought a minute. "I remember the insects. Brightest colors you ever saw. And I remember washing our clothes in the stream behind our house. I would get in the water and stomp on them before the servant wrung them out." She smiled at the memory. Spending so much time outside, she had come to love all the creatures that were her playmates and friends. She had found her calling early in life, just like me.

The only good thing about my lodging was the Jacuzzi. I would soak there with my sign language book propped against the faucets, practicing hand shapes and muttering the words. One night as I let the jets melt away the muscle cramps acquired from kneeling for hours in front of the observation window, I read that chimps can not only sign, they can make up their own expressions. A famous chimp at another sanctuary called the refrigerator "**open food drink**." When shown some alka seltzer bubbling in a glass, a chimp called Moja signed, "**listen drink**." A Brazil nut she called "**rock berry**." Another chimp named Lucy called a radish "**cry hurt food**" and a watermelon "**candy drink**." I wondered what Silvana or Moja would call this bubbling tub. Probably something like "**busy water**."

One of my magpie tidbits floated into my mind – the Navajo code talkers in World War II. To help Allied forces communicate in a code the Japanese wouldn't be able to break, the army had recruited Navajo men to use their native language for radio communications. Using Navajo words, the men created phrases for "battleship" and "airplane." The code word they used for "plane" is the Navajo equivalent of "bird"; for "bombs" they would say "eggs." Actually, that sounds a bit like regular military slang. In Navajo code, submarine was "iron fish" and a fighter plane was "hummingbird." Since my profession involves indirect communication, I looked up some of the other Navajo code words to use in one of my lectures. My favorites were "many shelter," for village, and "small whale" for cruiser. Hospital is "place of medicine." "Down to last" means desperate. That would be part of the code talkers' message when small platoons were isolated and under attack. *Please come save us. We are down to last…*

The Jacuzzi was soothing and my mind wandered. It was time to make a decision about the anti-smuggling job. I had learned that primates are valued as live cargo for pets, entertainment, and research. That there was a superficial system of permits and protection, under which thrived a black market which, like all black markets, was more profitable than the legal one. Could some lab-coated scientist be supplementing his legal allotment of chimps with an underground supply? Medical research is big business and scientists live and breathe grant money, not to mention insider information on profitable drug development. I remember hearing, in the early days of the AIDS epidemic, that there wasn't a single AIDS researcher who wasn't already a millionaire.

My week at Tucson was up. On the last day I made an extra donation to the sanctuary and promised Desta to keep her posted on the anti-smuggling project. We arranged to have lunch after she had settled in at San Francisco. When I got home everything looked normal, except this time there was no note from Terry.

Now everywhere I looked I saw animals. Squirrels on campus, raccoons scuttling industriously down the streets at night, lizards sunning themselves on the sidewalk. How did I not notice them before? I was becoming fond of furry creatures. Scalawag and Gambado had been my background; they had their own personalities, to be sure, but they were auxiliaries to my life, to cheer me up, to provide pleasure and diversion. It hadn't occurred to me that they were the protagonists of their own lives.

⟶ꞁ VII ꞁ⟵

This smuggling assignment was tempting, but I was still hesitant to abandon my writing duties. Partly to gather information and partly to delay making the decision, I resolved to check out one last thing: was this task force a genuine entity with authority to make things happen, or just someone's wishful thinking without a budget? My spies in Sacramento (who keep me informed of state budget negotiations on education) said I'd have to go to Washington, DC, where the real money is. Why can't I just call them, I asked – give me the phone number. Various sighs came down the line – ah, the innocence of civilians. "Go talk to them. Sit in their office. Look them in the eye. Use your own expertise to read their voices and faces." Good suggestion. Even if I got no documents, or fudged ones, I could assess the officeholder's personal veracity.

I'm just a citizen, but I have a modest civil service appointment as an associate professor at a public university. And as a taxpayer, technically I'm one of their employers and have the right to question them. Still, I had a queasy feeling about people in Washington. The elected ones have to lie repeatedly to crowds and reporters; the appointed ones are beholden to the elected ones and biding their time until they can quit public service and become filthy rich lobbyists. How could I, an academic, go toe-to-toe with seasoned liars? Maybe I could find one with a conscience, who was just dying to reveal the real budget figures... my own personal Deep Throat.

I said to myself, just imagine these people are my next set of research subjects. I've interviewed hundreds of people and coached dozens of students on maintaining a neutral expression while asking pointed questions and probing for contradictions. This role was a familiar one; just the setting would be new. After pulling a few strings, I scheduled half an hour with the deputy secretary of Centers for Disease Control, which has an office in the nation's capital. The red-eye flight from Oakland got me to DC early in the morning. After a shower and change of clothes at one of the airport's pay-as-you-go red carpet clubs, I was ready to beard the dragon in his den.

A secretary buzzed me in to a very well appointed, understated office, much sleeker than mine. My contact, a middle-aged white man, looked just like a hundred other administrators, well fed and well groomed. Lightning-fast pleasantries made me aware that, in this city, face time is a commodity hoarded as carefully as gold. His expression was a study in polite alertness as we went through the obvious agenda: who was I, what brought me here, what could he do for me, etc. With my best unexpressive bland face on, I observed his posture, gestures, face, and voice. He was giving nothing away. If this was the mask of a health administrator, I'd hate to interview the director of a spy agency.

I complimented him on how the agency had handled SARS and segued into avian flu. This was a topic to grip the heart of any health official. By now I knew enough about animals that I could with some fluency talk about crossing the species barrier, disease vectors, and so on. Suavely he reassured me that everything possible was being done about smuggling of wild animals.

"But what about funding?" I asked. "I presume avian flu is your top priority and gets the lion's share of your budget."

"For now, yes, the part of the budget for new threats. But we're not neglecting our other priorities." A boringly correct answer. I proceeded, "As I mentioned in my email, I'm concerned about other diseases crossing the species barriers. AIDS, of course, is the prime example. West Nile Virus…"

"Remind me of your interest in this?" he asked politely. "You're not on the medical side, I presume?"

"No, the behavioral side. Identifying the human vectors. Specifically, smugglers. Don Amberg of NIH in San Francisco is in on it."

I'd decided to drop that name. Don didn't know I was here but I doubted this bureaucrat would check. Why would he? I'd only requested half an hour and wasn't asking for any big favors.

"Ah, smuggling," he said as if it were an old friend. I could see the wheels turning. He became more animated and his risorius muscle relaxed. I saw that he was relieved I hadn't gone in another direction. There was some kind of worry he could now set aside.

"Yes," he went on smoothly, "We are aware of dangers to human health from exotics being brought in." He waited.

"Good. My piece of the puzzle is to identify the receivers, if you will. We're wondering what the budget is for this sector."

"I couldn't tell you without looking it up," was his answer. I was silent. Here was the stalemate I had been afraid of. If I was in on such an important project, how come I didn't know the budget? Shamelessly I improvised.

"We have some ideas for new approaches and are hoping there is more available than we've been told. Frankly, it's pretty difficult trying to get figures."

Pause. He would have to abandon his urbane pose if he declined to look it up.

"Just a moment." Good. I'd succeeded in calling his bluff. "Would you excuse me?" and he left the room. I looked around. It was rather antiseptic, as if he hadn't been installed there for long. I wondered how much of a revolving door this job was.

"Here it is," he said, plopping down on his chair and opening a folder. "For the next fiscal year, we have budgeted almost twelve million dollars to support stopping the exotic trade. Rough figures, of course. Some of that goes to administration."

"Oh, thank you," I said. We could use twice that much, but it was something. I could tell Anne and Norm that there really was money available. How did I know he was telling the truth? His forehead hadn't wrinkled once when he read me the numbers. His voice was steady, giving off no deception vibrations. To cover my tracks and use up the rest of my half hour, I asked some more questions about the twelve million dollars and about his role in the agency. I murmured a polite goodbye and left. No doubt he had forgotten the entire interchange before the highly polished mahogany door whispered shut behind me.

As a reward for all this unpaid sleuthing, I treated myself to a few hours of museum goggling. The Natural History Museum had an exhibit on the Ice Man, that ancient herdsman who had died high in the Alps 5,000 years ago and had lain frozen in a glacier until discovered twenty years ago. I was eager to see him, so I toddled along the Mall and went in. The Ice Man was shorter than I'd expected, about my height. I could have looked him in the eye if I'd encountered him in his Alpine homeland. Of course, this was only a model; the actual body is in a special refrigerated museum in Italy. His gear was fascinating. He and his tribe had done amazing things with the materials at their disposal. His cloak was made of reeds and he had an impressive backpack made of branches and fibers. His grass-lined boots were a respectable exhibition of leathercraft and he even had a modest first-aid kit –

researchers have determined that some of the plants he carried in a little pouch had medicinal qualities.

Imagining the lives of Ice Man and his people, I supposed that their guideline for solving problems was: use the materials at hand. They would be experts at noticing the rocks and trees and bushes around them, turning them to use, adding little improvements as the generations passed. Maybe even children devised some inventions that the adults then adopted. Use what's around you; watch the children. I made a mental note to pick the brain of someone in the paleontology department about this. What else did the kids invent? I've often thought that myths and religions were invented because children learned to ask "Why?"

Ice Man had been shot in the back – an arrowhead is still lodged in his shoulder blade. What kind of danger had he run from? Did he die from hostility within his own clan or from conflict with another clan? Could he have identified a traitor or an enemy if he had had my skills at detecting deception? I imagined him guarding his sheep, leading them up the mountain when someone sneaked up on him and shot him with that flint-headed arrow.

I stayed in the museum until they kicked me out. As usual, I was the last one to leave when the guards wanted to close up and go home. Impatiently, two of them rooted me out and shoveled me toward the exit. In each room we passed through, more guards fell in behind us until a whole phalanx of them followed me, their heels clicking on the hard floor. I felt like a drum major leading a marching band.

But I'd learned one thing from Ice Man: People have been killing each other for five thousand years. Nothing has changed.

~ ⁓

Next day I flew back to San Francisco. Because of the time difference, I arrived early enough to hold another powwow immediately. Anne and Norm were waiting for me at his office. After helping ourselves to tea, we settled around the table and I gave them the headline. "They're not lying. The money is there."

Norm was skeptical. "How can you be sure? They tell lies all the time. Politicians make promises depending on which city they're in."

I was exasperated. "Well, I can't guarantee it. Why did you tell me to listen to my Sacramento spies and go there if you weren't going to believe me? Besides, this wasn't a politician but an agency man. A health agency," I added virtuously. Norm snorted. Anne tried to smooth it over, but Norm continued fretting:

"Besides, there might be a change of administration. Or a new mid-level manager might be assigned and dedicate the money to…"

"And a meteor might hit tomorrow. Do you want to hear this, or not?"

Norm stopped pacing and plopped into a chair. I felt sympathetic. "I have a feeling these are the questions you have to ask yourself every day. Am I right?" Norm nodded resignedly and started flipping rubber bands across the room. Anne and I exchanged glances, glad we were not in his shoes.

"Some day I'm going to write a book about running a nonprofit," Norm sighed. "It'll be called *The Politics of Higher Begging*." We drank coffee and talking about our travels. Norm promised to take me to Palau, a Pacific island nation with fabulous diving. He cheered up after remembering the beauty of that faraway garden spot and was ready to hear my news.

"As I was saying, I think the guy was telling the truth," I said.

"Unless the bean counters lied to him," Norm said. Couldn't help himself.

"I tested that. I made small talk when I introduced myself and asked where he fit in the agency hierarchy. I'd already checked the organizational chart, of course."

"How did you do that?" Anne wanted to know.

"Friends in high places."

"You sly thing," Norm said teasingly. "You're not as gormless as you think you are."

"Then I griped a little about faculty politics, how they never tell us the truth about budgets, blah blah blah…"

"They don't?" Anne exclaimed in mock horror.

"…just to watch his orbicularis oculi muscles. Did you know you have three sphincters in your face?" I threw in the technical terms to squelch their skepticism. Any one of my students would have accepted my assessment of the bureaucrat without question. "He showed no suspicion of me. Ten minutes later I mentioned his boss again, just to check the same question in a different context, listening for inconsistencies. There weren't any. Either he was telling the truth or he remembered what he had said the first time. Also, I probed for distrust. Dislike and distrust are some of the most important emotions to detect, which you can do if you know about micro-expressions."

"*You* can detect them," sighed Anne. Norm had started practicing facial expressions, grimacing like Calvin frowning at Hobbes. I plowed on.

"The phone rang while I was there and his expression didn't..."

"Did you say I have sphincters in my face?" interrupted Norm.

"I thought you'd never ask. A sphincter is any circular muscle that can contract and close an opening or a tube. You actually have a total of six. Six major ones, that is. Three in the face."

"Mouth, ok. Gross, and I'll try to forget it as soon as possible. What are the other two?"

"Guess." Silence. "Eyelids. They're part of a circle of fine muscles around your eyes. That's why gunk that gets in your eye eventually ends up by the bridge of your nose, where you can get it out. Slightly eccentric circular motion of the orbicularis oculi. Neat, huh? So anyway, this official gave no signs of deception. Of course, to be sure I'd have to run a slow-motion tape to confirm the micro-expressions, but I'm fairly good at observable cues."

"Ok," said Norm mischievously, "Sez you. If you're so smart, what was I thinking when you said the feds had the money?"

"Surprise first, then hope, then doubt. But that was easy. Let me show you a harder one." I paused to think of a suitably unlikely cue to offer. "Winning the lottery," I said and watched him closely. "You just felt excitement, then scorn, then envy."

"Wow," Anne said.

"No way!" he exclaimed. "Scorn, for sure, and envy, but never excitement. I don't play the lottery. I don't believe in it."

"That's what you think! You've thought about it every time you see that billboard by the freeway." Norm blushed. He knew the billboard I meant, the one that tells you how big the jackpot is each week. I went on, "Half our true thoughts and reactions are fleeting, or unconscious, or both." It's hard to catch the fastest micro-expressions with the naked eye, but you can learn to do it. "And besides, we fool ourselves all the time. Think back. I said, 'winning the lottery.' What do you think about winning?"

"Silly adolescent ambition. Ball games. Slow steady work is better."

"Actually, I'd say you had a flash of interest first. Like, maybe you have hopes of winning *your* game – saving a million acres of rainforest, or whatever your metric is – but you've had to squelch it."

Norm looked thoughtful. "Egad, I'd better be careful around you."

"Too late. So anyway, I tested the CDC official three or four times, embedded in conversation, of course."

"But if the feds are as devious as you think…" Anne objected.

"As *I* think," interpolated Norm.

"…he may have fooled even you," Anne finished disconsolately.

"No." I said firmly. On the flight home I had replayed the interview in my mind a dozen times. I take mental pictures – and mental movies, too. They're not as reliable as videos for analyzing, but good enough for simpler evaluations. "Now," I concluded, "You could be right, someone's feeding him false figures. That I can't control for. But he was being truthful to me. So I think we should go ahead. Maybe we can finally put a dent in animal smuggling."

They looked at me with respect. Maybe they'd seen me as one more well-meaning amateur who was good for commiserating over extinctions, but not much use in actually stopping the slaughter.

"Gee, you're good," Anne said admiringly. "You could make a fortune finding out if people in the middle of a bitter divorce are squirreling away the cash." We laughed and dreamed up a few more lucrative ways to use my skill. Even Norm, the bruised warrior, permitted himself a little hope and we switched to dreaming up ways to spend the money, if we had the spending of it.

So the upshot of my trip was to find that smuggling of endangered species has finally gotten on the priority list of a few people in Washington, and a little money was being allocated. Randy and Melissa and Don and Gary would be glad – and impressed that I had taken the trouble to go pester the dragon. I made a mental note to call them and accept the gig.

But this was just a beginning. The Fish and Wildlife Service says (publicly anyway) that the laws are being enforced, pointing to the new officers they hired a few years ago. But a Yale study says that CITES is massively underfunded and can't even properly monitor the legal trade, let alone the black market. Bottom line: there are more resources than before, but still just a drop in the bucket. For now we'd have to be satisfied with this equivocal state of affairs. We toasted ourselves and went home.

It was strange, having two masters, I thought while weaving through traffic. Does this make me a double agent? How can I compartmentalize what I know and not let the government people know about some of the plans I was making with Anne and Norm? I recalled something Mark Twain said: "Always tell the truth. There's less to remember." This adventure was going to tax my memory. I hoped I wouldn't slip up.

⁓ ❧

The task force welcomed me to their midst. At my first meeting as a proper member, Randy assigned me to investigate the entertainment industry. They had heard of an animal trainer who was known for harsh methods. The chimps this man controlled weren't used in movies – Hollywood tries to maintain a good image on animal handling – but in commercials. Since animal rights groups regularly picketed his operation, he wasn't surprised to be confronted again. What he didn't know was that the Customs agent's silent sidekick (me) was willing and able to nail him for perjury about where he got his animals.

"Ok, Julie, here's the guy we're going to investigate. Not him, his business." Randy spun around in his chair and called up a video on his computer. It was an advertisement for a restaurant chain. A chimpanzee dressed in child's clothing toddled into the fast-food restaurant holding the hand of a human adult. The chimp looked pensively at the overhead menu and up toward the human's face, grinned, and was finally seen chowing down a french fry.

"Happy chimp, eh?" he said, and gave me a sarcastic scowl. "I don't think so. The trainer who rehearsed this little saga has been investigated twice for cruelty. It's time for us to go in."

"Yeah, but what's our pretext?"

"Don't need one. Just state our business: Where'd you get your chimps?"

I nodded and asked, "Who else is going?"

"I am. Wouldn't miss it. Besides, I like watching you in action." I blushed and changed the subject.

"Who is this guy?"

"Gene Hanson. His place is in Glendora, handy to L.A. We'll fly down on Tuesday."

On a hunch, I did a little extra-curricular snooping and found some animal training films our target had made that had been confiscated by HSUS. It was sickening to watch his cold-blooded lecture on how to break an animal's spirit. He even bragged about how fast he could do it. I played these tapes a few times until I knew his face well.

As Randy and I drove from the Palm Springs airport to Glendora, we went over our plan. He would ask the questions and I would, as usual, gauge the honesty of Hanson's responses. "Be sure to find a reason to get him moving around," I reminded him. "Sometimes you can catch people off guard if they're not planted behind their desks."

Hanson wasn't happy to see us; that was obvious from his expression. Grudgingly he let us into his office, which was in a trailer behind a barn. He hadn't bothered to hide the implements of his trade – a whip, a muzzle, and some other leather gear lay in the corner. Hanson was about forty, heavily tanned, with deep scowl lines around his eyes and mouth, and wiry of build. I could just see him dragging animals around and dominating the hell out of them.

"So what is it this time?" he said, staring at us. He made no effort to mask his hostility. Even his previous investigations for cruelty were on the table. He almost dared us to pick a fight.

"We're not here to bother you about how you do your work," Randy began smoothly. Hanson relaxed fractionally. "I'm sure it's harder than it looks to the untrained eye." I could see Hanson didn't totally buy this fake camaraderie. He waited.

"As I said on the phone, we have to check the titles to your exotic animals. Probably just a formality."

Just then a young man peered in through the half-open door. "Boss, what should I do about Coco? He's sick again."

The micro-expression on Hanson's face confirmed every suspicion: a fleeting glare of rage, quickly transformed into a calm stare. "Just give him the medicine like I told you," he said in that deliberately slow, distinct tone you take when you're letting the other person know you're smothering your anger.

The young man's face was equally revealing – sudden fright superimposed on longstanding anxiety. "Okay, okay," he said hastily and backed out the door.

"The paperwork?" reminded Randy politely.

"Waste of time. I get 'em from NIRS." This acronym was new to me but I didn't let on. Randy fielded this one.

"Good, good. Sorry, but we have to see the papers."

Hanson finally lumbered to his feet and went into a back room. I looked around, hoping to find incriminating evidence.

"Here," barked Hanson as he reentered and threw down a file. "Satisfied?"

"Thank you," said Randy evenly and opened the file. "This will take a few minutes. Feel free to go about your duties. We'll let you know when we're done."

Hanson didn't even reply but sat in his chair with his head tilted back. I've seen that before. Their downward gaze gives the impression that they're taller than you are even when they're sitting down.

Randy called his bluff, reading the papers slowly and carefully. I got ready.

"This one, the one you call Benny. How long have you had him?"

"Two years. Says so right there on the papers." He was not faking this answer.

"Did you pick him up at NIRS or have him shipped?"

"Shipped. Takes too much time to drive all that way and back." Randy posed a few more questions. Much as I hated to admit it, Hanson seemed to be telling the truth.

"I'd love to see where they live," I said conversationally. I wanted to budge Hanson from his fortress and see him moving and talking. At the very least, prod him into giving off more clues. No luck. Randy placed the file on his desk.

"You done?" the obnoxious animal trainer grunted, and showed us to the door.

Driving back to the airport, Randy and I sat in silence for half an hour. It was infuriating – there was nothing we could do. It's perfectly legal to verbally intimidate your staff and dominate animals under the guise of "discipline." Finally I said, "I bet he beats his wife. Did you see the wedding ring? Let's nail him on domestic violence. It's the least we can do."

Randy sighed.

"I'm serious," I went on. "I'll get my police pals to check out his record at the local cop shop."

"That's irrelevant."

"No, it's not. I thought I already told you that people who abuse animals are usually just practicing. Later they graduate and abuse people." My voice was antagonistic; I was taking out my frustration on Randy. I sighed and said, "Sorry. I just hate not being able to do anything."

"Don't you see that all the time in your work?" he wondered.

I growled under my breath. "Not really. Most of my time is spent on research and teaching. The violence feels more distant when you're describing a famous case ten years old. My officer friends call me on hot cases, sure, but this is different somehow."

Quietly I fantasized following up on Hanson. I could do the domestic violence check, grill the clients who paid for the ads he made, get the names of technicians who were on the set when they shot the commercials... Give up, I finally told myself. I have too many other jobs to do.

Now I understood why, on the day we first met, Randy had been so burned out.

After this success, the task force sent me on a series of verbal ambushes of other animal trainers. I caught a few and wished my assignment extended to throwing in jail the ones who didn't have illegal animals but who were cruel to their legal ones. After four weeks of this, I had scratched my itch to reel in the villains, at least for the time being. Half my summer break was over and I was longing to get out in the field. Not just my professional field of catching liars, but the outdoor field of savannahs, wild lions, and free flocks of birds.

VIII

So I went to Africa.

I hadn't taken a proper vacation in three years. The trip to Tucson had whetted my appetite and my passport was current. Anne said that one of the best places to study primates was Uganda, because it hasn't been touristified – you are actually allowed to get out of the van. Anne was coming, too. She had been straining at the leash and my project gave her a golden excuse to combine her knowledge with her passion.

Before locking up my office at the university, I notified my advanced students, for whom there is no such thing as a semester break, that I would be away for a few weeks. I ran into Jiang Li in the hallway; when she asked my plans for the summer, I said vaguely, "I'm going to London," which was true enough, as far as it went, since London was the stopover en route to Entebbe. Now look… I'm being deceptive toward my colleagues. Most of them don't know I'm taking this trip and the ones who do don't know the real destination. For some reason, I didn't want to say much about it. Something told me that I needed to learn secrecy. Maintaining boundaries, Carl would call it. Since he wasn't part of the university, I could tell him what I was really doing. Terry would take care of Scalawag and Gambado and bring in the mail.

Uganda is in east Africa near the equator. Thank goodness Anne would be there to open doors. She would take me to the best places and introduce me to a ranger who used to be a poacher. She had fallen into conversation with him on her last trip and sent him money to replace his worn and patched ranger uniform. She also told me how to find a doctor of tropical medicine, what shots to get, and which over-the-counter supplies to bring. At a store she recommended, I bought trousers with zip-off legs and a jacket with a dozen pockets and zip-off sleeves. I'm not a camera nut, but this outfit reminded me of famous field photographers who looked like lumpy walking department stores, pockets bulging with equipment and supplies. Once bundled up, I practically needed a map to show what stuff I'd put in which pocket. Every time I wanted a kleenex I had to frisk myself.

At the airport, Anne was a mixture of attention to immediate detail, excited descriptions of what we would see, and warnings. I imagined she had been equally vocal when bidding her husband goodbye, firing off reminders about the children's sporting events and dental appointments. She talked about her contacts in Uganda, who would be thrilled to see her again. After all, she had been sending them money and provisions for years. We were carrying medical supplies (some of them not quite legit for us non-physicians to have) and planning to leave behind most of our clothes on the last day before boarding the return flight. Our castoffs would be welcome.

I brought myself back to what she was saying. "And don't forget, Ezekiel has only been a ranger for a year.

Watch what you say about poachers. His cousins might still be doing it. Have you got the gear?" I was carrying some gadgets wildlife defenders couldn't get easily in Africa – GPS units, walkie-talkies, laser pointers, and so on. We were going to donate them to help the rangers communicate with each other, point to the smaller animals amid the dense foliage, and report to headquarters where the poachers were.

At security, I observed the inspection staff with professional interest. They had just a few seconds to check out each passenger while the bags went through the see-through machines. I noticed that there wasn't total consistency in procedure from one inspector to the next. Some looked closely at faces, while others focused more on the bags. I made a mental note to ask Randy about this.

The flight from San Francisco to London took eleven hours, so I had abundant time to read more about the exotic animal trade and learn a few words of Swahili. One of my books said that Swahili is an ancient language, but another called it a compound of Arabic and Bantu, with a dash of Persian. Everyone knows one word of Swahili: safari, which simply means "journey." Rafiki means "friend." Hatari is "danger."

Muttering quietly to myself, I practiced saying, "How are you?" "U hali gani?" Very well, thank you, is "Nzuri sana" and fine is "Sijambo." And you? "Na wewe, hujambo?"

My fellow passengers were sleeping. The plane hummed and droned as we flew over Canada and Greenland. After some fitful sleep, I awoke and looked out the window. We were nearing the English coast. The sparkling reflection of the sun on the water reminded me how small human beings are. I searched my Coat of Many Pockets and made sure my passport was handy.

Anne woke up and stretched. "I wish we had time to see London," she sighed. All we saw of England was the airport. People in motion, people sitting in rows of chairs waiting. I wished this airport had those little cubbyholes you can rent in Japan to take a nap in during long layovers – bed-sized boxes with blankets and televisions, stacked in rows and columns like a hatchery for voyagers. Finally we boarded the flight to Uganda on British Airways, which still has routes around the globe, last remnants of empire.

Once in the air again, I pumped Anne for information. She was going to introduce me to some rangers. I was wary when I remembered that most of them had previously been poachers. It was rather like drug dealers becoming narcs, I thought, or foxes hired to guard the henhouse. Anne firmly enlightened me.

"They're starving over there. I won't bore you with the history – colonials taking the land, modern medicine saving more babies, modern politics keeping birth control from women who need it… but face it, there are a lot of hungry people. A man can earn a year's salary in a week by helping a visitor shoot a gorilla or leopard or elephant. Ivory has been contraband for years – remember a few years ago when the president of Kenya burned a huge pile of it to show they were serious? But still the poaching goes on."

"I thought ivory was legal again."

Anne sighed. "There's supposed to be a quota. Fat chance. Not all the countries have quotas, and how can you prove where any one item is from? DNA testing is expensive, even if you can get a place of origin for your sample. There's a forensic wildlife lab in Oregon, but they're swamped. Anyway, we're glad when we can give local guys some work so they have an alternative to poaching. They're in danger, though. There's never enough equipment and the smugglers outspend us ten to one. So please respect them. They're risking their lives."

This was sobering. I resolved to sponsor one of them when I got back home. Twenty bucks to buy him a uniform, ten bucks to get decent rubber boots for traipsing through dripping wet vegetation – this would be the best birthday present I ever gave myself.

At Entebbe, we were soon speeding through the city in a dilapidated car piloted by a talkative driver who seemed more interested in finding out our plans than watching the road. Finally we arrived at the Uganda Wildlife Education Center, where orphaned animals rescued from the poachers were brought. The director, a Ugandan veterinarian, welcomed Anne enthusiastically and showed us around, proudly pointing out the improvements that had been made since her last visit. Anne called him Dr. Andrew and praised the improvements he had made. I didn't catch his last name. Then we set out for the chimp sanctuary on a small island in Lake Victoria, just outside Entebbe. Dr. Andrew accompanied us to the dock, where we got onto a small launch and pulled out into Lake Victoria for the twenty-minute ride to Ngamba Island. A small cluster of cement block buildings sat near the dock. Behind them a ten-foot fence stretched across to enclose the little sector that had been designated for human visitors.

Thanks to Anne's special relationship with Dr. Andrew, we were allowed behind the scenes, onto the preserve itself. There were almost forty chimps of all ages living there. They had been found and rescued separately, so they did not form the kind of family or troop that chimps naturally live in. So, Dr. Andrew told us, his first task had been to see if these strangers could live together. I wasn't listening very well to his enthusiastic impromptu lecture – too busy watching the chimps. We had arrived just as their morning food was being set out. About two dozen chimps were in sight and others arrived from the woods in a hurry as we watched. The biggest ones shouldered their way to the front and seized the best bits, and a certain amount of frenzied negotiating went on among the rest, like a church rummage sale. Some of them sat in small groups of two or three as they peeled their bananas or munched what looked like small meatballs.

"Monkey chow," said Anne, reading my question.

"The island isn't big enough to provide enough fruiting trees for all the chimps we're expecting," Dr.

Andrew explained. "This island has been a sanctuary only eight years, you know, so we have supplies shipped over from our headquarters in Entebbe." He continued, "Chimps mostly eat leaves, nuts, fruit, and so on, so monkey chow is made to contain the same nutrients. Sometimes in the wild they capture colobus monkey infants and eat them. Baboon infants, too. I know," he said, seeing me wince, "not pleasant, eh? But that's one more thing we share with them. Meat eating." I tried not to think about this and turned to look at the animals. Finished with their meal, they were taking up new activities. Some sat in pairs grooming each other, some foraged for leftover bits of food, and the youngest ones (or at least the smallest) chased each other around a tree trunk.

I suddenly felt grateful to be standing upright. Chimps always seemed to be hunched over.

"Tell me how they came to you," I asked Dr. Andrew, wanting to know more about the poachers.

"Well, you know about the roads, right? Oh." He backed up to start at the beginning. "Well, mining and timber companies are building roads back into parts of African countries so they can get at the trees and ore. This little guy," he patted a small chimp affectionately, "lost his mother when the guys building the roads killed her for meat. Not for themselves – they moonlight by bringing chimp and monkey carcasses back into town. Also pythons, duikers (that's a kind of deer), and pangolins."

Anne interjected, "Bushmeat. It's a whole market."

Dr. Andrew continued, "The babies might be saved for pets, either here or abroad."

I felt sick.

"For every mile of new road, a dozen chimp babies are orphaned. As far as we know. Maybe more. Plus monkeys, and the animals run over by the trucks."

"How…" I couldn't go on.

"Eight thousand chimps a year are killed for bushmeat. For every orphan we rescue, we figure ten others die."

So this was why chimps are endangered. This is how a species can go extinct. I wondered if this traffic was like most commodities trades, from food to coffee to opium – the people who did the dirty work got most of the danger and least of the money, and the people who got the money didn't care how many people or animals got hurt or killed. What kind of people was I trying to detect, how ruthless were they, and what kinds of deception would they use? Simple lying and denying, or the smooth persuasive double talk of stockbrokers and politicians? Dr. Andrew nodded goodbye and walked over to one of his assistants to take up the next in his endless round of tasks.

We stayed at the sanctuary two more hours. The chimps had worn narrow paths through the jungle. Imitating Anne, I picked up and carried a youngster. She curled comfortably into my arms and looked around, taking me for granted. She must be recovering well from the trauma of her capture. The forest was dense and I could see only a few yards ahead, but it was easy to follow Anne and the chimps ahead of me.

Suddenly, I spotted a huge spider the size of my open hand sitting still in a web four feet across, the distance from a tree on one side of the path to a tree on the other. Uh oh. Maybe I could duck it. Awkwardly carrying my new friend, I crouched down and crept underneath. Anne had assured me that there were no venomous spiders here, but I shuddered anyway. Around the next corner was another big spider across the path. Again I crouched, but this time happened to look up as I slithered underneath. I almost gagged. Layer after layer of spiders in their webs rose above me. There must have been dozens within a ten-foot radius. I froze.

Decision time. I could cringe from the spiders and retreat to the visitors' area, or I could enjoy a once-in-a-lifetime chance to play with our wild cousins. Anne and the others had vanished in the thick jungle ahead. I gazed at the spiders. They were busy catching their lunch. So what if the nearest one was two feet from my head? I forced myself to look at the webs. The looping threads looked as if they had been dusted with bright yellow pollen. These spiders spun webs of gold. I took a deep breath, hugged my chimp, ducked under the web, and put mouse-sized spiders out of my mind.

When I reached the beach, clusters of chimps were already there. They were picking up stones, lying along logs, and grooming each other. Anne was hugging one of them. I looked more closely, and saw that the chimp was nibbling her eyelashes. These chimps have lovely medium brown eyes. They nibbled our hands and wrists. One picked at my hair for a while, then sprawled in my lap and went to sleep. I caressed her ear, which was as soft as baby's skin. Some of them played along fallen trees. A few crabs moved slowly along the waterline. By noon it was hot. I splashed lake water on my hands and face.

Eventually, it was time to go. I looked up and down the small beach, trying to find the path. Finally I saw it, one footstep wide. After three steps, the lake vanished behind us. Anne told me later that this was the densest rainforest she had ever been in. The old nineteenth-century mighty hunter stories contain a lot of exaggeration, she explained. Usually in a rainforest you can see fifty feet all around. Not here. In this rainforest you really could step behind a tree and never be seen again.

As we hiked back to headquarters, I felt a brush against my knees. An adult chimp passed me to run on ahead. My youngster clung and nestled comfortably against me, nibbling and tugging on my collar, mumbling quietly to herself. A hundred yards from the station, something unexpected happened. One of the adult female chimps, who had been walking ahead of us, fell back in the queue until she was right in front of me. She looked up at the youngster I was carrying and held out her arms. The signal couldn't have been clearer. After a second's selfish pause, I accepted the message and let my little friend down to the ground. The adult turned around and the youngster climbed up on her back, just as she would have done on her mother. The pair ambled comfortably away. I couldn't help smiling. The family groups that Dr. Andrew had dreamed of for these lost strangers were forming as I watched.

~ ❧ ~

That night, I passed the time between dinner and lights out by practicing Swahili.

Let's go is "Twende."

Fine or okay is "Haya."

What do you call this? is "Hii inaitwa nini."

Can you help me? is "Unaweza kunisaidia."

Good morning is "Habari ya asubuhi."

It was a pleasant-sounding language, very different from English, but at least there weren't any tongue-twisting vocalizations. I never forgot my struggle in high school to learn German. My dad wanted me to learn it so my family heritage wouldn't be completely lost in the melting pot. In German, you can string together several words in one endless polysyllabic mumble: Geistesgeschichte (spirit of the times), weltanshauung (worldview), schadenfreude (guilty pleasure in someone else's troubles). Well, at least those actually get used sometimes in the English-speaking world. There are even worse obscure jawbreakers that never make it over the border, such as fortpflanzungsgeschwindigkeit, which means "velocity of propagation." Maybe my contacts at NIH were using it now as they worried about the spread of avian flu viruses. My all-time favorite is Kriegsgefangenerschadigungsgesetz. This means "law to provide compensation for prisoners of war."

I learned this in college and used it on my boyfriend of the time.

"So, you have a history exam coming up?" I asked him innocently. "I hope you've boned up on postwar diplomacy. I hear your professor is very demanding about kriegsgefangenerschadigungsgesetz."

He gave the only possible reply: "Gesundheit!"

Next day Anne took me to Chambura Gorge, home to a small troop of chimps. Chambura Gorge is a rift sunk deep into an otherwise flat plain. I didn't see it until we almost fell in. Paul Bunyan might have just passed by dragging his axe. At a tiny hut, two men in uniform held out their hands for money. Anne said under her breath, "They're legit. In other places the guys at the entrances are not really guards and probably half the money goes to local warlords." Well, whether you called it a national park or extortion, it proved that the animals were worth more alive than dead. People would let them live.

We descended a trail and entered a tiny world a hundred yards below the surrounding plain. After crossing a muddy stream by walking over a fallen log, we spotted a couple of hippos and what I knew by now were black-and-white colobus monkeys. The flowers were huge. I saw a really beautiful one and asked, "What's that one?"

"I don't know," she said casually and kept on walking. At the next stop, I asked, "And what's that one?" To my surprise, she seemed irritated at my interruption. Finally she said, "I'm not very interested in names." She glanced at me. "When you know a name, what have you really learned? That you can repeat some syllables." She shrugged. "I'm more interested in their lives."

That made sense. I'd always thought it was funny that there were diseases with names like "gastritis," which just means "stomach ache" in Latin. The naming fallacy, logicians call it.

This gorge was a perfect place to practice spotting animals in the dense foliage. Chimps are much heavier than the monkeys we saw scampering along the branches. They're easier to spot because they shake branches as they maneuver heavily along them, and they're big enough to make vague dark shadows up in the trees when they are resting. A cascade of leaves falling could mean that a monkey has just scuttled along a branch overhead. They don't always hide. Anne said, "Don't get underneath a monkey or a chimp that's overhead on a branch. They might pee on you, or throw something." I contemplated the message ("Go away!") and wondered if that qualified as animal-to-human communication.

The next day, we went to track gorillas in the Impenetrable Forest near the town of Bwindi. These visits are tightly regulated: once a day for one hour, six tourists with a small party of trackers and guides are allowed to visit the gorillas. The naturalists are very strict about the gorillas' health, too, protecting them from human germs. If you have a cold, you're not allowed to visit them, even if you paid for your very expensive permit months ago. To reach them, you trek for three hours to the remote area of the park where the last of the mountain gorillas live.

Anne and I joined four Australians who had planned this trip two years ago. They were starry-eyed and excitedly making last-minute checks of their cameras and binoculars. This is an all-day event, so food was being brought as well. The mountain gorillas are not confined or controlled in any way. The trackers follow the gorillas each night and radio their location to park headquarters, so the next morning the guides will have a good idea where to start looking for them. At the trailhead, we set out; porters carried our food, water, cameras, and other gear. Crossing a log bridge over a stream, we began hiking over a grassy plain, which gradually led to cultivated areas. Bananas were being grown. I was surprised at the appearance of the banana trees. They were not very tall, maybe ten feet, yet each sported huge bunches of young green bananas that seemed to hang upside down, the curves pointed upward toward the sky. It was hard to believe these modest trunks could carry all that weight, let alone nourish the bananas to make them even larger.

The gently rolling hills were covered by intense green. But the area of cultivation has gradually crept ever more deeply into formerly wild areas, and even the steepest hillsides were planted. The boundaries of the nature preserve were obvious. On one side of a ruler-straight line, there was a lush covering of rainforest. On the other side, the land had been cleared. It looked shaved.

Of course, I was as interested in our guides and trackers as I was in the destination, wondering which ones used to be poachers before this park was created and gave them jobs. They carried machetes and hacked away at the jungle when there wasn't a passable path. Occasionally one would hold a walkie-talkie to his mouth and speak into it quietly. Anne and I used a few Swahili words:

"Habari ya asubuhi!" (good morning).

Suddenly I started. A man carrying a rifle was talking to our guide.

"Don't worry," said Anne soothingly. "They're here to guard us."

"From what? You said gorillas are gentle. You said…"

"They are. It's people we have to worry about. Didn't you hear about the rebels?"

Oh, great. *Now* she tells me. It seems that in 1999 a group of tourists was attacked right here in Bwindi by rebels from the neighboring country of Rwanda who wanted to make a statement about foreign intervention in their country. Some of the visitors were killed. It was politics, not poaching, but it made headlines worldwide. It took years for the tourist trade to recover.

Later, after we had been hiking for several hours, I asked, "Tutafika saa ngapi?" (When do we arrive?). Mistake. I'd forgotten something I'd learned when traveling in Peru: don't ask a question in a foreign language until you've learned the words the person is likely to use in answering. Anne saved the day. She said something that probably meant, "We know only a little Swahili." Smiles and nods in response, and pointing at a wristwatch.

The path climbed gradually up and around the hills. Three hours after crossing the stream, we heard the long-awaited signal. "We've found them!" We put down our packs. Those who had brought cameras got them ready. Leaving our porters behind, we tiptoed closer, following the trackers, who talked quietly into their walkie-talkies or hacked away at the underbrush with their machetes. Then I saw my first mountain gorilla.

It was just a glimpse, a black hairy form up in the tree. We crept around and positioned ourselves to see. Several more shaggy forms appeared. It was a small family group: there were two youngsters, a silverback (alpha male), and two or three adult females. We were so close that I could have tossed them a banana. One adult sat quietly in its tree, looking around and chewing on leaves.

Soon the gorillas moved off, and we quietly followed, the trackers hacking a path for us. The gorillas settled into a little clearing and we were treated to an unobstructed view. One baby climbed a few feet up a tree, while the other rolled around on the ground. The two of them teased each other like any pair of toddlers, poking, chasing and tickling each other. One mother sat nearby feeding, occasionally looking to see what the youngsters were doing. The family watched us, too, looking calmly over at us, then just as calmly returning to their own affairs. The naturalists had prepared them well, habituating them to these brief visits from the strange pale apes with their shiny little boxes that made whirring noises.

Eventually the guides gave us a signal that our hour was over, and we began the long hike back. Anne's eyes were shining. "Did you see when the silverback disciplined the juveniles?" she asked excitedly. "He just pulled one away from the other and kept them apart for a moment." She was assimilating these observations so she could pass them along to her docents and the zoo-going children and their parents.

I too was enthralled. The rare gorillas, the chimps we had played with the day before, our closest relatives in their natural world – *This* was what the project was all about. I redoubled my determination to help the task force protect them.

Anne doesn't enjoy reciting names on command, but she enjoys the sound of them. As we hiked back to the camp, still exuberant from our gorilla encounter, she told me some of her favorites: snakelocks anemone, long-billed scimitar babbler, barking gecko, jeweled frog beetle, aoudad, Malachite kingfisher. My favorite name is for a magnificent New World bird, the resplendent quetzal. There's a stuffed one in San Francisco's science museum. It's tall and iridescent green, with long tail feathers that trail sixteen inches behind its body. In flight it must have been magnificent; resplendent, for sure. I hoped there were still some alive, flying majestically over central Mexico. Not in cardboard tubes.

That night, as we packed in preparation for an early-morning departure, I thought again about people who steadfastly deny the intelligence of animals. Thirty years ago, when Jane Goodall discovered that chimps make tools (stripping twigs to make straight implements to dip into termite mounds), her mentor, the famous paleontologist Louis Leakey, said, "Now we'll either have to redefine human, redefine tool, or include apes as humans." Some people weren't willing to adjust their definitions, and clung ever more desperately to the idea of our specialness. They called it the "discontinuity" between us and the rest of nature. One hilarious example was their response to Goodall's termite-fishing discovery: "Ah, but humans use tools to *make* tools, while chimps just use their hands and teeth." You could almost hear them breathing a sigh of relief when they thought up *that* distinction. When it was incontestably proved that chimpanzees can use sign language and that bonobos (formerly called pygmy chimps) can use computer pictures to communicate, they pooh-poohed the length of primate sentences – they don't contain *grammar*, after all! The skeptics kept upping the ante again to suit the emergency. They reminded me of cult members desperate to protect their illusion.

Our last stop was the Burundi ranger station. The clerk in the tiny souvenir stall said that Ezekiel was out in the bush. We thanked him and walked fifty yards to headquarters, a small building at the border of the national park. Anne chatted in Swahili with the young woman who was on duty there. I looked around at the exhibits. Local children had made signs and cards with animal drawings, just as they do at home. The heat of the day waned. Finally I heard some talking and footsteps, and several men arrived, taking off their hats and tossing them onto the tables. One of them smiled broadly and greeted Anne.

"U hali gani?"

"Nzuri sana," she replied as they shook hands.

"Sijambo."

"Na wewe, hujambo?"

Anne stepped back to admire him. He smiled bashfully and thanked her for his fine uniform. He said it helped a little to convince locals that there really was an effort to stop the killing. The well-armed international smuggling rings, of course, weren't deterred by a thin line of men carrying antiquated rifles, but one had to start somewhere.

"Julie, this is Ezekiel. Ezekiel, my friend Julie," Anne introduced us. We had brought some drinks from the camp we were staying in, which Ezekiel and the other rangers gratefully accepted. They told us about their day. Every morning, they came here, put on their uniforms, and conferred by walkie-talkie with the trackers who followed the gorillas' movements. The trick was to communicate with each other on frequencies that the villains can't eavesdrop on. They changed code words frequently. Some days nothing much happened. They removed a lot of snares, the wire traps set to catch animals. They had a program for buying snares from locals as a way of recruiting an informal cadre of helpers. Of course, they had to make sure that they didn't pay too much, or the hungry people would build snares, or even set them, so they could claim the rewards. A fine balancing act. I hadn't realized that saving animals was so complicated. Every hopeful solution was immediately beset by disadvantages. It was like trying to make peace in the Middle East.

After about an hour, most of the rangers had gone home (after we tactfully left the room so they could change clothes). Ezekiel knew that we wanted to speak to him, and about what. He was solemn and a bit reticent at first. To put him at his ease, I thanked him again for guarding the animals and told him about my pets.

Anne said, "Julie wants to help save animals, too. Her job is to catch the buyers of the animals." Ezekiel looked interested. "Which animals?" he wanted to know. Anne was a good explainer and I began to feel like part of a team with Ezekiel and the other rangers. Suddenly I didn't want to know so much about the lives of poachers. Having seen the muddy villages, the half-clothed children (too many of them), I didn't need any further explanation. But we had come all this way and asked for his time. I couldn't back out now. Maybe I could sign to Anne, "**let's go**." But if we left now, he might think we were rude, and who could blame him? At the very least, it would be ungracious. So I just kept steering the conversation toward techniques, how poachers got their catch to market.

Ezekiel was thirty years old and hoped to go to the university in Entebbe. He knew several people who had done this. The school fees were low, but more than he could earn by herding cattle or growing fruit. When some men came and offered him much money to lead them to game, he agreed. If these people wanted to catch and export some animals alive in cages instead of shooting them, it was no business of his. White people had come hunting in Africa for over a hundred years. It was an old tradition to lead them to the game. It reminded him of the honey-guide birds who lead honey badgers to beehives. The badgers tear open the hives to get the honey, and the birds get the leftovers.

I had a brainstorm, embarrassed I hadn't thought of it before. Instead of collecting information from him for later analysis, like some astute anthropologist, I would simply ask him for advice. Why should the white person be the one to do all the strategizing? As soon as I recovered from my shame at this blunder, I asked, "Ezekiel, if you wanted to talk to the head man who pays others to catch animals, how would you find him?"

Ezekiel perked up. He explained who the smugglers are. It had started locally – hunters arrived from America and Europe and wanted help finding game. I was beginning to hate the word "game." Since Ezekiel and his cousins knew how to find them and had even done a little bushmeat trade on the side, they helped the men. Their satisfied customers told their friends, and like any enterprise with an eager market, it grew. One foreign hunter arrived after the season was over and bullied Ezekiel into breaking the game regulations. Another wanted to hunt animals that were protected by law. When Ezekiel needed the money, which was most of the time, he agreed to help them.

These muzungus (white people) were crude and heartless – the kind of men who wanted gorilla hands to make into ashtrays. Eventually an entrepreneurial muzungu eliminated the haphazard nature of it all and set up a standing organization. Ezekiel didn't know if they smuggled anything else. Maybe, he said, his cousins could start listening to their talk. Even today some white people never believed the locals had any brains, so they talked freely in front of them as if they were furniture. To reach the head smuggler, we would start with good old-fashioned eavesdropping.

To cement our alliance and bring the business portion of the conversation to a close, Anne offered to take pictures of Ezekiel and his family. In a charming mixture of pride and shyness, he led us to his house, a cement block structure with a thatched roof, surrounded by a dirt yard. He called out for his children, and four little ones pelted out the doors, screeching in English, "Hello! Hello!" We had seen this everywhere we went in Uganda – eager kids rushing up to practice their words. Sometimes as our car drove through a hamlet without slowing down, the children would stand by the side of the road, wave, and shout "Hello!" Proudly Ezekiel and his family posed in front of their house, holding a scrawny dog, with a goat and a few chickens in the background. Anne took pictures. She showed them the tiny versions on the viewfinder, which excited the children, and promised to send prints to them, in care of Dr. Andrew at the wildlife center in Entebbe.

There was only one down side to this whole adventure. I couldn't publish a journal article about it.

⸺✎ IX ℰ⸺

Anne had to go back to the U.S. Grateful that I hadn't agreed to teach a class this summer, I stayed in Uganda, promising to send her detailed emails about my discoveries whenever I could get to one of the cybercafes in Entebbe. Ezekiel took charge of me, arranging for me to stay in one of the tented camps for tourists. The tents were quite comfortable – tall square affairs strung over a fixed frame; probably military surplus. We even had hot showers. The camp's staff would heat the water at the kitchen stove. Five-gallon buckets would be tied to a pulley and hoisted up so the water could be poured into a tank installed on the overhead beams in the corner of each tent. Gravity did the rest.

When Ezekiel was on duty, obviously I couldn't go with him, but he kindly took me on private safaris on his days off. He introduced me to local people and must have asked them to look after me, for I always got a friendly greeting when I stopped to buy a drink at the tiny shacks that served as stores.

Ezekiel patiently taught me more tips on how to spot animals. In the trees, get the sun behind them so their silhouette stands out. Notice branches shaking. Keep your eyes on one spot, even though you don't see an animal immediately. This was a familiar trick; as a kid I'd noticed that the best way to find ants in my yard was to stare at one spot on the grass. Almost at once my peripheral vision picked up the movement of any bug in my visual field. Of course, I hadn't known the term "peripheral vision" at the time.

Now I was learning to pay attention to dark blobs in trees. It could be a bird nest or it could be a chimp. Ask yourself, are there large birds in this area? Wait long enough to see if the blob moves. Did it move slowly or quickly? Learn to distinguish the different chatters and screeches. Locate the water sources and wait near them. Know which time of day each species is out and about.

I had neither the authority nor the courage to research poaching by taking part in a hunt, even if I could find one. Apart from my repugnance at the trade itself, horrible visions of being shot or arrested as a poacher danced in my head. But I could lurk around as an innocent tourist and simply collect Ezekiel's descriptions of the men he or his cousins met. This time, at Anne's urging, he would ask his cousins to remember what language the hunters were speaking, what kind of crates they brought, and how many animals they took.

One day about two weeks after Anne left, I asked Ezekiel, "Do you ever feel tempted to let people escape? I mean, the people you catch trying to take animals?"

"Oh, sure," he said in his languid way. "My job is protect animals. If peoples run away, okay by me."

This Dogberry approach was very sensible for Ezekiel and the other rangers. They had enough to do, removing snares and putting up the equivalent of speed bumps in the path of the animal smugglers. They shouldn't have to die in the bargain.

But I did have an itch for justice. Wouldn't you just love to catch these people and put them behind bars? Let them see what it's like to be caged. I was surprised by the strength of my anger. But, as Anne had made me repeat before she left, we were not there to catch people but to get information. The experts would take the next step. Amateur vigilantes need not apply. So I occupied myself by spending time with each new batch of tourists. They came in groups large and small from Australia, Germany, Brazil, and Japan (some of the greatest primatologists are Japanese). Since I had already been to the places they would most likely want to go – Bwindi, Chambura, Mountains of the Moon – I was able to give basic trail advice and recommendations about where to eat and what time of day was best for spotting which animals. It felt odd being seen as an old-timer in a country I barely knew.

All told, I stayed nearly a month in Uganda. Whenever there wasn't a full complement of six visitors for a gorilla trek, I cadged the extra ticket for myself. They were much cheaper at the last minute. I even briefly went over the border into Tanzania to visit Gombe, where Jane Goodall made her discoveries, but it made me nervous to remember the Rwanda civil war when neighbor killed neighbor. A few miles away in Congo, killing was still going on. Even Uganda wasn't immune – Anne had sternly warned me against going into the northern part of the country, where a local religious fanatic, Joseph Kony, was kidnapping children – *twelve thousand* of them so far – and turning them into his private army of killers.

I wasn't sure if it made me feel better or worse that humans slaughter each other as much as they slaughter animals. If Mom had known how close I was to the religious fanatic and his kid army, she would have fainted. But it's odd: here and now, the visible houses and trees and paths were so normal, so comfortable. Danger seemed abstract and far away. Before I moved to California, the threat of earthquakes made it seem an insane place to live. But once I got there, each day's commonsense reality pushed aside thoughts of future danger. Still, I stuck sensibly close by Ezekiel and the other people Anne had introduced me to.

Meanwhile, Ezekiel was quietly gathering information. His cousins were willing to help us, to watch and listen with more attention than before and to meet Ezekiel every week to tell him what animals they'd collected. One hunter they especially disliked. He was always hurrying them and calling them cowards when they said they had to proceed carefully because of hippos or lions in the area. He usually wanted chimps, they told Ezekiel, but he would also take monkeys. Once they saw him throw a crate at a man who didn't move fast enough. Brutal treatment of a man… and of the monkey inside the crate.

This lout was an American, they were sure. His name was "Riceler" or something like it. He was arrogant to everyone; his favorite insult was "ignorant." I made Ezekiel repeat the man's name several times. It sounded vaguely familiar.

One evening, as we sat in the camp chairs in front of my tent, I decided to learn more about Ezekiel and get an answer to one of my original questions. We were drinking some of the local beer, which is quite good after a hot day on the trail, and listening to the villagers singing in the distance. "What made you decide to become a ranger?" I asked finally. He looked at the floor and consulted an inner conscience. After a moment he said, "Two years ago. Last time I went on safari with animal takers. White man was in big hurry. Maybe the same man my cousins talk about today. Not enough chimps any more in Bwindi. Told us to go into the north. Too far north. Close to Kony. Kony's slaves were there, the boys with guns. They do not like people to come near their place. My friend Ndoko was shot."

I was sorry I'd asked. I felt like an intruder. "My second son was born. I see too many sons without fathers." A pause lengthened. I respected his foresight and was glad he had gotten out of the trade, for whatever reason. But I was puzzled. Wasn't he just exchanging one danger for another? Anne had impressed on me how dangerous his job was. There was more to this story, but I would probably never know it all.

One day when we were sitting in the little cement block building that served as the town's gathering place, Ezekiel introduced me to Ndoko, who was lame now and couldn't work as a ranger. All over northern Uganda there were men and women living with mutilations after Kony raided their villages and ordered his army to take the children and hack off the hands and limbs of the adults who tried to stop them. It was humbling to think that Ndoko could count himself lucky to have both legs.

Infuriated by this senseless brutality, I started ranting about closed minds and people who think they have The Answer and cram it down your throat or kill you if you disagree. Ezekiel worriedly tried to shush me until he realized I was talking about American cults. "It's true," I said aggressively, "They rope in young people and take their money and sexually exploit them and…"

Everyone in the little market stopped talking. Ndoko looked at the floor. Everyone in the room was listening. I sat in a surly mood and gulped down my drink. One person in the corner looked sad and slipped away. After the evening was over and we were walking back to camp, Ezekiel told me the man had moved here from northern Uganda and had probably seen many atrocities

"Oh, no," I said, "How awful of me to bring it up like that. Can I make it up to him? You do it – go visit him and tell him I'm sorry." Ezekiel promised he would. In doing so, he found out more. The man's grandson had been forced into Kony's army. In one of its occasional forays against the rebels, the real Ugandan army had captured the group the boy was in and brought him safely home. He had been a captive soldier for three months. His family was torn between joy at his return and fear at what he might have become. But with some counseling from both the village elder and the nearest Anglican mission, he settled back into his old life, horsing around with the other twelve-year-old boys. Then one afternoon without provocation he walked over and killed his eleven-year-old sister.

I groaned inwardly. How many thousands of children had been shanghaied and turned into killers just like this one? How could this small country cope with such a lingering time bomb? How many decades would it take for the scars to heal? And Kony hadn't even been stopped yet. His expansion had slowed, but he still carried out raids. Whole villages were emptied every night as the villagers fled to a town big enough to shelter them. They were called "night commuters."

Once I was invited to the home of the man in charge of the tourist tickets. He had gotten used to seeing me stroll up to the office looking hopeful. Whenever I was unlucky, I would sigh and hang around talking to him as the six fortunate trekkers gathered their gear and walked off down the trail with their little posse of guides and armed guards. He was an incurable extrovert and knew everyone in Bwindi. After I had been there two weeks, he invited me to his home to join a celebration for the birth of his first grandchild. There were about twenty people there, some inside the small main room and some spilling out onto the front entry. They were polite and friendly. The ones who could speak English were happy to practice their skill on me. The conversation turned to the different people who came there from all over the world. To one man the topic was not interesting. He said with a shrug, "Foreigners come here since my grandfather heard about them from his grandfather."

I waited politely, though I was burning to ask, "Which foreigners were worse – the empire builders or the missionaries?" To lead up to my question, I told them more about the cults in my country, how religious manipulators can be subtler and more devious than men with guns. Some of the local teachers spoke English well and translated for the rest. There was an echo to my monologue, as my words trotted after me in another language.

"In America," I explained, "they lure you with sweet promises – you'll be loved, you'll go to heaven, you'll be special in God's eyes." I told them how the recruiters then isolate their victims, overworking them and depriving them of sleep and food, preventing them from having any contact with their families and the outer world. I explained brainwashing, how this deprivation and the constant preaching made the recruits doubt their own senses, how the cult's creed was pushed as the Truth that explained all their disappointments until finally the exhausted people gave in. This gave them a sense of relief so strong it fed them for years.

The Ugandans could hardly believe people would willingly remain in prisons without walls. I tried to say how beliefs can be twisted and sealed against reality, how anyone who doubted was blamed as a sinner. I told stories about various cults that had predicted the end of the world, "So you see," I concluded, "people's minds can be taken prisoner even if their bodies walk free."

Then I remembered the grandfather who had moved here from the north. Furtively I peeked around to see if he was present. I was sorry I had upset them just to relieve my anger. I tried to explain that some people do escape.

"Some people do get out. Their doubts finally grow too big or they can't stand seeing their young daughters being taken into the leader's bed or sometimes they just run out of money to give."

"Do they just walk away?" someone asked.

"Oh, no. If they actually live with the cult, they have to plan for months. They have to pretend they still believe, but secretly they're thinking ahead, deciding where to go and what they can take with them in one suitcase."

Sadly I added, "It's not always a permanent escape, though. Sometimes people go back to the cult they just escaped from. The world they've been away from for so long just seems too strange." They were looking at me solemnly. I tried not to sound too much like a visiting white blowhard, so I asked respectfully,

"What do your people do when someone has... lost himself?"

Eagerly they told me about their ways, how they held ceremonies and gave the troubled person a talisman and composed a special song for him or her to chant. I nodded. A sensible solution, really. Ritual is powerful, even for supposedly rational people. The doctor's white coat is the vestment of the high priest and an unspoken promise of power. Taking a pill is a ritual. The placebo effect does much of the healing. There have even been experiments with sham surgery, complete with fake incisions, *and it works*. The patients say their knees hurt less afterwards. So I listened with respect as my Uganda friends told me about their ways.

Bwindi is only a few hundred miles from the zone ruled by Kony, yet people here go about their lives, growing bananas and coffee, raising kids and cooking meals. Well, it's the same in the U.S. Inner-city gang wars go on two miles from the suburbs.

I wondered what happened to the rescued boy who killed his sister.

～♪♫～

Three days later Ezekiel came to me with a troubled look on his face. I had been sitting just outside my tent, watching the sunset and listening to the sounds of animals settling down for the night. He walked up slowly and sat on the camp chair next to mine.

"What is it?" I asked. Ezekiel had a naturally solemn countenance which lighted up magically when he smiled, but even for him he looked serious.

"Miss, I hear something today I don't like. In village, I am buying some food when white man comes in. I am wearing my own clothes so he does not know I am ranger. He is very loud man. Abel and Nguri say they have worked for him before. He asked store owner who is the white lady asking so much about rangers and hunters."

This felt weird. I'd realized from the beginning that I'd obviously stand out as one of the few white people who stayed in Bwindi more than a few days, but it gave me an eerie feeling to hear that people were talking about me. Ezekiel looked me in the eyes now. Wordless worry, and not just for me. I was putting him and his fellow rangers in danger, too, asking my questions and drawing attention. Protecting wildlife is dangerous business. In California Judi Bari was bombed for defending the redwoods. Chico Mendes and Dorothy Stang were killed by ranchers in Brazil. Here in Africa, even Richard Leakey, from a venerated family of paleontologists and prominent for his own research, was not safe. His private plane was sabotaged and crashed; he lost his legs. Gorilla defender Dian Fossey was murdered in her camp in the mist. I forced myself to stop remembering the list, and asked Ezekiel, "Is this the same man you told me about, the hostile over-educated jackass who hates everyone?"

Ezekiel nodded. "Then he set his gun on the table and said, 'I don't tolerate being interfered with'." I was impressed that Ezekiel remembered the threat word for word. He added, "There is hatari."

Danger. I must back off to undo the mess I was close to making.

"Ezekiel, thank you. You have done so much for me. I have learned much. It is time for me to go back to U.S. Asante."

Ezekiel seemed glad that I had understood so quickly and was ready to heed his hint. I wondered how often he made quiet negotiations like this. What was his work really like, day in and day out? He nodded and walked back to his home.

The evening, so suddenly to be my last, passed slowly. I wasn't exactly afraid, yet I alerted to sounds I would have ignored before. When the camp's cook was putting away the pots, the familiar sound was reassuring. There was only one other tourist group in the tent camp this night, some Japanese I'd encountered once or twice in the village. I wondered if I could make an impromptu visit to their tent. But I kept delaying, not exactly whistling in the dark and trying to be brave, but just… delaying.

I tried to think what Ezekiel's news meant. I knew people already thought me unusual. On my gorilla trek day, the porters asked to carry my camera and were surprised I didn't have one. The locals probably called me "the lady who doesn't take pictures." Oh, great, another little mannerism that set me apart. My longer-than-usual stay in the tiny village, my lack of a camera, my questions… I had been about as subtle as a chemo patient at a hairdressers' convention.

Ezekiel sent Abel to drive me to Entebbe. That was smart of Ezekiel, not to be seen with me again. I wished I'd had a chance to talk with him more. He was an interesting man. As I'd intended, I folded most of my clothes into a neat pile and gave them to Abel to give to someone in the village. There was no false pride on his part, or need to be thanked on mine. It was simply the natural thing to do.

My plane ticket had been open return, and fortunately I didn't have to wait too long at the airport before a standby seat became available. While waiting, I wandered up and down the craft stalls inside and outside the airport building, buying artisan wood carvings for friends and relatives to bring home in my now-empty suitcases. I still have a pair of earrings I got there.

※

Back home, I greeted Scalawag and Gambado and glanced at the mail. Terry's message read, "I've discovered my new career – geloscopy." She won this round. I needed my biggest dictionary to learn that geloscopy is a kind of fortune telling: "determining someone's character or future by the way he or she laughs."

In a few days, after I had readjusted to Pacific time, I set up a meeting at my house. Norm and Anne were as committed to this project as I was and I automatically thought of us as a team. I continued my work with the task force, interviewing possible receivers of smuggled animals, but it was much more exciting to hatch plots with Norm and Anne. I reported my Uganda discoveries and they blended my news with their deeper knowledge to devise the next step. The obvious strategy would be to discover all the players in the smuggling web – everyone in the chain of custody, the police would say. Catch them in the act and interrogate them. But my foray in Uganda had reaped only limited results and tipped off our adversaries. I shuddered to think what information they were collecting about me and what they might do with it.

"Don't think about that," said Norm decisively. "We need to concentrate on our next move."

"Well, should we continue to track the animal collectors at this end?" Anne asked.

"How would we do that?" I wanted to know. "Shall I call Gary Brown? He may have caught a few more culprits by now."

"Yes, but I think that's premature. Besides…"

"Or what about your NIH contacts?"

Remembering the advice of the real Deep Throat, I suggested, "Follow the money."

We batted that around for a while, but finally concluded that we weren't equipped to do it. International finance is incredibly complex, let alone the underground laundered variety. I wasn't sure I wanted to get that close to the villains. But sharing a bottle of wine brought out the gumshoe in all three of us. Soon we were hatching schemes that would have landed us in very hot water. My Buddhist friends would say I'm getting too attached to form, caring about species and their survival, instead of accepting ceaseless change and loss.

Very well, I'm attached.

Norm suggested, "Infiltrate the labs."

"No," I replied, "too hard. They hire medical students who are so brainwashable that as soon as they're interns two years from now, they'll let themselves be enslaved. You know what I mean. They'll work a hundred hours a week, and even defend their own servitude. I've heard them do it."

"It does work, though. Infiltrating, I mean."

Anne said, "Sure, in proving cruelty charges. But it takes ages. And how do we know the lowly lab techs know where the animals come from? Are you suggesting we have them break into the files in the laboratory's office?"

I grimaced. The medical industry is *very* wealthy. Pharmaceutical companies always post the highest profits of any industry. Any legal one, anyway. Their full-time legal departments could run us into bankruptcy just filing pre-trial motions. "Too risky. They'd sue us, or have us arrested, or both. We'd be locked up in cages ourselves."

Norm sighed. "Ok, let's go after the sellers in this country. Another step along the pipeline."

"How?" Anne and I asked at once.

Norm gave a wicked grin. "We pretend to be a buyer."

I laughed. "Oh, like a mystery shopper!"

Anne was dubious. "I don't think you can pose as a chimpanzee customer. I bet you have to identify yourself, and be a laboratory, or know someone."

"Besides," I added, "What if they actually sell us one? Then where are we? Do we take delivery? Then what if customs catches *us*? That would be a fine how-do-you-do. Like the Catholic priest who had a heart attack in a brothel – at the emergency room, he kept *insisting* he was there carrying the Lord's word to fallen women."

Norm grumbled, "Gee, we're doing a great job of eliminating the impossibles. Any minute now, we'll hit on the one that works." He paced around the room. We were in my living room and decided to take a break from all this brilliant brainstorming. Anne phoned home to see if her kids were doing their homework. Scalawag was dozing in the corner. Gambado stretched and padded across the room to snoop in Anne's capacious purse. It was so big she could have gotten lost in it. But at least pets can be traced. Suddenly I shouted, "Hey!"

Norm and Anne almost jumped out of their skins. I told them my idea.

"How about installing an identification chip in every chimp in Africa, the way they do with pet cats and dogs in case they get lost?"

Their reaction, after they had gotten their blood pressure back to normal, was less than enthusiastic. Anne said, "No, it would be too expensive. Besides, it would be traumatic to anesthetize them. And how could you dart even one of them without scaring the whole troop into running away?"

Norm had questions. "Who would run the tracking machine? How would you transport the chimp to the place where they have the chip-reading machine?"

I stalled. "Maybe there are portable machines by now. I had Scalawag's and Gambado's chips put in years ago."

Anne's next question was all too pragmatic. "Who pays for the portable machines?" We didn't even know if these existed.

I had an answer to Anne's first question. "We find a way to shoot the chip under their skins so we don't have to anesthetize them." There was silence. Anne broke it.

"Boy, you really are free associating." I had taught them that term, and lived to regret it.

Norm disagreed with her. "No, this is a good idea. On top of identifying the chimps, this way we can also flip the hunters – get them to use their skill on our side." Anne looked puzzled. Norm said, "Hire a hunter to use the dart gun."

I was pleased that someone liked my idea. "Yeah, that has promise. Like turning them into rangers. That works, doesn't it?"

Anne kept her skeptic's hat firmly in place. "Aw, come on. Even the best sharpshooter in the world can't guarantee to zap a bullet – excuse me, a chip – into an exact specific place on an animal's body."

Norm and I spoke at once. "Want to bet?" "How do you know?"

Anne persisted. "And besides, who exactly is motivated to identify a chimp? The poachers don't care."

"Customs!" I said triumphantly. "This gives them ammo against the medical labs. You know how the labs claim they get all their chimps from captive breeding? This way we can prove an individual chimp came from Africa. It'll be faster than DNA."

Anne finally showed a spark of interest. Thoughtfully she said, "I suppose this could speed up the time it takes to get them to a sanctuary..."

Norm agreed. "Yeah! No more waiting in quarantine while labs and other assorted creeps fight over their provenance."

So we spent an agreeable half hour devising harebrained ways of protecting the primates by inserting identification tags under their skin from a distance. Eventually we sickened of the idea of turning living animals into one more kind of trackable commodity. It was disheartening. How could we defeat these animal traffickers without becoming like them?

—✎ X ❧—

Desta and her charge, three-year-old Kijana (Swahili for "young boy"), were acclimatizing to the San Francisco Zoo. The other keepers had helped her find a place to live and Kijana had an enclosure to himself for the first few weeks, where Desta spent hours playing with him so he would not feel abandoned. Then he was moved to a room that shared a chainlink wall with the big room, so he and the other chimps could see and hear and smell each other. When all of them seemed compatible, he would be let in with them one at a time for a little while, and then for gradually longer periods and larger groups until the introduction was deemed complete. Eventually Kijana would be allowed to use the overhead tunnels that connected the different enclosures to each other and to the central large room where the chimps slept each night. These tunnels had been built so the chimps and gorillas could travel from one indoor enclosure to another without having to be caught and crated.

I shared my Uganda experiences with the Randy Carstairs and Gary Brown. It confirmed what they suspected: an American was out in the field at the start of the smuggling pipeline. At least we now had contacts among the poachers who might send us more information through the offices at UWEC.

Randy and Gary sent me on another lie-catching mission, this time to investigate a furrier they suspected of selling furs made from forbidden exotic species. I protested that I knew nothing about furs and would gag at the thought of pretending to buy one. "Fine," they said, "Pretend you're nouveau riche. Engage them in making long explanations. That'll give you plenty of data to analyze."

I heaved a sigh and agreed. Randy had already researched this high-end dealer and gave me a thorough briefing. To look the part, I borrowed a sleek silk dress and stylish accessories from Jiang Li. "I refuse to wear the fancy stilettos," I said firmly. "Anyway, I'll bet nobody will notice what shoes I've got on."

"Well, if it comes up," she said darkly, "Say you're on your way to get some Christian Louboutins." I memorized the name and promised to give her a full account of my visit to the land of the rich and the home of the chic.

Hoping I looked convincing in this getup, I set out for the expensive shopping district near San Francisco's Union Square.

"In the same location for forty years," Aubertin's sign proclaimed. I took a deep breath and pushed open the heavy front door. A well-dressed gentleman looked up from his mahogany desk and smiled at me as if I were the answer to his prayers.

"Good day, madam," he said smoothly, rising to meet me. "How might I assist you?"

"I'm looking for something a little out of the ordinary," I replied. "Everything I have is so tired. I really must have something more distinctive this time."

"Ah," he said with a deferential nod, "A pleasure. Would you be thinking of evening wear?"

"Of course. The season begins in just a few months." I didn't tell him what season, just to see what kind of answer he would give.

"Opening night?" he asked suavely.

"No, the gala, you know."

"I see, madam. Shall we begin here?" he said and gestured to a corner lined with rows of tailored jackets made of fur.

"Oh, please," I said with a haughty sniff. "What do you have in the vault?" His smile deepened and I could see him calculating the upgrade in his commission.

"Right this way, madam," he purred and led me down a hall. Far down the narrow silent hall, at least thirty yards from the front of the store, stood a cold intimidating floor-to-ceiling metal door. He used two keys to open it and waved me in. Quickly, I scanned the entire room and then turned around to face him with a bored look. "Well?" I said, daring him to wow me. The silence was oppressive. The air was chilly.

"Perhaps something more in this line?" he asked hurriedly and led me to the rack with the fanciest stuff on it. I pretended to look over the swanky wares he brought out. I browbeat him a bit more, and started to enjoy it. Served him right for being so smarmy. By now he was probably cursing himself for not getting my name the minute I walked in. It was too late to retreat from his hello-darling manner. Behind his smooth face I could tell he was racking his brains, trying to figure out who was this well established and lucrative customer, and what I would expect to be shown.

Eventually I couldn't indulge my social malice any longer, since all the pieces he showed me came from legally killed animals. Time to raise the stakes. "Really," I said with a little sigh, "Monsieur Bechard will be so disappointed you couldn't do better for me."

His sharp intake of breath said my remark had hit home. Bechard was the current owner. In a tone of silky veiled threat I said, "Why don't you just call and see if he's at home?" (Randy had said that the owner always stayed in close touch with his staff). If Bechard actually hurried over to take over from the underling, I would say airily, "Why hello, Jacques. My dear friend DeeDee said you would be sure to take care of me."

Fortunately, that wasn't necessary. "Oh, of course, silly of me," said the king of smarm. "There's one more salon over here." With a condescending nod, I followed him toward the darkest corner where a second forbidding door loomed. Using two more keys, he opened it, swinging the heavy door outward. I swallowed and went in to the small closet-sized room. It was even colder than the last one. This would be an ugly place to be locked in accidentally... or on purpose, if they found out who I was and what I was planning to do to them. I brought my mind back to business and looked around.

Pay dirt. Two racks, one above the other, lined each wall. These furs were made of animals that were strictly prohibited. "Excellent," I purred in my turn. Squelching my real feelings, I oohed and aahed, trying on a dozen or more, asking questions and memorizing the species while filing away his facial signals.

Remember the mirror, I said to myself. Be sure to look at yourself in the mirror; that's what a socialite ready to spend serious money on a fur frock would do.

Finally it was time to go. I acted indecisive about which cloak to buy and gave an effusive promise to come back soon to make the purchase. Actually, I was feeling cramped and nervous in this claustrophobic little animal cemetery and just wanted to get out. A few gushing compliments to smarm-face – his actual name was Ian – got me to the door, out into the larger vault, and into the front room. With a gasp of relief I regained the sidewalk and hurried over to Randy's office.

Seeing the expression on my face, his secretary let me in right away. I plopped into a chair and said to him, "Yes, they're selling furs from endangered animals," and I listed the species. "The second-in-command knows exactly what they are, because he made me jump through hoops to get into the inner sanctum."

"Did you get any incriminating statements?" he asked eagerly.

"Well, that wasn't easy, either. Talking like a rich person committing a crime is pretty oblique, you know. Hints and code words. But I did find out that Bechard himself does the buying; that explains all the travel he does. Ian was hiding some species identities but he was clean on that statement about his boss. So you've got the green light to prosecute these guys." I stood up. "Call me if you need me to vet Bechard. Now I just want to get out of these clothes."

~⁓꘎⁓~

Ever since returning from Uganda, I had been cudgeling my memory for the name that Ezekiel's cousin had overheard... Riceler... or was it Riley... Why did that name keep nagging at me? Then I had an idea: contact Interpol, the international police organization. Early in my career I had thought of Interpol as either a romantic entity in a James Bond tale or a grim faceless Cold War bureaucracy operating mysteriously to carry out the plans of ruthless dictators. Actually, Interpol is the world's second-largest international organization, after the U.N., with 184 member countries and many programs for collaborating to catch criminals who crossed borders. Was it too far-fetched to hope they would deal with endangered species? I brought up Interpol's website on my computer. Jubilation! Interpol has a whole department dedicated to stopping crimes against wildlife.

Let's see, do I know anyone at Interpol? One of my former students had gone on to work in criminal detection; she had written me a note shortly after getting the job. Was it at Interpol? Would she still be there? If she had kept connected to the university's alumni organization, I could locate her quickly. Backup plan: Check out her dissertation topic, snoop on the Science Citation Index to see who had cited it and what his affiliation was. That would be a long shot, but one lead is better than none. The boring old telephone directory, even in its new nationwide electronic incarnation, might not help because her name was so ordinary, even assuming she hadn't married and changed it. Some women still do that.

My search for her didn't pan out. I could ask Randy to start the handshake chain, but it would be more fun if I could make the contact myself. Maybe Anne or Norm would know someone who knew someone at Interpol's wildlife group. I put all these threads on my to-do list.

Then I got some unsettling news from Anne. Ezekiel's cousin had contracted food poisoning while on a shooting expedition. This made us both uneasy. Anyone can get food poisoning – America's own food supply is far from sanitary, especially the meat – but the news didn't sound good. What if the smugglers had discovered the cousins' link to Ezekiel, and to Anne and me? There was no way to know.

One day about two weeks after my return from Uganda, I went to the San Francisco Zoo again. I just couldn't stay away, not while there was a signing chimp to admire. I even found a sign language instructor on campus and began lessons so I could communicate with him. So on that Wednesday, Desta arranged for me to meet her in the night house. This is where the animals come in to sleep and where their medical procedures are done. As I entered, she was signing to Kijana, teaching him to use the overhead tunnels.

"**Open**," she said and made the sign that matched the word. She always spoke aloud when signing. Just to keep in practice, I made the sign for "**open**" with my own hands. "**Wait here**" was Desta's next instruction. I wondered if the other chimps, who had never been taught to sign, were interested in this odd hand-waving behavior. They could watch through the chain link barrier from their own room. I wandered over to look at them, turning the corner. The phone rang and Desta answered it. "Oh, hi, Susan," I heard her say. "Yes, Kijana is here. We're ready for you to come and give him his inoculation."

Just then I heard heavy footsteps. There were some words I couldn't understand in a deep man's voice. Desta responded, "I'm sorry, sir, this area is off limits. Hold on a minute, Susan," I heard her say. Some more deep voice. "What do you want? I can't understand you," she said. More baritone rumbling. Then Desta's voice again: "No, really, I can't show you. I'm working now. Perhaps one of the docents…"

Probably just another lost zoo visitor. But for reasons I'll never know, I stood still and listened instead of meandering back to help Desta handle this intruder. "What – what are you doing?" Desta cried. A sound like a person being shoved against metal lockers. Then I heard an odd popping sound, a scrambling falling noise, and an ominous silence. Heavy footsteps went out the door. I never saw the man who made them.

"Desta," I whispered. Something had happened, something not good. I was afraid to go into the next room. I peeked around the corner. Kijana loped toward me. All I could see of Desta were her legs and feet splayed out on the floor. I made a small tapping sound to get Kijana's attention and signed to him to be quiet. "**Quiet**," I signed. Please, let my signs be correct. "**Come**," I added, and hoped he would follow me back to the other room. He did. We reached the other room. God, I think Desta has been killed.

Dead silence. Then footsteps approached from the other entrance. The attacker had come back – or someone had come back – and was looking around. I looked up at the overhead tunnels. They were big enough for me to get in. Maybe we could reach them. I signed to Kijana: "**We go. Up**." Kijana looked at me calmly and began scratching himself. Come on, *come on*, I screamed inwardly. "**Up, up**," I signed. Uh oh, don't stare directly into a chimp's eyes – that's a threat signal. Keeping my gaze downward, I signed, "**tickle chase**." Kijana laughed to himself and began to run – luckily, away from the men. I dodged after him and caught him for a tickle, trying to nudge him toward the tunnel. Please don't pant hoot, I thought.

Now I knew what it felt like to be hunted.

The mesh door leading to the tunnel was standing open.

"**Hurry**," I signed to Kijana. "**In. In**," and gestured to the tunnel door. He sat still. Maybe if I led the way – I scrambled into the tight space and gestured fiercely. I couldn't wait any longer. Hunched over, I duckwalked along the tunnel, leaving the door open. Looked straight ahead – where would the tunnel lead? I prayed for a corner, so if the attacker looked into the tunnel I wouldn't be visible.

A creaking sound. What was that? I held my breath, too afraid to turn around and look. Someone was following me. Then I heard the panting sound chimps make when they're nervous. Kijana was behind me. I sighed in relief and squirmed sideways, made a play face so he would keep thinking this was a game, then turned and scuttled along the tunnel. Kijana followed.

Praying the metal stairs wouldn't creak, I tiptoed up the ramp to the overhead portion of the tunnel system. "**Come**," I signaled. "**Tickle Kijana**." To my relief, Kijana followed me up the ramp. How much had he learned about this tunnel layout in his short time here? I looked around. Just ahead there was a corner where two solid metal plates met. That would make some slight shelter and block us from view from most directions. I nudged Kijana and we reached the corner. Uh oh. Now he would want to be tickled. Please forget I said that, little friend. Your giggles are too loud.

Huddling there in the metal corner with Kijana, I had a sinking feeling. I knew what this was all about. This is not a random attack. I tried to calm myself, thinking they're not really going to kill us. Maybe one of the attackers had been hasty with the gun and the rest were furiously shushing and containing him. Maybe they had already left. Maybe they wouldn't want to leave too many corpses in their wake. Then

I remembered: these people are experts at hiding and moving bodies.

Oh, boy, we were *down to last*. I hoped we didn't end up in the *place of medicine*.

I tried to remember the tracking tips Ezekiel had taught me. Get the sun behind them. Look for falling leaves. This advice was no good inside a tunnel in a chimpanzee night house. I waited. Should I try to get out of here, or would that be the worst thing to do? Now I understood why people become paralyzed in a crisis. At any given instant, you're not dead yet. The slightest action could change that, fast.

I huddled at the back of the walkway, trying not to shiver. We'd only been up here two minutes but it seemed a lifetime since the gun went off.

I'd never been shot at before. What made me think it was gunfire? One short popping sound in the room where Desta had been working. Maybe it was just Desta slamming a locker door, or dropping a box of supplies. We'd laugh about it later. I should just climb down right now and…

My body didn't believe me. I stayed put, leaning against Kijana, holding my breath because my body told me to. Please, Kijana, be still. Now is not the time to play the alpha male.

Were they coming closer?

Kijana began to fidget. I had to make him stop or they would hear us. Don't look him in the eye, I said to myself – he doesn't like that. Gingerly I put my hand on his hairy arm and gave a little shake.

It worked. I leaned against the wall and tried to be small. Found you can survive on almost no air.

A second voice spoke, higher than the first. "Kwa nini wewe tenda?" The cadence was familiar. I could almost recognize what it meant. Deep voice replied.

"Niache." It was Swahili.

Somehow I'd gotten my arms around Kijana. He hugged me back. He trusted me. I was thankful. He squirmed again, making me slide toward the railing. "**Kijana**," I used his language. "**Stay here. With me**."

Voices in Desta's room again. "Wapi a?"

"Labda kule." High voice became more insistent. "Wapi a?"

Deep voice replied. "Sijui." A door opened and slammed. A third voice spoke.

"Quit your babbling, you two. Where is she?" Footsteps stopped. "Oh, shit, what have you done? Who is this?" Pause. The bullying voice went on, "You fools. You can't do *anything* right. You got the wrong one. I *told* you she had blond hair."

Oh, god. They knew I was in the building. The third voice brayed on, interrupting deep voice's excuses, "You *imbecile*, you weren't supposed to *shoot*. We'll have everyone within miles on top of us in a minute. Can't you get it through your thick heads that we want her alive?"

Please don't play the hero, Kijana, I begged silently. He could jump down from this catwalk in one bound and tear the man apart. For a moment I indulged this fantasy. But no – even Kijana, robust and made of pure muscle, was no match for a man with a gun, a man who had already used it. Let alone three men. "**Stay here**," I repeated.

Suddenly I had an awful thought. Suppose the men were looking for him, too? By now I'd recognized the language the men were talking. Maybe I could catch the next words. I strained to hear them. The braying man spoke in Swahili this time, angrily emphasizing each word.

"Na nilete sokwe mtu. Yeye azizi." I'm pretty sure that meant: "And bring the chimpanzee, too. He's valuable."

They wanted both of us. Hurrying to find us before someone responded to the shooting, they would search the human offices, and then the chimpanzee quarters. They must have knockout drugs in their pockets and a cage for him in their van. Surely they just want him as part of their usual trafficking. Surely they don't know he can speak sign language. Oh god, let them not discover that. Because he witnessed the attack on Desta... if they know he can talk to us, they'll kill him for sure.

Kijana and I huddled together, hugging. Tunnels are like the tree highways that monkeys and chimps travel in the rainforest. If we scuttled too fast or too noisily, the hunters would spot us, just as I'd learned to spot monkeys clambering overhead.

Keep still. Breathe softly. To keep Kijana busy, I made meaningless gestures with my hands. At least I thought they were meaningless. Anyway, it worked. He looked puzzled and kept watching my hands.

Time passed. A door closed. Had the attacker left…
or come closer?

I sat with Kijana and breathed and hugged him. He
hugged me back. We rocked and gradually my mind
cleared. I could hear announcements over the loud
speaker. "Dear visitors. We are having an emergency.
Please make your way to the nearest exit. Thank
you." This was repeated several times. Someone had
responded.

I still didn't know what my pursuers looked like.

"**Scared**," signed Kijana.

"**Me, too**," I responded.

There was nothing to do but wait. I wondered what
Glenn and Carolyn would think of this close contact
I was having. Kijana took to it naturally. I wasn't
afraid of him – he was saner and friendlier than a lot
of men I've known. I had played with chimps on the
island in Uganda. Besides, you can only be afraid of
one thing at a time. Remember that moment on the
path at Ngamba Island, I thought; put the spiders out
of your mind and play with your chimpanzee.

There was a creaking sound. I held my breath.
No, it was just a locker door swinging shut. Was that
a cross-draft, or was someone there? Maybe we should
move to a new hiding place. I wondered if Kijana had
ever had to hide from other chimps in the fractious
chimp community at Tucson. Chimp battles include
a lot of running away. Maybe taking the better part
of valor wasn't strange or stressful for him. "**Groom**,"
I signed, and bent my head. He gently touched my
hair. I tilted my head so I could keep a lookout below.

I desperately wanted to get out of there, to get in my safe old familiar dented car, to run to Terry or Carl and sit on a normal chair in a normal coffee shop. But I couldn't leave Kijana here. He had witnessed the shooting.

Then came one of the voices. They were back.

"Harakisha!" No one answered. The voice became more insistent. "Ni muhimu!"

"Ngoja kidogo."

Then the third voice spoke.

"Keep looking. Where is she?" The bullying voice went on, "We don't have much time."

Suddenly I realized who he was. It was the angry American, the one who bullied his crew of poachers, the one who had thrown a crate. Riceler, or Rensler, the name that had sounded familiar. He must have come all the way from Uganda. They wanted me – alive. They must think I had discovered a lot about their operation, not just the crumbs and bits of information I'd managed to pick up. They probably wanted to know if I'd shared it with anyone. I debated whether to get out of this cramped hiding place and hide somewhere better. But where? Desta had showed me all around. Let's see... the nearest buildings are the small primate house and the lemurs, and then... Aha! the commissary, the central kitchen where workers prepare the food for the zoo's six hundred animals. It has big storage rooms, with huge bins and stacks of boxes in cold storage rooms. It would be a good place to hide.

Then I remembered the knives.

Knives scare me. I've always been afraid of them, ever since I nearly cut my thumb off on a camping trip, and I'm convinced a knife would be useless in a struggle. It could easily be wrested away and used against you. You would have exactly one (small) chance to use it. And even if I ignored the knives lying all around, my pursuers might not. They had already been chastised for making so much noise. A nice quiet weapon, lying so handy... Forget the commissary.

Footsteps and creaking sounds. Held my breath. Urged by their truculent boss, the shooters would come back any minute to find the blonde one. We had to get out of here. Where do the tunnels lead? Just into other enclosures, or are there exits? If they found us in a tunnel, we would be caged, literally. Maybe we should just keep one step ahead of them, double back, and hope they miss us.

Uh oh. Where was Kijana? He must have wandered away from the tunnel when I was listening to the men. He was down on the floor. I could see part of his black back around a corner. I was about to call out and run to him when I heard sounds that froze me in my tracks. Heavy footsteps. "Get out of here, your filthy beast," growled the American voice, and then there was a thud that sounded like a kick. Kijana howled. Oh please, don't let them realize he can sign. Kijana, be still.

"Keep looking. She's here somewhere."

The men were still moving around loudly. They were either totally reckless or feeling safe that crowds of zoo visitors stampeding toward the exits would cover any sound. Where was all that vaunted chimpanzee strength when you needed it? I excused him. Kijana was young, had been outranked all his life, and wasn't going to start swaggering now, especially since the chimps in the large chamber were upset and making a lot of noise. Suddenly my perspective switched. I entreated, oh, let the men be looking for me, not for a chimp. I can run away, I can call for help, I can drive a car.

A small wailing sound sounded faintly in the distance and slowly grew louder. I hardly dared to hope. So this was what people mean about not breathing in a crisis. After an agonizing wait, the sound turned into an ambulance siren. I heard the men cursing and they slammed their way out of the building.

Suddenly the room looked different, normal. Things were normal again. An ambulance was coming. Soon I would be talking to the authorities. I rallied myself and tried to prepare what I would say to them. "I heard voices and then an odd popping sound. I saw Desta on the floor, and ran away." That didn't sound very heroic, but who would expect more? I was just an ivory tower egghead, and I was alive.

My relief was short-lived. The siren didn't seem to be coming closer. I tracked the sound as fervently as I'd ever tracked any sound in my life. Who had called 911? The struggle and shots had been so brief. It would be too lucky if someone had detected the emergency. The wailing sound stayed the same – still the same…

Finally, the siren came closer and then stopped. Silence. More footsteps. The door banged open.

"Right, you get this room, I'll check the back." Blessed California voices, matter-of-fact, men at work, looking for injured bodies to save. "Here," I croaked. "We're up here." They didn't hear me. Footsteps came and went. "Here she is," one called and footsteps came again, stopping in the room where Desta lay.

"Ok, adult female, bleeding from chest, pulse 85, respiration labored. Intubating."

Breathing. She was breathing. Desta wasn't dead. I remembered to breathe, and slumped down against the tunnel's chain links. Hugged Kijana and felt weak. The ambulance guy kept barking out brief sentences into a transmitter, or maybe it was to his partner.

"Entrance wound in chest. Prep IV. Bullet may still be in there. Advise S.F. General E.R. Estimated arrival 20 minutes." I hadn't even gotten all the way down to the ground and they were already whisking her out on a gurney. "Wait," I gasped, wanting to jump down and get into the ambulance with them. Then I didn't want them to wait. Hurry. Go. Get her to the hospital. I leaned against the wall and tried to breathe. Hoped the attackers weren't hiding somewhere, waiting to return.

Another faint wail sounded in the distance. Ahhhh, let it be the police this time. Please let them get here fast. I promise I'll donate blood every six weeks.

Once again, my heart rate began to slow. As soon as the second siren was definitely, absolutely near, I let myself down from the tunnel and slumped to the floor. "**Kijana**," I called weakly. He was in the medical examination room, mumbling to himself. I closed the door and waited for the police.

Now what would happen? The police would see the blood and my shocked expression and draw conclusions. Surely I looked innocent. But the zoo people here did not know me, probably didn't even know of my existence; I hadn't joined the zoo, just visited Desta when she was on duty. The helpers would not arrive saying, "There, there, miss, safe to come out now."

Well, deal with the police first. More footsteps.

"Is this the place?" an official-sounding male voice asked, brusque and businesslike. A distressed female voice answered, "Yes, the chimps live here. Our new keeper was shot somewhere in – oh, my god… it must have been right here." I imagined them standing there, staring at the blood on the floor. After a long pause, the female voice said haltingly, "I was on the phone with Desta and I heard an interruption. Voices. Male voices. She was trying to stop them from doing something. Then I heard… I heard…"

I got to my feet and staggered around the corner. I looked at them. No words came.

"Did you see it happen?" the policeman asked me impersonally, as businesslike as before. A second policeman brought out his pen and paper, ready to write down whatever I said. What an anticlimax.

I must look like the last survivor of a shipwreck and he was unflappably on the case already. I croaked out a few words:

"Yes. Well, almost. Are they gone?"

"How many? Did you know them?"

"I didn't see them. I know who one of them is, though."

Because while I was waiting and hiding with Kijana, I had remembered that name: Rensselaer.

$$\sim\!\!\mathcal{I}\,\mathcal{C}\!\!\sim$$

The wrapup took hours. The police sealed off the night house. Photographers came and took pictures from every possible angle. Fingerprint experts dusted and lifted invisible marks. A sample from the blood on the floor was collected. Desta's co-workers hovered anxiously in the background, urging the officers to hurry so they could begin calming the chimps, who were vocalizing loudly and banging on the chain link partitions. I had no idea what was going on in the rest of the zoo grounds. I felt very tired and sat in the light metal folding chair in a tiny service area near the tunnel entrances where I was being interviewed.

"No, I don't know them personally. I think two of them were Ugandan. They spoke Swahili." I explained how I knew this. "The other guy was American. He was bossing them around. I think he's the same one I heard about in Uganda."

City police officers deal with a lot of mayhem, but animal smuggling is not one of their routine adventures. Every time I tried to explain that this was about animals, they kept bringing attention back to the three men. Well, I guess in a way they were right. Ultimately, it was about humans and their love of money.

"Rensselaer, if it is Rensselaer, was a prominent medical re-searcher." I spelled the name and pronounced it: "Ren-sa-leer. Not in my field. He studied cancer in Harold Vincent's lab in Sunnyvale. About six years ago he was caught fudging his data. It was in all the academic trade papers. Of course Vincent fired him at once and Rensselaer lost all his funding. The journal had to publish a retraction. They hate to do that."

"The perpetrator, miss."

"Oh, yes. Um, yes, academic disgrace. Of course it was reported in all the trade publications as well. So Rensselaer was *persona non grata*…"

"He was who?"

"Unwelcome. Not able to get another job. Not in any scientific field, anyway. That's all I know about him."

"What made you remember him?"

I told them about Ezekiel's cousins and the clues we were trying to put together about animal smuggling in Uganda. They shook their heads disgustedly as I described my doings in Uganda. I could almost hear them thinking, "Amateurs!" I resented this and said, "Why don't you call Frank Halloran?" I asked. This was a San Francisco officer I'd helped out a time or two with fraud cases. "He knows me."

"Yeah, maybe tomorrow. Back to this Renster guy…"

"So ever since I heard the name they tried to repeat to Ezekiel, it's been haunting me. Then they kept describing him as a bully, loud, obnoxious, always in a hurry. I'm not a therapist, but I'd think if you'd lost your career you'd be angry and if you're trying to start over in a new line of work you'd be in a hurry. Just a guess."

They didn't write down my guesses but they did take his name. "What's he look like?"

"I don't know. Never met him in Africa, and didn't see him today." They chewed their pencils, and finally one asked,

"So how would he know who *you* are?"

"I published something about him."

Rensselaer had been Vincent's top disciple and probably wanted to co-author some papers and be accepted as an equal by his famous mentor. Rensselaer's research findings were so provocative because they suggested that metastatic lung cancer could be treated by simple injections. The big pharmaceutical companies eagerly backed his reasoning and showered him with grants. Heady stuff for a youngish researcher. He probably thought that soon he would have his own lab.

Hmmm…like my own fantasies. An uncomfortable reflection. Maybe my own undisciplined scattershot idea-hopping wasn't so bad, compared to laser-like focused ambition. But Rensselaer's meteoric rise began to stall. A study run by another institute to confirm his findings came up blank, and then another. A persistent graduate student kept going over Rensselaer's numbers, trying to understand them. She told her advisor, who couldn't figure them out either and got the funding agency to demand to see Rensselaer's raw data. He delayed for as long as he could, but finally he had to produce them and it all came out. Faked research, the biggest crime in academia. Vincent fired him and that was that.

This all happened one year when I was studying academic fraud and it seemed a classic case of dishonesty fueled by inflated ego. Rensselaer's downfall made a good illustration of some of my ideas, so I began to include it in my lectures. It also served as a cautionary warning to my students, I might add, in case they were ever tempted to fudge their facts. A while later I included it in a paper I published in the *Journal of Perception and Cognition*. I hadn't thought about it in five years.

Had he heard about my publication? That was probably a grandiose thought – *The Journal of Perception and Cognition* is prestigious, but has only a few hundred readers. Still, it just takes one. After all, a few months ago I had outed Mr. Oily Man based on (faked) publication information. Maybe my article had made a difference in Rensselaer's life. Maybe he had been trying to rehabilitate himself and my article repeating the old scandal and calling it a clue to his character was the final nail in his academic coffin.

That alone would be enough to start a grudge in the heart of an ambitious cheater. Hearing that I might also break up his new line of work would be the last straw.

I was pretty sure that my article about Rensselaer's character listed only my university office information, not my home address. Still, he could have tracked me to the university and then followed me anywhere – the zoo, home…

Oh, god, home. What was happening at my house? I was as eager as anyone to help the police solve this bloody attack, but I needed to make sure my home was safe. Fortunately, the police were done with me for the moment. I handed them my card and got out of there just as the zoo staff was allowed back in to the night house to take care of Kijana and the other chimps.

Driving too fast across the bridge, I fretted about what could have been happening at home. Suddenly I banged my fist on the steering wheel and cursed myself for not asking the SFPD to get their Berkeley counterparts to check it out. Too late now. I drove cautiously up my street and parked a block away. But everything was quiet. All the cars I saw belonged to my neighbors. When I opened the door, Scalawag and Gambado greeted me as usual. A note from Terry lay on the hall table: "Troglodyte called."

I laughed in relief. No harm had occurred at home. I re-read the note. An oddly perfect word; troglodyte means "cave dweller" and is used to insult people, but it's also the scientific name for chimpanzee. I hurried downstairs to find out whether the troglodyte was a student or a telemarketer. Fooey. No Terry. Using our sesquipedalian word code, I hurriedly composed a note warning her to leave the house immediately: "Exigency! Nefarious malefactor in the environs. Eschew the domicile forthwith. Felid and canid are under my aegis. This is veridical." I was grateful for our quirky word game. Now I could warn her right out in the open to leave the house. If any nefarious malefactors broke into the house and snooped, this bizarre note would mean nothing to them.

And I was not going to stay here to find out. I picked up the phone and made a call. It was early evening by now. Thankfully, he was home.

"Norm," I said. "May I stay with you for a few nights? I'll explain when I get there." I didn't want to be in this house until I'd had a chance to collect my wits and strengthen my defenses. Bless his heart, he was willing to take me in without asking for a reason. He even said I could bring Scalawag and Gambado. It was unthinkable to leave them behind to face the music without me.

—⁊ XI ℂ—

We raced down Marin Avenue toward the freeway. Scalawag and Gambado were in the car with me, two morsels of furry normality. Scalawag picked up my fear and whined gently, sitting upright in the passenger seat. I closed the windows to keep Gambado safely inside. Along with her usual car-ride shrieks, she kept walking around the car, over my arms and down by my feet, dangerously near the brakes. When we stopped at the toll plaza, I scooped her up and deposited her unceremoniously onto the back seat.

Norm had said to park in his driveway. I crept down the narrow streets crowded with parked cars, found the house with the porch light on, and pulled in. He opened the door before I could even ring the bell and guided Scalawag up the steps as I carried Gambado in my arms. I hadn't thought to get her carrier. I introduced them. "This is Scalawag. He fits his name. Gambado means to prance or leap fantastically, like gambol. She was like that as a kitten." Extraneous babble. Funny what you think to say when you're scared witless.

"Here," he said, "let's put them in the back room," so we did. He led me down a narrow hall, through a kitchen, and into a comfy-looking room that probably was where they watched tv, if they had one. Scalawag began investigating while Gambado cringed in my arms, then leaped down and hid under a desk.

Leaning against the door, I blurted out the headline: I'd witnessed a shooting probably meant for me. "Norm, it was awful. I froze. I was no help at all. Desta was in the next room. Should I have rushed in? But my CPR training was years ago. I could have…"

"Stop, stop. Tell me what happened from the beginning." He shut the door and steered me back to the living room. It was odd that he wasn't surprised. In fits and starts I told the story, circling around to the thing that was bothering me most, now that the immediate danger had passed: what I had done wrong. Finally he interrupted.

"Julie. Listen. You heard someone get attacked in the next room. It took ten seconds. It was done before you could even have gotten in the room. If you had rushed in, well, they would have popped you, too. What good would that have done?"

"But after they left, I hid. I hid with Kijana. I thought she was dead, it was no use to come down…"

"Exactly. You thought she was dead. Why *would* you come down? No one would expect you to. You did the exact right thing and you're alive to tell the tale."

"Yeah, maybe that's a good thing…"

"Maybe!? Whaddya mean, maybe?" Norm was truly shocked.

"I mean, I'm able to help track them down."

"Not yet, you aren't," Norm said firmly. "Who put you in charge? Maybe you can help later."

Norm was right. This wasn't my job. When I was hiding, I did think Desta was dead. Only afterwards, when I heard the medics say she was breathing, did the guilt come. But it wasn't my fault. Norm saw I was coming back to earth and gave me some brandy to smooth the process. The phone rang and he went to answer it. I sipped some brandy, caught my breath, and went in to the back room to make sure Scalawag and Gambado were ok. Scalawag had taken advantage and was curled up in an armchair. Gambado was draped above him along the top of the chair arm. I budged Scalawag over and sat with them, stroking their fur. This room was real. I was safe. Desta was being taken care of in the hospital. Police were in charge at the zoo. It could have been worse. Everyone was going to live.

I went back into the living room. Norm returned and so did my anxiety. I needed to talk.

"So anyway, the police are in charge and Desta is at S.F. General and I may be in danger." I began to get worked up again. "I shouldn't have brought danger to your door. Shall I leave? Will you keep Scalawag and Gambado? They're no trouble. They..."

Norm shushed me. For some reason, he was unworried. "You're staying right here." He ushered me to the sofa. "So you mixed it up with some big game hunters, eh?"

"Game, my foot. They were after me – they said so. 'Get the blonde one'."

"Julie, you're not the only blonde in San Francisco." This was not comforting.

"But I was in Uganda. Just a few weeks ago. Snooping about smuggling."

"And you're not the only blonde who ever went to Uganda." Norm was making tea. "Sugar? Lemon?"

He was right. There were other blondes besides me. Anne, for one. But for some reason, Norm kept acting as if he knew I was safe.

"Quick, let's call the hospital and see how Desta is doing," I urged. Without waiting for an answer I grabbed his phone. I got through to the emergency room but the hospital authorities refused to answer my questions or even identify anyone who was a patient there.

"See?" said Norm. "There's nothing you can do. Now sit down and calm yourself." Norm's wife Leslie was away in the Mojave Desert on one of her research expeditions, so he distracted me by telling me all about her research. I fixed my gaze on him and tried to listen.

"See, two years ago she was at Kelso Dunes in the Mojave observing blister beetles – *Meloe franciscanus*, if you want to know," he began. "She noticed the beetle larvae clumping together in little heaps. She found that when the larvae crawl out of their underground burrows, they swarm up to the top of grass blades and then cluster into wriggling masses."

I looked at Norm through glazed eyes and tried to follow what he was saying. This was important science to him and to Leslie, but today I had nearly been shot and had escaped with my life. Wriggling masses of beetle larvae – who cared? Well, maybe he wasn't expecting me to absorb all this. Maybe he was just hypnotizing me… His plan was working, because I was calming down.

"So she kept noticing that bees would land on the masses and then fly away. After she saw this dozens of times, she captured the bees and found they were all male *Habropoda pallida*." Norm paused. This was supposed to mean something. I tried to guess.

"So the bees needed someplace to rest? It was too hot on the desert floor?" A question would show I was listening. It was only polite.

"No, actually they thought they were having a hot *date*. The heaps of larvae just happen to look – to a *habropoda pallida*, anyway – like a female bee."

"Are you serious? Is this some trick to see if I'm awake?" I kicked off my shoes and put my feet on the sofa.

"No, really, it's true. This is evolution at work. The larvae clumps are about the size of a female bee. So the male bee lands on the clump. See, the larvae get something out of it. A free ride. When the bee lands, most of them jump on his thorax and hang on."

"They want a ride? How do they know where the bee is going?" This whole scenario was incomprehensible. Norm was unperturbed.

"Then the male bee flies away and meets a real female bee, and whoopee. In the act, some of the larvae jump off him and land on her." Sexually transmitted parasites among the insects. Sheesh. Norm continued.

"Then, when she lays her egg, the larvae jump off the female bee into the bee nest she made for it, and presto, the beetle baby has bee egg and pollen to eat."

Gee, biology. You don't even need to take drugs to blow your mind. I said thoughtfully, "Oh, I see. Interspecies romance."

"Not exactly. More like hitchhiking. This is the first time this was ever recorded. Leslie got it published." He said proudly, "In *Nature*."

I picked up my ears. "Really? In *Nature*?" That is one of the most prestigious science journals in the world. I'd give my eyeteeth to be published in the top psychology journal. My interest in the mysterious Leslie went up exponentially. I wondered if she would be interested in helping us detect. She would be perfect... a trained observer, patient, noticing patterns, collecting evidence, probably able to write complete sentences...

I brought my attention back to Norm. He was saying, "She's down there in the Mojave now, following up."

"By herself?"

"Yeah, this time. Sometimes I go with her. I'm a bug man too, you know. But I have a big meeting with a donor tomorrow, so I couldn't go."

Norm was on a roll. I forced myself to stop thinking about the last few hours and listen to some of his adventures in the field. It was an odd contrast. I knew Norm as a slightly harried nature lecturer and fund-raising environmentalist. Now there's this other Norm, the intrepid explorer, who knows animals, knows how to get out of jams in tropical countries, how to think on his feet. Yet here he is, running a nonprofit in the middle of a big city. I know enough about NGOs to know that mountains of administration are required to fulfill teaspoons of the dream. I wondered if he missed being in Palau or the Pantanal or Costa Rica.

If Norm was afraid that I had brought enemies to his door, he didn't show it. I began to unwind. He told one story after another about dangers in the field and how he had escaped. But the uncomfortable message seeped through: People don't like their livelihoods interfered with. When you set out to save nature, you risk your life.

We went back into the kitchen and Norm fed me a midnight snack. I was still distracted and I had no idea what I was shoveling into my mouth. Maybe it was nasturtiums. I called to leave a message on Terry's cell phone. In the middle of speaking, I had an appalling thought. What if she'd left her cell phone in the house and my pursuers broke into the house and stole it? Whatever I said they would hear. In mid-message I choked back Norm's phone number and didn't mention the note on the table. I said only, "Terry, it's me. Leave a message at my office. I'll call you back."

Was that protection enough? If they stole her phone they could try *69 – no, that would connect them to this number but not identify it. Anyway, how could they retrieve her messages without her code? I gave up. This was exhausting. I would make a terrible secret agent.

Norm was disgustingly excited and decided to do some snooping tomorrow. Just then, a knock came on the door. Oh god, had they followed me after all? Norm gave me a reassuring look and opened the door. It was Anne. He had called her while I was en route and forgot to tell me. As soon as my heart rate went back to normal, I went through the whole story again for Anne's benefit.

"See, and then the one man said to the other man – there were two of them, two speaking Swahili, I mean. One voice was farther away. And another voice interrupted him."

"Do the smugglers know about SaveNature?" Anne asked. She had snuggled into the roomiest armchair and made herself comfortable.

"Sure they do," Norm said. "In Brazil one time…"

"No, I mean Julie's smugglers. Do they know the connection?"

"I doubt it. SaveNature isn't on most people's maps yet. Ten more years, I figure."

The phone rang. I jumped. "Oh hi, Leslie," Norm said. "Guess who's here? Julie Heidebrecht." He retold my adventure in abbreviated form. Oddly, I could tell from hearing his side of the dialogue that Leslie wasn't making him repeat anything, the way you do when you're shocked out of your socks. She was used to the dangers faced by naturalists.

After two more hours of rehashing, Anne went home. Norm helped me open the foldout sofa in the living room. Norm and Leslie don't have a guest room. I'm learning that conservationists don't earn much, and if they do, they immediately spend it on animals. For Christmas and birthdays they give each other certificates adopting endangered cheetahs. Note to self: find someone at the university who has connections, and get them nominated for a MacArthur genius award.

Scalawag and Gambado, released from the back room, settled down with me. Scalawag, of course, wanted to explore the entire house. Norm had to restrain him from slobbering all over his mementoes with their fascinating smells. Drums, baskets, feathery fans, bowls, knives, fans, musical instruments made of gourds — artifacts of many travels. Gambado was happy to snuggle next to me. Just before I fell asleep, I suddenly thought about Terry. Would she be safe? Was my note on the table believable? I shouldn't have said "eschew." It was too late now… or was it? Should I drag myself out of bed and pick up the phone? No, this is ridiculous, I'm panicking unnecessarily. No one's going to break into the house. I'm all tucked in now. Relax. Nothing will happen. Anything I do might make it worse. But the moral dilemma didn't fade. I fell into an uneasy sleep, dreaming of overhead tunnels and sabotaged planes.

～っe～

Next day I tried to make amends to the other person I had drawn into danger. I tiptoed into the hospital room. Desta was sleeping, or still under anesthetic. I sat down and looked at her. Her hair was messy. Machines were hooked up to her in various places.

"What should I have done differently?" I muttered. "I'm so sorry."

"She won't answer you," a voice said sharply. "Can't you see she's unconscious?"

I hadn't even noticed the other patient in the room. A cross-looking older woman lay in the other bed by the window. She must have been 75 years old. Piles of toiletries, books, and magazines filled her nightstand and the moveable tray table, showing that she'd been here a while. Her bed had been raised to a seated position so she could survey the room. Under a cloud of fluffy white hair, sharp blue eyes scrutinized me.

"I said, she's unconscious," she repeated more loudly, as if I were deaf.

"I can see that."

I was Desta's second visitor. One off-duty zookeeper had already been here. Norm and Anne would come later; for now, only one visitor at a time was permitted. Desta had spent only twelve hours in intensive care before being moved to this room. That's a good sign, I told myself. If she were on the brink of death, they would have kept her in intensive care. For some reason, I decided to feel safe at the hospital. There had been so much in the news in recent years about emergency rooms being like war zones (staff attacked by drugged crazies or criminals with bullet wounds or wife batterers pursuing their fleeing victims) but I hoped that the upper floors, at least, would be secure.

A medium-height man with curly brown hair entered the room. He wore a name tag but not a white coat. He came straight to Desta's bed and checked her vital signs.

"She said something half an hour ago," said the elderly lady.

"Hi, Minnie," he said.

"You must be new," she announced with pursed lips. "I am not called by my first name until I grant permission."

"Ok, Miss Manners," he replied jauntily. He continued doing his little tasks for Desta. He didn't notice me at all – the opposite of Minnie, who obviously noticed everything.

"How is she?" I asked, feeling inadequate. The man glanced at me.

"Do I have permission to tell her?" he asked Minnie mischievously.

"Certainly not. I don't know. I don't know who she is."

"Downstairs they told me she'll live," I hinted. "Did they get the bullet?"

"Oh, yeah. Paramedics did a great job. Few units of B positive, few weeks of rest and she'll be back raising cain."

I'm glad he's the expert, I thought faintly. If this is what he considers a routine case, I don't want to know what else he deals with.

Minnie was eyeing me sharply and said to him, "Maybe you shouldn't tell her all this. For all you know – did you say bullet?"

"Yeah. Who are you?" he said to me, continuing to take notes and do medical things. Like all hospital personnel I'd ever known, he didn't introduce himself. I made a point of taking a few steps closer so I could look at his badge.

"I'm Julie Heidebrecht, Nicholas," I said. "Do you mean the *paramedics* got the bullets out?" I didn't think they were allowed to do things like that. Speeding ambulances and all. He must have meant the trauma surgeons in the ER. Meanwhile, Minnie was obviously on the horns of a dilemma. The strict etiquette of her generation forbade her to eavesdrop, but this was too juicy to ignore. She was miffed at Nicholas, but he was the only one with the information we both wanted. For a moment, she and I were on the same side. I tried to look like someone who had the right to know.

"She'll tell us eventually anyway," I prompted.

"Now, now, no wheedling. I'll see if you're on the list," and he disappeared.

Well, he wasn't much of a barrier if he didn't even ask for more than my name. Desta stirred slightly. I still didn't know who got the bullet out or where it had lodged. Suddenly that mattered. You'd think that knowing your friend was alive would be enough, but I wanted to know where she was hurt, to reconstruct what had happened just out of my line of sight in that night house. Then, somehow I wouldn't be so afraid, so vulnerable. If I knew the sequence of events, it would be a story, with a beginning, middle, and end, not a confused jumble of sounds and images and guilt and fear.

I remembered why this urge was so powerful. Trauma experts say that it's really important for people to tell their stories. Telling the story reinforces that they survived, that the peril is over. They tell their story over and over, and gradually the horrifying event becomes more and more distant. It becomes history, and maybe eventually a source of pride. After World War II, reporter Ernie Pyle rode home from Europe on a demobilization ship, and wrote that as the men sailed over the Atlantic, day after day they talked to each other, telling their stories: in Ernie's words, "gabble gabble gabble." It was too soon for Desta to gabble, but when she was ready, I would listen.

"Not next of kin," said Nicholas, who had reappeared soundlessly, like Jeeves. "Officially, you're an unperson."

"Would it help if I told you I was there when she was… injured?" I asked, partly to see how Minnie would react. That magazine she'd propped up was a thin disguise. Funny how you can tell if people are listening in on your conversation. They give off some kind of invisible waves. I should get one of my graduate students to look into it.

"No shit," he said amiably, as if I'd offered to show him my Elvis albums. "So how'd you get away from the bad guys?"

"She was really brave," I said, not answering his question, and suddenly realized how fond I was of the animal people I had met over the last few months, Anne running programs to awaken zoo-going children and their parents, Norm saving acres of rainforest, Glenn and Carolyn breaking ground with chimp language, the courageous Ezekiel fending off poachers, and Desta, lying here in a hospital because she'd had the misfortune to meet me.

I continued, "This happened at the zoo. You knew that, right? I don't know how much information you get on what causes the emergencies." Nicholas nodded as if he knew, but the white-haired roommate was transfixed.

"Desta is a zookeeper, new here. She came from Arizona with Kijana just a few weeks ago. Desta was talking with Kijana. He's a signing chimp. I was…"

"A what chimp?"

"Signing chimp. You know, sign language. He's still learning, though." They looked dubious. "I was in the other room looking at the other chimps. Some men came in and tried to get past Desta. I couldn't hear what they were saying, but she tried to stop them." I was doing my own gabbling cure.

Nicholas and Minnie listened intently.

"I think they were after me." Their eyes grew rounder. It seemed egotistical to put myself in the spotlight, but there was no way around the next part. "I'm part of a group that's trying to stop the smuggling of endangered species, including chimps. Anyway, I think the guys who did this were looking for me. I'm a threat to them – I know who one of them is. Desta just got in the way."

There was a silence as they stared at me. The unspoken message was, "And you've brought your dangerous ass *here*? Thanks a lot."

"The police are on the case," I added hastily. I didn't mention that I was avoiding my own house. Surprisingly, both of them took it calmly. Nicholas had probably seen everything in his line of work, and Minnie... I would find out about her soon enough. Nicholas spoke.

"Well, she won't be climbing the monkey bars for a while, but no permanent damage. Unless you count the scar. I'm Nick."

"I'd like to be able to talk to her, Nick. When will she be..."

"Compos mentos? Probably tomorrow. Come back in the after-noon."

"Mind if I just sit here a little while? I won't try to get her to talk."

"Who did you say you were?"

"College professor." I corrected myself, "Associate professor. I know how to sit in the back row and be quiet."

"I never saw you," he said conspiratorially and shimmered out.

I tried to figure out what to do next. Somehow I could think more clearly when Desta was there, even though she was still asleep. I asked myself, what had she seen, what did she know? Would she be able to describe the men?

"You're not going to start smoking, are you?" It was Minnie, abruptly pulling me out of my reverie.

"Smoking? This is a hospital. They haven't allowed smoking since before the moon landing."

"You had that look." Oh, I get it. The only way she knows how to make contact is to be abrasive, even if the gibe is forty years out of date. Suddenly I thought of something.

"Has she said anything? When did they bring her up here from the ICU? You said she said something half an hour ago."

"I thought you knew all about this."

"I had to stay and talk to the police. It took hours." I left out the part about making sure that Kijana was safely stowed and the rest of the chimp house searched. "And I don't smoke, by the way. Never did. You have to be pretty dumb to start smoking."

The joy of one-upmanship lit her eyes. "Or continue it once you've started."

"There is one good thing about smoking," I said meditatively. I just wanted to provoke Minnie to see if she could top me. She promptly did so.

"Yes, I know – it kills people. The problem is that it takes so long."

"Yeah. They live long enough to reproduce." We smiled at our shared prejudice. I don't often voice my heaviest judgments, but she started it.

"Did she say anything?" I repeated, using the exact same tone that I used the first time. I've found it helps if you don't change your intonation when repeating a question. Don't add any sardonic or impatient tones that could push the conversation in a whole new direction.

"No, she did not. I was reading." And she suited action to word by picking up her magazine. How would I find out what Desta had seen just before the shooting? Was the attacker someone she knew? Unfortunately, some people who have been traumatized have no memory of the trauma, or even of the hour leading up to it. I hoped against hope that this wouldn't happen to Desta. I sat there staring, as if her very body could give clues, or by act of fiercely focused will I could extract the answers from the air.

The sound of rustling bedclothes made me look up. Minnie had reached over and pushed her buzzer.

"What do you need?" I asked, just to be doing something. There's only just so long you can stare at someone sleeping.

"You can't get it," she said.

"Shall I call a nurse?" I asked.

"I just did. They're so slow here. I think they're using untrained orderlies and calling them nurses."

I could see that the sun beating through the window cast a glare, so I offered to close the curtains. She nodded grumpily. Finally Nick came back in.

"Took you long enough," Minnie complained. "They shouldn't give you so many people to look after."

"I completely agree," he said imperturbably. "I'll get them to change our workload. Then I can spend more time with you." He winked at her.

Minnie harrumphed. "Don't you dare call me dearie, or anything like that. I'm not your dearie."

Nick leaned over her bed and said to Minnie in a loud stage whisper, "It's okay to pretend you don't like me. In fact, that's a good idea. Don't let them know we get along famously. They might give me a raise." She stared at him inscrutably.

He looked at her chart. "Time for your pain medication?" She nodded. He pulled the traveling screen over and, I presumed, gave her an injection. I gazed moodily at Desta. Minutes passed. Nick left. Minnie drowsed. I sighed and decided I couldn't do any good here. I wrote a brief note telling Desta I would be back and included my home phone number in case she wanted to call. Her purse and daybook were probably still at the zoo or in police custody.

"So, she didn't bite your head off," Nick said with mock surprise as I emerged. I looked at my watch. I'd been in there half an hour. I looked at him, feeling forlorn. He became serious, too, and said,

"I know. She's really a duck. She's just afraid."

"Afraid? She isn't even awake. Oh, you mean the battleaxe. Afraid? She doesn't act like it. She's not afraid of a tyrannosaurus."

Nick shook his head. "Can't live alone any more, not with that hip. She could easily fall again and not reach the phone next time. Once those sutures come out in a week or two, we can't keep her any longer. Then where will she go?" I wondered why Nick was telling me this. He seemed to want to keep me in conversation. Well, that was ok by me. Here was another man in the healing arts, like Carl, and had no ring on his finger. Maybe he was available.

"Doesn't S.F. General have a rehab wing?" I asked. "Couldn't she go there?"

"Not permanently. Our social worker is trying to find her a place. Minnie was living on her own, you know, doing her own shopping and gardening. Not bad for someone nearly 80."

In my short acquaintance with her, Minnie seemed so indestructible, so privileged. She probably had a DAR chapter named after her. But that didn't meant her life was good now. Maybe she had outlived her friends. Maybe she didn't have a family. And now to have no one… to have to give up her independence and know that her life would be in the hands of strangers… I'd be afraid, too.

It does give you pause. Desta had just nearly died in her twenties. My father lasted until 74, but who could say what his last five years were like? He seemed to recognize me most times. The staff at his nursing home seemed nice enough, but how much could they really do? How can you really tell if someone knows it's you? Are there other subtle signals that tell whether an aged or comatose person perceives anything? I should have visited more often. It wouldn't have ruined my budget to buy a few more airplane tickets.

~9 XII 9~

I left the hospital. After the rush of relief and gratitude subsided, I realized that Desta's survival was just the beginning. Now I had to deal with police, maybe even ask for police protection, make sure Kijana was safe, and deal with all the phone calls that would pour in from worried friends and colleagues at soon as my own part in this drama hit the news. So far the media reports hadn't mentioned me.

How would I explain this to them? That I'd made enemies so evil that they came from Africa to capture me? I should have realized that the hint from Ezekiel (about the man he overheard asking about the white-lady-with-no-camera) suggested more than a passing precaution, like swatting a fly out of the way. Rensselaer knew there was someone who was curious about his doings. Now he was tracking me, just as he tracked other primates.

After Kijana had wandered away from me, he had seen the shooter and heard his voice. If he was someone Kijana knew, he could tell us. This gave me an idea. I telephoned the chimp sanctuary in Tucson. Oh dear, this meant being the bearer of bad tidings. Couldn't be helped. She answered on the second ring.

"Hello, Dr. Madison?" I said. Secretly I'd hoped they wouldn't be in, but now I had to plow ahead. "Um, this is Julie Heidebrecht. Oh, fine, thank you. He settled in well. Yes, I can see why you miss him. He's a bundle of mischief. How are Silvana and the others reacting to his being gone?"

Sooner or later I'd have to get to the point. "Um, Carolyn, I have some… um, there was an accident. No, no, to Desta. Kijana is ok. She's in the hospital. No, he didn't attack her. Actually, it was humans. Carolyn…" I wanted to stop her flow of anxious questions. "We think it was some smugglers. It was in the night house. Some men came and tried to get in – well, it may have been an accident but she was shot. Yesterday morning."

Hard to believe it had been less than twenty-four hours ago.

"Yes, I've been there already. She was asleep. They're not too worried about her. She's already out of intensive care." Gad, what a way to put it. Escalate the anxiety, why don't you? Luckily, Carolyn said the very thing I was hoping for. "I'm on my way." She would jump on the next plane.

"Oh, would you? I was hoping you would. She'll be so glad. The people at San Francisco Zoo are wonderful, but they hardly know her yet. Here's my phone number." I recited it. "Can Glenn come too? Let me know your flight. I'll pick you up."

Whew. I was partly relieved and partly troubled. Now I'd have to explain it all again, with that renewed stab of guilt. What should I have done differently? But here were allies who cared as much – what was I saying? who cared about animals ten times *more* than I did – and had done for thirty years.

I went back to Norm and Leslie's and let myself in with the key he'd given me. Scalawag greeted me with his usual bounding joy but Gambado was under the couch.

Before the news about me got out and the onslaught of worried questions could begin, I phoned Carl. Besides, I had an idea: There must be another way to investigate this. I was sure that Vincent, the famous researcher, and his assistant Rensselaer were involved. Top researchers rarely work alone – they have lab assistants, junior colleagues, secretaries, graduate students… Jiang Li was out of town at a conference. I reached Carl right away, and asked him to track down someone, anyone, who used to work with Vincent and Rensselaer.

"What for?" he asked in a puzzled tone. I replied, "Oh, some complications are keeping me away from my computer for a few days."

"Are you off on another mad quest?" he asked. "You'll never make full professor unless you park on one idea and follow it up."

"Squat on it, you mean," I replied. "Not my style. Thanks, pal." Then I realized he could do another favor. I knew he had enough computer savvy to do it. Was my article on Rensselaer ever cited in the medical research press? Who outside my field would know I had written it? I asked Carl to run down the citation index clue, too. "I can't spare the time." Anxiously, I added, "And don't tell anyone."

"Don't worry," Carl said with a smile I could hear down the line. "Confidentiality is my middle name."

~ ೨ c ~

When Norm came home from his SaveNature office that night, we powwowed until late. He wanted to get Desta's family's phone numbers and call them, but I thought we should leave that to Glenn and Carolyn. Besides, by tomorrow she'd be better and they could call with a less frightening message.

Norm had an intuitive sense of the gabble technique of trauma recovery, because he asked me to repeat my experience in the night house several more times. He listened carefully. "I wonder if Kijana saw the shooter directly," he finally asked. "Do you suppose he could describe him?" Norm knew about chimp signing, of course, but didn't know how extensive their vocabularies were.

Just then the phone rang. It was Leslie, calling from the Mojave for an update. While Norm filled her in on our doings, I thought she must be as brave as Norm. There she is, out in the desert alone. Admittedly, her targets weigh a tenth of a gram but I still think she's brave. Rattlesnakes, scorpions, off-road bikers with guns...

Which are more dangerous, animals or humans?

Norm was now talking to Leslie about their other concerns, home repairs and property taxes. As soon as he got off the line, I'd pick his brain again. I was thankful to have someone to talk to who understood the gravity of all this, who would try to help me figure out what to do next. We didn't know if the shooters realized they had been seen and that Kijana could communicate with humans. If they did, they would surely try to eliminate him.

Before Norm could hang up, I said, "Put it on speakerphone. I want to get Leslie's opinion." He complied and I mentioned my worries. "Suppose they know Kijana can talk to us?"

Leslie's voice came over the speakerphone. "Maybe we should get him moved, just in case." That gave me a sinking feeling – the villains wouldn't know one chimp from another. They're all just cargo to them. God, would we have to move them all? That would be impossible. Chimps have permits, like passports, and their movements are closely monitored. Anyway, where would we take them?

"Where?" I asked stupidly. I felt sick. Instead of protecting wild chimps, I had brought danger right to their captive cousins.

"Let me think about that," said Norm.

"Besides, how would you ask what he knows?" I wondered aloud. "How do you talk to a chimp about the past? Are there tenses in sign language?" I wasn't sure whether a chimpanzee understood the concept of "yesterday" or "before." Or whether we would have to wait till the shooter showed up again so Kijana could sign, "**That's the one! Book him!**"

Leslie interrupted my ruminations and brought me back to the present. "Do you know about the National Fish and Wildlife Laboratory? It's in Ashland, Oregon. They track down and convict poachers."

"You mean the whole lab is dedicated to stop poaching?" I had a vague memory of hearing about this.

"And other wildlife crimes. Say an officer knows a certain population of a protected species is dwindling. And suppose they catch the guy. The lab uses DNA to prove that the meat in his freezer matches the guts and bones he left behind at the kill site in the woods."

We contemplated this. Leslie added, "I have a friend who works there."

"If only they had this lab in Africa," I sighed, thinking of the untraceable ivory.

Norm asked me, "Does Gary at Fish and Wildlife use this lab?"

"I suppose. But remember, he doesn't know how far I've gone with this."

"Well, he'll know now," said Leslie ominously.

Norm said, "Yeah, it's almost ten o'clock. Let's turn on the news." I silently hoped my name wouldn't be mentioned. Leslie hung up and Norm turned on the goggle box. It was weird, after a lifetime of watching news accounts of elections and liftoffs and assassinations and Olympics, to see if I would be added to the parade of faces that flicker through a million living rooms. At least my story would be local. I hoped.

After a few minutes of attentive impatience and boring irrelevant stories, a picture of the zoo's entrance flashed on the screen and the announcer said, "More on yesterday's shooting at San Francisco

Zoo, right after this." We groaned and fidgeted during the commercial. Finally a local beat reporter was shown doing a standup by the zoo entrance.

"Yesterday a mysterious shooting occurred in the primate section of the San Francisco Zoo. A keeper, whose name has not been released, was shot in a service area of the chimpanzee building. No motive has been identified. There was no immediate danger to the public but the zoo was closed for several hours after the incident." Some pointless sound bites were given from zoo-goers who had been evacuated and stayed around to be interviewed. We listened eagerly, hoping one of them had seen the shooters escape. No such luck. Thankfully, there was no mention of the police finding and questioning me. I hoped my incognito would last and that tomorrow would be a busy news day, blotting out the Case of the Clobbered Keeper.

～っc～

At baggage claims, I spotted Glenn and Carolyn looking anxiously around. They brought almost no baggage (people after my own heart!), but that was the easiest place to find each other at the crowded airport.

"Hello, Julie," Carolyn said graciously, her manners outweighing her obvious worry.

"Tell us exactly what happened," Glenn said almost simultaneously. As we walked to my car, I went through the story for the tenth time. I was sure I was losing details as the complex sensory experience morphed into a narrative. The words I'd used when telling the story before came back effortlessly and the words began to seem more real than the fear I'd felt while hugging Kijana in the tunnel. I guess that's how the gabble effect works.

Once we were in the car, Glenn said, shaking his head, "We knew it was dangerous to interfere with wildlife trafficking," he said worriedly, "but we never thought they would attack someone in this country. They must be desperate."

"Yeah, either that or crazy," Carolyn added under her breath.

"Well, that's more likely than you might think," I said thoughtfully as I drove through early Sunday traffic leading out of the airport. "I've got an idea who the leader might be."

"Really!" They were astounded. After all, I was a neophyte in their field.

"Well, listen to this." I told them about the disgraced researcher whose name just happened to be the same as that of an obnoxious American in Uganda who was collecting chimps and monkeys.

"These are the species that are used in the kind of research he was doing," I said. I had used Norm's home computer to use my university password and look up Rensselaer's work.

Carolyn said doubtfully, "But if he's banned…"

"Exactly. He can't work in a lab now. But he knows what the researchers need and he knows who they are. His name in the old boy network may be mud, but the network still exists. And it still needs animals. Maybe he went on a collecting expedition himself in earlier years and knows the ropes. Who knows? Maybe that's how he's making a living now." The police hadn't been interested in this trail, but the Madisons were.

The subject was dropped temporarily as I pulled up in front of the hospital and let them out. I parked the car, locked it with their luggage in the trunk, and went upstairs to Desta's room. Nick wasn't on duty today, or at least not at the nurses' station. Now that Desta was awake more of the time and visitors were allowed, I didn't have to sneak in.

Desta was tearful, moved that Glenn and Carolyn had flown so far to be with her. Her eyes were wide with slightly nervous pleasure, as if she were afraid she couldn't hold up her end of the conversation. So Glenn and Carolyn started out with their news and the bedside reunion became a Silvana-Dougou-Patty-Zanzibar update. Eventually we turned to the present situation.

"What do we do about the media?" Carolyn wanted to know. "It was even reported in the Tucson paper. We picked one up at the airport." Oh, great.

"Did they say there were any suspects?" I asked. "Maybe they'll catch them now."

"Don't get Desta all worked up," Glenn said. "The main thing is for her to get well."

"Thanks, Glenn," she said softly, and I saw that indeed this was too much excitement.

"We can talk about this at my house," I said boldly. "You'll stay with me, I hope?" Now that we had numbers on our side, my fears began to seem exaggerated. I wanted to go back home. This was a free country. Foreigners, even ones with U.S. accomplices, can't just march around killing people in their beds. So we made sure Desta was comfortable and drove to my house in Berkeley. There was no note from Terry.

While Glenn and Carolyn were settling into my guest room, I phoned Norm to tell him I was coming back to San Francisco to pick up Scalawag and Gambado. When he heard about my guests, he jumped on the opportunity. "I'll bring them to your house!" he volunteered decisively. "I've wanted to meet the Madisons for years. Then we can decide what to do next." Before I could object, he dragged my address out of me and arrived within the hour, pets in tow.

~ ୨ ୧ ~

The four of us sat around eating pizza and strategizing.

"Well, the first thing is obviously to find out what Kijana saw," Glenn said. I was quietly pleased to hear it. My hunch about asking for the chimp's evidence hadn't been crazy after all. "I'll talk to him this afternoon. He doesn't have a great vocabulary yet, since he's only three."

Carolyn said, "Then what? So we get a description – he's never met these guys before…"

Glenn burst out, "Was Kijana-cam on? Maybe we have them on film." We sat up with a shiver of excitement. Then I remembered something: "Yes, it was probably on, but it points only in the direction of his enclosure."

"Always?" Glenn persisted. "Don't they record him when he's in the examination room?"

"I'll check, but let's not get our hopes up," I said, and made a mental note to talk to Desta's supervisor. I went on with a new thought. "How did Kijana come to you? Was he captive bred?" I asked.

"Oh, I see where you're going with that. Yeah, it would be poetic justice if they were the ones that had captured him and he ended up putting them in jail." We reveled in that vision for a moment.

Norm added, "If his evidence is accepted in court." We guffawed, so relieved at Desta's survival and her good spirits that we got a bit daffy.

"Yeah, can you see the bailiff swearing him in? 'Do you promise to sign the truth, the whole truth…'"

"Anyway," Glenn answered my question, "Kijana came to us from Coulston's, the lab that was shut down for cruelty." I remembered Anne had been talking with him about it when we were in Tucson. "I'd have to look up his history before that, but I don't think he was taken in the wild. We accepted him to give him a chance to acclimate safely to other chimps under our supervision before he was sent to a zoo." Pause. "Also, it helps shut down labs if the feds know the chimps will have some place to go. We've been on the list of sanctuaries for years."

"We can check his status this afternoon," I said. "I presume you sent his records with him?" So in two cars we drove to the San Francisco Zoo to visit with our hairy friend. Kijana was still in an enclosure by himself, as the zoo staff had decided that the recent commotion had upset everyone too much to proceed with introductions right now. They were so concerned about his mental state that once they met Glenn and Carolyn, they let us into the enclosure with him. Kijana was lying on his back kicking the hammock over his head.

"Hello, Kijana," Glenn and Carolyn said and signed in unison. Screams of joy issued from Kijana and he threw himself into their arms. They laughed and fell in a tumbling heap on the floor, rolling around and tickling. Kijana was still a kid. Roughhousing was his nature. Kijana jumped up and down, pant hooting. Glenn and Carolyn hooted back.

I wished the skeptics could have seen this.

After fifteen minutes of joyful reunion, we got down to business. Using Desta's ASL name, Glenn signed to Kijana, "Who hurt Desta?"

Kijana signed, "Desta hurt."

Glenn replied, "I know. Who?"

Kijana signed, "Desta."

This was a logical answer but it wasn't what we meant. Glenn and Carolyn tried for another few minutes, but no usable information came of it. I think Kijana was still distracted by seeing Glenn and Carolyn after a few weeks apart. He kept wanting to show them his toys.

I felt drained, in a not unpleasant way. The terror at the night house, the exhaustion of the police interrogation, the guilt and then relief about Desta's injury, and the joy of this reunion had successively washed through me. I waited for an hour while the three reunited. We finally tore ourselves away. Back in Berkeley, I told my guests to make themselves at home while I took a nap. Norm had left from the zoo in his own car to go to his office; I wondered how he could concentrate, but I guess the wheels of NGOs never stop. He promised to come over this evening so we could continue our planning. Leslie was still in the Mojave. Why not make the party complete? I thought, and phoned Anne.

She was home and said she would come, too, after she fed her family.

Over a dinner of leftovers foraged from my fridge, Norm, Glenn, Carolyn, and I brainstormed. It would help if we could trace the Ugandans who had been with Rensselaer. They knew enough English to understand the bullying American, but not enough to speak it well back to him.

"How did they get into this country? Did he smuggle them in, too?"

Glenn laughed. "That wouldn't be likely. No, I doubt if they would put up with it. Besides, there wasn't time after Julie returned from Uganda to route them through Mexico in a car trunk."

"Look," Norm said impatiently. "They wouldn't need all this rigmarole. They simply came in with him on a tourist visa using their passports."

I looked blank, and then had a rerun of the insight I'd had when hanging out with Ezekiel. Africans are not just chattels serving as porters and foils for bwana; they have their own lives and talents – and careers.

"Good trackers are valued, especially during high season," Norm said emphatically. "They shuttle back and forth to Kenya and Tanzania all the time. Of course they have passports. Ones who are old enough, anyway. The three countries now have an economic union, like Europe, but adults would have passports from before."

Glenn said, "I think Rensselaer is going to abandon them. They got violent when there was no need and he's pissed at them. Julie heard it. He doesn't need them here any more, if he ever did."

"But won't he need his experienced trackers when he gets back to Africa?"

"Well, maybe they weren't trackers."

A thought came to me. "Is this whole shooting thing going to be more than just a one-day wonder?"

"Why?"

"I don't want my face all over the news." They looked at me in silence.

Then Norm spoke. "So don't give interviews. Forego your fifteen minutes of fame. Let the zoo officials handle it."

"They will anyway, but that's not enough. The zoo's press officer will probably mention my name in the next briefing. Practically an eyewitness, you know." Now I was scaring myself. I explained: "Reporters are skilled at using online materials. They'll get my portrait from the university website and stick it on the front pages. That'll help the villains recognize me next time." There was a silence. Maybe I should go back to Norm's.

Norm wanted to get back to the pursuit. "Well, then we can either track Rensselaer or track the Ugandans. I have to feel like I'm doing *something*."

I felt hurt that my safety was so cavalierly set aside. Carolyn noticed and said, "You'll be safer if we can catch them." Well, that was true. I tried to focus on that.

We cogitated. "We don't have descriptions of any of them, not till Desta can be debriefed, and maybe not even then."

Anne arrived, talking on her cell phone as she came through the door, orchestrating her family life. Hanging up, she greeted Glenn and Carolyn, and said, "Hey, did you know it's still on the news? I heard it on the car radio."

"Did they mention Julie?" asked Norm.

"Yes. Mispronounced her name, of course." I groaned. The conversation shifted back to the Ugandans. The police would be checking their list of translators. The Bay Area has so many ethnic minorities and immigrants that in some school districts there are more than a hundred languages spoken. Undoubtedly there are networks of bilingual citizens, but the two men from Uganda wouldn't know this, or how to find them.

The Ugandan consulate wouldn't help us. The men wouldn't go there to hide or escape. Even if they did, the consulate would be obligated to side with their countrymen until guilt was established. We didn't have that kind of time. Still, Glenn said, "I say we go after the men first. Maybe they're sick of being poachers and are ready to flip."

Carolyn retorted, "Are you dreaming? One of them just shot Desta, unprovoked. Ready, my foot."

"Well, don't bite my head off."

"Besides, for all we know they *do* have friends or contacts here and could sink out of sight," she added.

There was a pause. Then Norm asked, "Well, then, do we go after Mr. Big?"

It was odd how we were assuming it was up to us to catch the gunmen. In fact, there were others involved, professional crime fighters and law enforcers – the local police, customs... I made a note to call my friends on the SFPD.

What about CITES? Interpol? But we didn't know what any of the agents were doing. Everyone in the room except me had spent years crossing borders and tackling a kind of wrongdoing that some people didn't even consider to be a crime. It was exhilarating, in a way, to be part of this little cadre of rescuers. In the background was an alphabet soup of other cadres. Maybe we should call in the pros; I hadn't been in touch with Melissa or Randy or Gary or Don in weeks. But now to call them up while I was in trouble? Surely they would be angry or disgusted. I found out later they would gladly have helped, but my pride got in the way. I didn't call them.

"Julie, you said you knew who he was," Norm reminded everyone. So I explained again about the defrocked researcher and my hunch that he was now the bullying hunter in Uganda and the shooter's boss in San Francisco.

"His name stuck in my mind because it's an odd one. I have an unusual name, too, so I always sympathize."

Norm said, "So, does he know who you are?"

"Maybe. I'm in a different field. His case was widely reported and I mentioned it in one of my papers. I told the police that might be the connection, but now I'm not so sure. I suppose if he was a masochist reading articles about academic fraud he might have come across it. No, I think he just traced me from my snooping in Uganda." Until Carl called back with information from the Science Citation Index, this would be my theory.

"You quoted his scandal?" Anne squeaked in horrified delight.

"Yeah, well, I used his case of academic fraud to show how pressure to publish can be as powerful a motive for deception as greed is. Mostly I do forensics. And college sophomores." That world of classrooms and dissertations seemed far away. Then I remembered a possible enemy I'd made in academia: that researcher I'd blocked from being hired by the university, Mr. Oily Man. I tried to remember what he was studying – something about toxicology. Those people experiment on animals by the hundred, and always need new ones. They have a research standard called LD 50, which means "lethal dose 50%" – half the experimental animals die of whatever chemical you gave them. Would he remember me from that meeting on campus? I had been introduced, he had repeated my name...

Anne said, "Something just occurred to me. Maybe it was that cult leader – what's his name? Kony – who sent someone after you."

I hadn't even thought of that. Oh, great. Enemy #3. Cult members with guns. My mind raced as I tried to remember the attack. Did the shooter's voice sounded deep, a man's voice, or like an adolescent boy's? The thought of Kony pursuing me was so appalling that I squelched it as fast as I could. "Come on, Anne," I said. "He's busy running an army. Even the government of Uganda can't eliminate him. Why should he be afraid of me?"

Norm said, "Well, you did tell people about how to stay out of cults. You told me all about it."

"Oh, sure, big threat. Don't you suppose Ugandans have been thinking and talking about that for ten years? Besides, I was mostly bitching about how people get sucked into American cults, not about how to get out. And he doesn't recruit people, he captures them." Still, I was uneasy to think that I had made not one but two powerful enemies in Uganda. Matt would have loved it. Damn the man. Where was he now that I needed him?

I kept trying to talk myself out of the Kony worry. But Norm was right. I had told people in Uganda that some people escape from cults, but I hadn't said how. In my paranoia, I imagined a ghastly game of Telephone, in which the message gets farther and farther from the truth. Maybe the grapevine told Kony about the white lady who knew how to liberate his zombies. As in a bad dream, I morphed into a declared enemy of Kony. He and his lieutenants were even now plotting to get me… they would kidnap Scalawag and phone me saying they had him and lure me to a dark spot…

I phoned my police friend and got him on the case. He said he'd set me up with protection and agreed to meet me the next day after his shift was over.

We raided the fridge again. I felt shaky but lucky to have Norm and Anne, Glenn and Carolyn on my side. No one made a move to leave. Finally Norm said, "What about this wildlife lab? They could map the smuggling network…"

"Jeez, not now. We have to keep Julie and Desta and Kijana safe first."

The phone rang and I interrupted the powwow to pick up. "Julie, is that you?" It was Carl. "I just heard about the zoo." Carl sounded more upset than I'd ever heard him. "Is this anything to do with your latest mischief? Why didn't you TELL me?"

"Oh, hi," I said, and signaled to the others that I would take the call. "Yes, I was there. No, I'm ok. I just had to talk to the police for about a million hours. I didn't tell you because… because…" I couldn't think of a good reason and trailed off.

"Julie, I hope you're going to be smart enough to stop this, whatever it is," he said with a touching mix of anxiety and authority. "I don't know what you're up to, but this isn't funny any more."

I looked around at my allies. Norm and Carolyn were at the fireplace, talking earnestly. Carolyn had Gambado in her lap and Scalawag sat between them, looking from one to the other and hoping for a handout. Anne and Glenn were in the kitchen. Frank Halloran was on the case.

"Relax," I told Carl. "I'm in good hands." He protested a bit more. To reassure him, I added, "I'll call you if I need more help."

When I hung up, Norm and Carolyn looked at me intently. I could see they were sharing the same thought.

"Ok, you two, what is it?"

"The Ashland lab," Carolyn said.

"Match the DNA of chimps with their lineages," Norm said.

"Trace individual chimps?" I responded. "I thought you'd never ask." They had realized that the fastest way to keep us safe was to discover who was smuggling chimps from Uganda into the U.S., and to start at the buyer end of the chain. So Carolyn contacted her friend at the wildlife forensics lab and persuaded her to accept the samples of chimp DNA.

Now just one small hurdle. Collect the samples.

◝ XIII ◜

"Yo, girl. Danger past? Lay some info on me. Your &%@*#$# adventure scared the vocabulary out of me."

A note from Terry. She must have stopped in briefly when I was out this morning. Rats, I'd forgotten to tell her the coast was clear. Instantly I rang her cell phone and left a message telling her to come home. I'd have to make it up to her, since she must have been sleeping on a friend's sofa for days. A few hours later, she arrived, parked her car in the driveway, and came in. I went downstairs to her flat and explained the whole thing. I was amazed by her response: she began to cry.

"Julie, I was so scared," she said. "Not for me – I got out of the house the second I read that note you left." She laughed a little through her tears. "'Eschew,' honestly." We laughed. "I was scared for you. I know you mess around with police cases and track down psychopaths, but you're always so calm about it all. I try to keep it out of my mind. But now it seemed like trouble had finally found you. I was so scared." She cried again. I put my arm around her and made soothing sounds and felt guilty. Who knew what she had been going through? I tried to remember what I knew about her. Father left when she was five, mother died of breast cancer when she was nineteen, her only sibling in the military far away… she was more alone than I'd realized. I was someone stable in her life, the friendly landlady upstairs who invited her to my faculty parties and was always available to drive her to the repair shop when her aged car broke down.

I stayed with her for an hour until the worst of her jitters had subsided, and went upstairs. Terry's reaction sobered me. I'm in way over my head. I should have called Interpol when I'd thought of it. If only I had... Maybe Desta wouldn't have been shot, wouldn't be in the hospital, I wouldn't feel this scared and guilty... Recriminations are wrenching. I could use a really good rationalization. I thought of one: maybe even Interpol couldn't have prevented the shooting. They're the experts, but they can't be everywhere. Why don't I just call them – throw myself on their mercy, put the whole thing in their hands, endure their sniffs of disdain or outright finger-pointing. They'll know what to do. They'll know who the smugglers are and how to arrest them and keep them away from Berkeley.

I was feeling just the way I had felt as a kid when I'd gotten into trouble. I just wanting Mom to fix it, make the nightmare go away. But Mom couldn't keep me safe from criminals who saw me as a threat. I hoped Interpol could.

But can you just call up the second biggest international organization in the world? It had to be done, so I would try audacity and luck, trying not to look like a ninny who got into trouble and expected them to clean it up. At the very least, I should compose myself and convey a coherent story so they can make sense of it. Ok. Right. So... I'm in Uganda seeing the animals and yes, I'm interested in wildlife smuggling, everyone's heard of that (small lie) and I have a professional interest and behold! I encountered the villains and brought them home with me.

No, try again. Hello, this is Dr. Julie Heidebrecht and I have a lead that can help you solve one of your cases. That's better. Now I just needed to track down Interpol's organizational chart and learn the names of their current projects and get the right person on the phone. If I had the time, I'd also read the proceedings from their conferences, learn their lingo, approach them as an equal. Maybe I could invite myself onto a task force. Maybe Norm would let me represent SaveNature. Then there's the university – check with the biology department to see if they have any projects I could horn in on. I now had half-baked plans to try later.

Then I worked on my self-image for a while. I got out my pile of publications and conference programs to remind myself that my peers published and respected my work. My neglected ideas gazed at me reproachfully from the page, reminding me of all the research topics I could have taken further and turned into fame and fortune. Well, too late now. Here I am haring off after another new one. I admired my resume and began to believe I would be welcomed by Interpol as a valuable resource. I would offer them a workshop on my area of expertise, facial expressions and vocal frequencies in forensic settings. Wildlife defenders are always operating on a shoestring anyway; who would turn away free expertise?

According to its website, Interpol has a standing committee, the Interpol Wildlife Working Group, which has had some spectacular successes, especially in collaboration with other agencies. One of these, called "Operation Jungle Trade," took three years, involved 42 offices around the world (including Fish and Wildlife and Customs in the U.S.), arrested 40 smugglers, and rescued 660 animals, not to mention saving the other animals the smugglers would later have captured. This was encouraging.

Suitably prepared, I got on the phone, worked my way along the chain of responsibility to what I hoped was the right person, and after initial introductions, offered my services. He said in a friendly fashion, "Call me Jeff."

"Thanks, Jeff. May I ask who screens likely suspects for you? How much time could you save if you had an expert on voice and face? That's my area of expertise."

"Hmm, that's an interesting angle. We don't have a psychologist on staff. What exactly would you do for us?"

"Mostly interviews. I review taped interviews and testify for you if it comes to a trial. Maybe help you secure a confession and avoid the expense of a trial. I've already worked with U.S. Customs; you could ask Randy Carstairs here in San Francisco. I helped his team on an animal smuggling case." Now that I had established my credentials, I brought up primates and Uganda. "Actually, that's why I'm calling. This is a new area for me and I'm really interested in going deeper. I know of a possible suspect you may not have on your list."

"Really?" I now had his full attention.

"This is confidential, right?" I wanted to avoid enraging Rensselaer further, not to mention a slander suit if Interpol flubbed the case. "If I give you a name, what happens to my tip? Will he find out who snitched on him?"

"No, of course not. We'd never get anywhere if we didn't protect our sources. Who is it?" His voice carried conviction and honest vibes. I decided to trust him.

"Derek Rensselaer." I spelled it for him. "I have two reasons for thinking he might be involved in animal smuggling. One, he used to be a medical researcher, defrocked now, but he knows the medical underground. Two, I'm almost positive he was the one who tried to shoot me not long ago."

"Shoot you? Where? Are you sure?"

"Jeff, I'm sure he – or someone – was trying to capture me. They ended up shooting someone else who got in their way. I work with police on cases, but I don't have any public recognition. Well, not until this week." I described the whole story, including my fifteen minutes of fame. Jeff listened intently and said, "This sounds like a lead we should look into. Could you write this up and send it to me? I'll forward it to the primate department." He gave me his contact information and I promised to send him a summary.

I hung up and heaved a sigh of relief. Just knowing that someone on the international stage knew about this project made the world feel a little safer.

___୨ ୧___

"**Boat**," signed Kijana. "**Boat**."

"**No, it's a car**," I signed, but then I turned around and looked at the street. Sure enough, a passing car was pulling a trailer with a boat on it. Now, how did Kijana know that was a boat? He'd only seen photographs of boats in water. I was impressed. Clearly, he was able to transpose things from one context to another and translate from photograph to reality. This fit with what I'd been hearing in recent months – that a chimp has the intelligence of a four-year-old child.

We were standing on a grassy spot behind the north wing of the hospital. I'd never thought my harebrained scheme would work, but once I suggested it, all the keepers had gotten together and stormed the administration until they gave us permission to bring Kijana here for a surprise visit. Desta was a relatively new co-worker, but they rallied round after her injury, like police officers who travel hundreds of miles to attend the funeral of a cop they don't even know. While negotiating permission for this little trip, Glenn diplomatically reminded the zoo administrators that Kijana's transfer paperwork wasn't completed. He never actually threatened to take Kijana back to Tucson if they didn't allow this jaunt, but I think they got the hint. He and Carolyn had stayed behind to sign more papers taking responsibility and were coming to join us any minute. Three keepers came in on their day off, borrowed the zoo-mobile, emptied out all the stuff that usually gets taken to the elementary school presentations (hedgehog carrier, parrot stand, etc.), and maneuvered Kijana into it. Now we were standing in a little knot and hoping we wouldn't cause a car accident from drivers craning their necks in disbelief and giving themselves whiplash.

I looked at my watch. Nick was supposed to casually encourage Desta to look out the window at exactly three pm.

"**Stay**," I signed to Kijana. "**See Desta soon**." I still had to think twice about which signs to use, but Kijana seemed to understand me anyway and began to jump up and down, making excited hoots. I hoped he would be able to recognize her from thirty yards away.

"There she is!" exclaimed one of the keepers.

"**Look**," I signed, and pointed. Desta's face appeared in the window, looking to her left into the distance. "Hey, Desta!" I shouted and she looked our way. When she saw Kijana, her expression was worth a million dollars. Her eyes widened. She laughed aloud and began signing. Kijana gibbered in excitement and before we knew it had scrambled over the driveway and reached the building. Oh, shit. I just hope they get to say hello before security comes out on the double. I ran after him. One of the keepers quickly moved the zoo-mobile, blocking the view from the hospital's first floor. Pant-hoots came thick and fast. I looked up. Desta beamed with a smile as wide as Carol Channing's.

"**Desta happy**," she signed. "**Kiss**." She paused to make sure Kijana understood. "**Desta come soon**."

"**Hurry hug**," signed Kijana.

Desta kept signing "**Kijana stay**" from the window so he wouldn't keep trying to get closer. Glenn and Carolyn drove up just then and joined us. The level of sophistication in the patient-visitor conversation went up dramatically.

I hadn't felt so happy in weeks.

"**Yes, Desta in big building**," Carolyn echoed Kijana's signs, and added "**Desta can't play now**."

"**Desta bad girl?**" Kijana asked. Awww, he was worried that she was being punished.

"**No, Desta hurt. Doctors helping Desta. Desta good girl**." Carolyn replied.

"**Good girl**," Kijana echoed.

We stayed outside Desta's window for twenty minutes until, as if by telepathy, we all looked at each other and knew it was time to go. Glenn and Carolyn left with Kijana and the keepers to take him back to the zoo. "**Bye**," I signed. But Kijana was busy talking to Glenn and Carolyn. I sighed and waved as the two-car caravan pulled away.

When I reached her room, I was in luck. Desta was still smiling and Nick was still there. So was Minnie. The social worker must have had no luck in finding her a placement.

"Oh, Julie, thank you for bringing Kijana!" Desta's eyes were big and she collapsed giggling onto a chair. "Oh, it was worth it," as she winced and leaned on the arm of the chair. "Don't make me laugh." A doctor arrived. It was time for Desta's two-minute daily checkup. As he examined her stitches, she signed to me, "**hurt**."

"You should be resting," the doctor said to Desta innocently. He must have missed the show in the yard outside. "Your heart rate is up. I'm sorry, miss," he said to me, "You'll have to go soon." He pulled the traveling sheet screen and Desta was soon hidden from view. Unspeakable medical acts would be performed behind it.

Life went on. Nick handed Minnie a 7-up, saying with mock severity, "No burping allowed."

"There's nothing wrong with burping, young man," she said frostily. "As long as you're discreet. What did they teach you in nursing school, anyway?" Would wonders never cease – Minnie defending natural functions. Maybe she was just being oppositional.

"But think what you're missing!" He had that mischievous grin again. He was kinda cute. I wondered where he spent his evenings.

"Missing? What do you mean, missing?" She looked suspicious.

"Every time you burp, you cheat yourself out of a good fart."

Minnie compressed her lips to keep from laughing, but a small snort gave her away. She rattled her newspaper in front of her to hide her smile, but I wasn't fooled. She sat even straighter. "She's awake now," she told me unnecessarily from behind the front page. Poor old dear. I bet no one had come to visit her.

"Hi, Miss Manners," I greeted her and immediately wished I hadn't. Why rub it in? "May I call you Minnie?" I hastily added, contritely. "I'm Julie."

She came out from behind the newspaper. "I know, I know. Desta keeps telling us how you're saving the world."

"Minnie," I said suddenly. "Could you help? We need to find out how much she saw of the men."

"This is a hospital, not a detective agency," she said, keeping up her cynical front. But her face said her heart wasn't in it and I knew that one more nudge would get her on our side.

"Did you get to see Kijana just now? Oh, right, you can't get out of bed…"

"I'm supposed to be walking. The physical therapist tells me to. I happened to be by the window, so yes, I saw him." She gave a small smile. "Desta was very pleased," she added in a major understatement.

"Isn't Kijana clever?" I enthused. "He knows over a hundred words already."

"How can you be sure?" she asked, but not in that arrogant tone of the skeptics. She seemed dubious, but honestly curious.

"Well, you saw them signaling, right?" Minnie nodded. "Remember when Desta made this sign?" I made the sign for "**stay**."

"Not really," Minnie said with a furrowed brow.

"It means '**stay**'," I explained. "Desta was telling him not to keep running toward the hospital."

"Oh, yes, now I remember. He was coming forward, then he stopped."

"Exactly. He did what the word says." I made the sign for '**stay**' again. "See? It worked."

Minnie nodded thoughtfully. I hoped it was safe to repeat my request. "If Desta wakes up, can you ask her what she remembers? I'll come tomorrow. You give the message to Desta. Ok? Then you can tell me what she says if she's asleep next time I visit." I hoped the prospect of having both a visitor and a mystery would be too tempting for her to resist. As I left, I gave her a wink and signed "**stay**." She laughed and didn't try to hide it.

───── ✺ ─────

To keep up Desta's spirits, I visited the zoo regularly so I could bring her news of Kijana's doings. The young chimp was exuberant and curious, keeping the enrichment staff busy coming up with new toys and activities. He had fully joined the existing troop; after being cuffed once or twice by the alpha male, he located his place in the dominance hierarchy and obeyed the rules of chimp society. This includes frequent interactions and a lot of deception. Like every self-respecting chimp, Kijana played tricks on the others: pretending he didn't know where treats had been stashed, mischievously poking a sleeping animal and then running away looking innocent. I loved watching the ancient roots of human deceptiveness being played out right in front of my eyes.

I ran back and forth along the front of the enclosure, inducing a decent imitation of chase and tickle. I learned new signs: **play, not now, wait**. He asked over and over, "**Where Glenn? Where Carolyn?**" He missed them. Talking to Kijana regularly, I improved my ASL and began absent-mindedly signing basic phrases like "**thank you**" to students and store clerks.

I even began signing secretly to Nick. "**You're hot**," I signed once. "**Wait, I get you alone**." Of course he didn't notice, but it released the tension of my secret. Once, as he left the room, I signed to Desta, "**beautiful man**," and she smiled mischievously. I scowled at her severely and added one more sign: "**Mine**."

Next day at the hospital I passed Anne in the hall. She was leaving just as I came in. We commiserated and promised to reconnoiter later. A new nurse tried to stop me from entering, saying that Desta couldn't take any more visitors.

"But I'm here to see Ms. Montrose. Isn't that right, Minnie?"

"Yes, it is. We were just going to discuss my exercise regimen," Minnie improvised with a straight face. "Did you bring the dumbbells?"

"No, but I brought the enema," I said and pretended to grope in my handbag. I looked over to see if she was flummoxed. I should have known better.

"Oh, the same kind you use?" Minnie said tartly. She was entering into the spirit of our game. She would have been a champion at Fictionary. Or maybe she had been a spy during World War II. Vanessa, now in seventh grade, had told me once that there were dozens of women secret agents. She was doing a report on them.

Finally the nurse left. Minnie said instantly, "I told her what you said. She said to contact Ezekiel." Minnie was leaning forward, speaking in a conspiratorial tone and doing a poor job of not looking excited.

"She said that? Contact Ezekiel?"

"Well, not exactly. She just said Ezekiel would know." That was a good clue, actually, in the few words a wounded sleepy gunshot victim could say. That meant I was right, that the attackers were Ugandans speaking in Swahili. Desta must have been a good listener to remember Ezekiel's name from my traveler's tales.

Desta had already fallen asleep, worn out by the excitement of Kijana's visit, so Minnie and I chatted about travel and danger and animals. Finally Desta stirred. I scuttled over to her bed. When her eyes opened, I asked breathlessly, "Is it ok to ask you about the – you know. Do you know who did this?"

Desta was tired but game. "I think there were two of them. Two black guys. They were nosy and opening all the doors looking for something or someone. I was afraid they would let the chimps out." What a relief. She remembered.

"Did they say anything?"

"Not to me. They were talking to each other. I couldn't understand it. I was already on the floor by then." So she had been conscious for a moment before blacking out.

I was eager to hear her tell the whole story, but I didn't want to tire her out. The police report would tell more, if I could get access to it. After Glenn and Carolyn had returned to Tucson yesterday, I appointed myself the unofficial town crier and relayed news to Anne and Norm. Leslie was back from the desert and joined our deliberations. Leslie is like Norm, practical and dedicated. Unlike me, she was unafraid.

"Julie, is that you?" It was Randy on the phone. "You're late."

Oh my god, today I was supposed to testify against Bechard, the furrier. I'd completely forgotten. The grand jury would be furious if I wasn't there to give my evidence.

"Oh no, I forgot."

"I thought you might, with all you're going through. That's why you were supposed to meet me at my office an hour ahead of time, remember? I wanted to go over your testimony with you."

"Oh shit," I said and ran my hand through my hair. "What time is it? I'll get there as fast as I can."

"Come straight to the courthouse. Use the police parking lot. I'll tell the attendant to let you in."

"I'm on my way," I said and was out the door.

Crossing the Bay Bridge with my mind racing was becoming a habit, but at least this time my life wasn't on the line. I screeched into the police parking lot and raced up the courthouse steps. Randy was waiting. "This way," he said and we strode down the echoing hallways to the grand jury room. Now that I was here, my mind slowed down and I rehearsed my answers. No, I hadn't known Bechard before. Yes, I went in to the store under false pretenses but didn't break any laws. No, I didn't see him on my first visit to his fur boutique, but I did when Randy and I met him in his office, having made an appointment in my own name. All this ran through my mind as we entered at the back of the grand jury room and took our seats. I caught my breath and watched the proceedings. Eventually it was my turn.

"And did you determine through your expertise in reading facial expressions that he was in fact lying when he denied selling illegal furs?" The prosecutor was questioning me.

"We don't determine with facial expressions if someone's lying, but we can read their emotions. Mr. Bechard showed a micro-expression of panic when I named all the species his employee Ian had shown me."

"And he knew the purpose of your visit? That is, the visit when you were accompanied by Mr. Carstairs?"

"He did after the first two minutes. We identified ourselves and our intention."

I was grateful that grand jury proceedings did not require the presence of the accused. Bechard was a slimy type and I didn't want to see him again, at least not yet. If the grand jury indicted him, I would have to face him at his trial. But I've looked villains in the eye in courtrooms before.

"So what made you conclude that Mr. Bechard was lying?"

"Characteristics of his voice. The facial expressions give us an idea if someone is trying to hide something." I spent the next half hour explaining the science and left the chamber feeling I had done a really good day's work.

~ ♪ ℭ ~

Over the next week, I visited Desta almost daily. She begged me not to say any more funny things, as laughing strained her stitches. I always spent some time by Minnie's bed, too, asking her about neutral topics or places she had visited. So I learned about Minnie. Her husband had died in the Korean War, before they had had a chance to start a family. Later she was a mystery shopper for department stores in the 1950s, traveling from one city to another and trying to catch pilfering employees, not just inattentive ones. Minnie spoke about these times with quiet dignity. She remembered all the cities she had seen.

A few days later, a severe-looking nurse was repressively discouraging conversation with frowns and ostentatious glances at the wall clock. I tried to give hand signals to Desta, but my vocabulary was still too small. I couldn't convey much about our mission with "**open**," "**drink**," and "**tickle me**." Even when Nick caught me trying to communicate with Desta, he frowned and shook his head warningly. So when no medical people were in the room, I simply talked to them both. When a nurse or dietician showed up, or when Desta was asleep, I gave messages to Minnie, asking her to pass them on to Desta. I found out when we compared notes later that she was very good at this, very precise and accurate. Desta didn't tell me till *much* later that Minnie also imitated my mannerisms to a T.

The second week, Minnie said suddenly, "You should look for the buyers, not the sellers."

"What?" I hadn't heard her at first.

"I've been thinking about it. If you keep tracking down the smugglers themselves, they're bound to strike back. You see what they've done already," and she gestured to Desta, who was asleep. I shouldn't have been surprised. Minnie was sharp and had nothing else to do all day.

"And furthermore, you should look for the person who pays Rensselaer."

Desta woke up at this point. "Say what?"

"Look for the person who pays Rensselaer." Minnie continued with her suggestion. "Who manages the network in this country while he's over there collecting… specimens?"

Desta adopted this idea immediately. "I get it. We follow the pipeline upward beyond Rensselaer. Ooh, Julie, that's good." I didn't want to spoil the mood by saying we'd already considered this strategy.

"And look here." Minnie was on a roll. She picked up a magazine that had been on the nightstand between their beds. "See this monkey? Look at its eyes."

It was a photograph of a lab monkey in a story about animal research. The monkey was looking directly at the camera, apparently calm. There were no visible wounds or machinery bored into its skull. I didn't see how this picture could help us locate smugglers. I looked quizzically at Minnie.

"Do you know northern Renaissance art?" she asked. Uh oh, she was going to lose her train of thought, just when I was sure she was the sharpest old person ever. "Do you remember that famous painting of the Arnolfini wedding? The skinny pale guy in the ridiculous hat and the woman in the long green gown, holding hands?" At each question she looked at me intently, waiting for my mental image search to catch up with her. "On the wall behind them, there's a curved round mirror hanging on the wall." She stopped, as if mission accomplished. Realizing with some disgust that mission was not accomplished, she went on, speaking slowly as if to a child: "Reflected in the mirror are the backs of the couple, the rest of the room that is assumed to be behind you, the viewer, and the artist with his easel." She smiled at us triumphantly.

Desta was looking the way you do when a forgotten word has almost resurfaced. I didn't get it at all. Minnie pointed to the magazine photograph and explained.

"The reflection shows you what's behind the camera!"

Bingo! The photograph of the monkey's eye would give us a peek into the room he was sitting in.

Eagerly we examined the photograph of the monkey to see how much of the room was reflected in his pupil. The picture was a decent size, about six inches by four, but the pupil was smaller than my pinkie's fingernail. Even so, you could make out reflected shapes. I was excited.

"Let's get this blown up. Who knows what we'll be able to see?"

Desta asked, "Which magazine is this from? Who took the picture?" We practically fell over each other turning to the story's credits.

"It's from *Animals and Nature.* That's a publication of the AZA. Anne must have left it for you."

Minnie promoted herself to full team membership and asked, "How can we get the negative?"

Desta explained, "Better than that. It's probably a pdf file. If we can track down the photographer he can just send it to us online."

I was elated. "Oh, man, this is good. Then we can blow it up instantly. Any scale we please."

It took a little trouble, but we pulled all the strings we had. In less than two days the file landed in my computer. I couldn't resist peeking, but heroically resisted making a thorough examination. I loaded it onto my tablet and headed for the hospital.

Desta was asleep as usual, so I turned on my tablet and called up the photo so it would be ready. Minnie was almost as excited as I was. Just then Anne arrived.

We shut the door and whispered so we wouldn't be caught with too many visitors in the room.

"Desta, wake up! It's here!" Anne whispered loudly. Desta opened her eyes. I rested my tablet on the rolling tray table between the beds. Desta sat up. We devoured the picture with our eyes.

"Ok, I'm zooming in on the pupil," I said, matching action to words. After a few more zooms there were sharply defined but puzzling shapes. We had to mentally flatten out the images that were reflected in the monkey's curved eye.

"It looks like a box, or hallway. Have we got it wrong? Is this a door?"

"Look, what's that line? It goes up from the middle of that frame, or whatever it is." I zoomed in. The line was a chain. I followed it upwards and it ended in the ceiling. I followed the chain back down and zoomed around the picture, enlarging first one area, then another. Now the whole perceptual puzzle fell into place. The square shape was a cage suspended off the ground.

"I've heard of those," said Desta sadly. "The cage is a steel box, about five feet by five feet by maybe seven feet high. The monkey lives there its entire life. The lab operators hang them from the ceiling." We looked again, with a shared sick feeling. The excitement of the successful hunt faded. We gazed despondently at each other. No one wanted to imagine the monkey's life.

"So in the reflection is the hanging cage the monkey usually lives in. See, there's another one just beyond."

"So to get the picture they just set up a corner of the lab and threw down a rug and a toy. Probably drugged the little fellow, not too much, just enough to hold him still. They do that all the time. And then they probably propped him in a corner and poked him with a stick to make him open his eyes."

We looked at the dungeon. I asked, "From this layout, can we detect which lab this is? Then we can demand to know if their chimps are legitimate. We could use the Freedom of Information Act."

Anne let out a heavy sigh. "You don't ask much, do you?"

"Well, can we?"

"I don't know. I hate those places. They pretend they're helping humanity and maybe they are. Do we have to think about this?" The long silence was her answer.

"Ok," she sighed again. "Oh, man, this means working with the animal rights people. They don't like us too much."

"I know. Well, my enemy's enemy is my friend, you know. Let's get started."

⟶꣸ XIV ꣸⟵

While Norm and Anne worked on tracking down the lab we'd seen in the photos, I investigated Vincent and Rensselaer so I could give more information about them to Interpol. With Carl's help, I found the link we needed – a lab assistant who had been dragged down with them, Sonya by name. Meeting her at her house, I looked her over. My deception detector was on high alert and I hoped my own mask was securely in place.

"So you worked under Harold Vincent for… how long?"

"About five years. Last year of medical school, internship, residency, postdoc." Sony was about 35, with circles under her eyes and a defeated, surly expression.

"What was your position?"

"I was his lab assistant on the NIH grant."

"And your duties?"

"I ran the actual tests. Standard bench work. Not very challenging." Uh oh, another budding narcissist. Or maybe she was just trying to downplay the incident, get some distance from the humiliation and loss.

"Did you interact with the chimpanzees yourself?"

"No, I just read the slides of the blood work and wrote up the results. A guy named Tucker took the samples and did the preparations." I remembered that to lab scientists, a living creature that had been subjected to an experimental procedure like implanting electrodes or severing its spinal cord wasn't called a mouse or a rhesus monkey. It was called a "preparation."

"What was it like, working for Vincent?" I asked conversationally. Sonya grimaced and shifted slightly in her chair. I judged these were not signs of impending deception but of unpleasant memories. She was choosing her words carefully. Finally, she said, "Driven." Pause. I said sympathetically, "Long hours?"

She laughed grimly. "*Oh* yeah."

"Gee, that must have been frustrating, keeping you from your own research." She relaxed fractionally. Maybe she was pleased someone finally noticed that particular sacrifice.

"I thought it was worth it at the time."

Carl had located Sonya with some clever sleuthing. As Sherlock Holmes once said, there is no better source of inside information than a discharged servant with a grievance. When I asked him to get more dirt on Vincent and Rensselaer, he figured that someone whose career had been derailed would be willing to talk. I didn't know how he found her – are names of lab assistants public information on grant applications? Anyway, he did it somehow. I was fairly straightforward when I called. "I'm Julie Heidebrecht at the psychology department at Berkeley, looking into the fallout from academic fraud. Would you be willing to talk to me?" After some hesitation, she agreed. Maybe she needed the gabble effect, too, even after all this time.

Sonya hadn't taken the fall with Rensselaer when his faking was discovered, but her career had suffered. Five years slogging away for Vincent and then the main project she had been working on couldn't be published. It was a crushing blow.

"Vincent kept us at it constantly," she said in answer to my question. "Hurry, hurry. Rensselaer wasn't like that at first. We used to order Thai food late at night and talk about our ideas. Then Vincent became more demanding. I got divorced during this time, did I tell you? But I believed. How I believed. Just one more data run, one more tweaking of the research protocol. Vincent kept reminding us that people were dying every day. As if we weren't thinking about that already. But I don't care any more," she said with defiant disgust. I knew she was now working as a pathologist. Useful medical work, but not directly saving lives. A far cry from her youthful hopes.

"You said Rensselaer was an ok guy when you first met him."

"Yeah, but that didn't last long. He and Vincent used to hole up in Vincent's office for hours, days. Rensselaer wormed his way into Vincent's good graces." She snorted disdainfully. "I was jealous at the time."

"When did you suspect something wasn't right?" I asked as neutrally as I could.

"When the results began to look *too* good. At first I thought it meant I wasn't smart enough, that I had to work harder to make the same progress Rensselaer was making. I never would have spotted it, frankly.

That graduate student from Johns Hopkins did, though."

"Do you know if Vincent or Rensselaer ever interacted directly with chimps?"

"Not really. I don't care. Look, I don't romanticize nature. Predators eat prey, parasites live off hosts, big fish eat little fish. As Woody Allen said, nature is just one gigantic restaurant."

It was time to bring this to a close. Sonya was not an accomplice, just disillusioned. One more casualty of academic ambition. At least she'd given me another link in the chain – Tucker, the lab guy who did the procedures on the chimps.

I passed our speculations and observations along to Interpol and to the officials who got me into this whole venture: Don (NIH), Randy (Customs), Melissa (AZA), and Gary (Fish and Wildlife). They would now follow Rensselaer's contacts in Uganda. So the trade was being tackled at that end. We found out later that they caught one ringleader red-handed; this gave some welcome encouragement to the rangers and pride to the agencies. Meanwhile, we tackled this end.

Thanks to Minnie, we decided to follow the idea we'd rejected earlier and track the buyers. Medical labs are the biggest legal buyers of primates and we suspected they tapped the black market as well. Anne would get the names of the most active animal rights organizations and I would ask them for their list of labs they suspected of taking contraband chimps. The awful place we had seen reflected in the monkey's eye would be a good starting point.

Anne guessed it was the Northern Industrial Research Supply. NIRS had almost 400 captive chimps and was currently facing ethics charges for mistreating them. Maybe conditions there were so appalling that animals died all the time and the experimenters kept having to replace them. I remembered that this was where that nasty animal trainer from Southern California had gotten his chimp.

To link NIRS to smuggled chimpanzees, we would need blood samples from chimps that we suspected of being in this country illegally. Fortunately, Vincent's lab was right here in the Bay Area, the biotechnology industry's epicenter. If anyone was in possession of smuggled chimps, it would be he. Maybe Nick would come with me into his lab to extract samples secretly. There was a certain romantic allure to have him sneak in with me, share the fear, escape dramatically, breathing heavily in relief upon escaping. I got quite carried away by this fantasy. But it wouldn't be fair to ask him – breaking into a lab could risk his nursing license. Besides, what if he *liked* this adventure? What if he became like Matt and wanted more scary adventures? Better plan: have him show me how to draw blood by practicing on an orange, the way he learned. Say it's just for fun. But maybe later he would resent being used. That could sour our relationship…

I finally admitted that getting closer to Nick was as important to me as catching smugglers.

Luckily, while snooping on the Ashland lab's website, I discovered that you don't need blood to get DNA. A hair pulled out by the root works just as well, since there's living material in the root. But how could I get into the lab to pull the hairs? Time to contact Tucker, the technician at Vincent's lab that Sonya had mentioned. Maybe he could get us in. Better yet, have him get the samples and hand them off to us. No break-in needed.

Now to locate Tucker. Sonya wouldn't help; she didn't care. But maybe this would be easy and he would still be at Vincent's lab. Not everyone changed jobs every year like Terry. I would tell him I have my own research lab but that I'm having trouble finding good assistants. I'd heard about him from a friend and wondered if he could give me some advice on how to hold on to good help. There was enough truth in that story that I could sustain it for half an hour.

Vincent's lab south of San Francisco is a renowned one easily found in the directory, so I just picked up the telephone and asked for Mr. Tucker. Sure enough, he was there. At least one thing in this whole operation was easy.

As I'd hoped, Tucker sounded burned out and ready to leave. Too bad for him, but it played into our hands. He was happy to meet me after work. If lab techs have a confidentiality clause in their contracts, he was long past caring about it.

As I drove to the rendezvous, I rehearsed my approach and tried to imagine the lives of lab technicians. What was their workday like? What would touch them? What would make them rebel? Would the fact that they are inflicting pain harden them? What psychological defenses did they use? One of my graduate students did her research on how butchers can live with the memory of what they do all day. She found that emotional numbness is the main defense; not having feelings at all. That was probably the main one for lab techs, too. Or they could idealize their work, visualizing the human lives they would be saving. Another common technique is to exaggerate the less-desirable habits of the animals, thinking of them as obnoxious, calling them nasty names... After all, demonizing the enemy is how we teach young people to go to war.

If Tucker was a cruel man he wouldn't need any defense mechanisms. Then I'd have to appeal to some other motive, perhaps resentment at being underpaid. But I hoped he was a decent person who had just wandered into a lab job and never gotten around to leaving, staying on year after year, squelching his sadness and guilt. I hoped he would still have access to what was going on and have all the keys, yet be disillusioned enough to help.

One more rendezvous at yet another coffee shop. This was getting to be a habit. It was like blind dating all over the Bay Area. Tucker was about my age, fortyish, with long-ago acne scars and a throaty growl for a voice. We exchanged pleasantries. I came to the topic in a roundabout way. I could tell he was getting curious by the way he held his head at an angle. We talked about faked research, harm to humans caused by badly tested drugs, animal suffering, and Vincent's personality. I watched his eyes to see which topic set off those dilations of the pupils that reveal deep interest. Finally it happened when we were talking about researchers' willingness to cheat.

"Yeah, I really think faked research should be exposed," Tucker said disgustedly. "The federal agency just can't keep up. It's even worse overseas. You know the Korean cloning guy? Hwang? Same story. Blind ambition. They'll even fudge their data. They get away with it, too. I say get 'em on whatever charges you can find." I breathed a sigh of relief. He would help.

Ten minutes later, I could tell he was curious about me. Good thing I had at least told him my true profession when I'd first called; less backpedaling to do. So before he could suspect he was being strung along, I revealed the real agenda.

"Look, you've been really helpful. And this is making me feel a bit guilty – I'm not really looking for an assistant in my lab, not right now, anyway. Please don't be mad at me for lying – it's in a good cause." Hastily I plowed on. "What I'm trying to clean up is the way they're using animals from the wild and pretending they're captive bred." I could tell this didn't light his fire, so I told the whole truth. "Actually, it's about smuggling. I'm trying to stop smuggling of endangered species."

"But chimps aren't endangered," he said, puzzled. "There are still thousands of them in Africa."

"Not for long. They're being killed for meat or sport or smuggled here for research. AIDS, hepatitis – you know."

"Oh." He looked at me speculatively. I explained some more. Tucker began to lean forward. When he finally had both elbows in the table, I knew he was in. Tucker was not a scientist, but he was shrewd and made good guesses about how the faking was done. Once he overheard Vincent and Rensselaer talking about it and even saw them altering records.

"Really? You did? Could you get me copies of those actual research results, not the published ones?"

"Nah, that won't work. Ever since I caught them at it, they got more secretive."

He was willing to pull some hairs, though.

I had one worry. "What if the animals scream or bite you?"

"They scream all the time. No one pays any attention." I gulped and forged on. "What if they bite you?"

"Oh, I'll do it when they're anesthetized. How many do you want?"

So we discussed how many samples we wanted. I had carefully planned this with my allies. There were several species being used in Vincent's lab, but we'd start with chimps. Maybe later we'd tackle species that were hard to breed in captivity, used for the most promising medicines that would bring the biggest profit, or used for the most dangerous experiments.

These were the animals that researchers constantly needed to replace. But for now, chimps.

Tucker and I set a date for next week for the handoff. That would give him enough time to get hairs from twelve chimps. He would carefully label each envelope with the supposedly accurate pedigree that was in each animal's file. Such a pedigree should link the chimp only to gene lines that had been in this country for at least 20 years. If we identified just one that had come from Africa instead of the stated genetic line, we had a case.

As I drove home, I thought uneasily about Karen Silkwood, the plutonium plant technician who died in a mysterious car crash on her way to give evidence that her company was breaking safety regulations and poisoning people. Surely that wouldn't happen to me... I would set up the meeting in broad daylight, meet Anne and Norm immediately afterwards, and run to the post office to send the evidence to the Ashland forensic lab.

On the appointed day, Tucker appeared at the cafe. He sat down and pulled a small case out of his inside jacket pocket. Inside were a dozen envelopes, almost flat, each labeled with rows of details. I was so excited I forgot to be afraid. "Oh, how can we ever thank you?" I gushed.

He was solemn, almost grim. "Just don't ask me to do it again." He gave me one weary stare, and lumbered out of the room and out of my life.

The DNA results took less than two weeks to arrive. Two chimps were definitely from Africa.

We sent the test results to Dr. Andrew in Uganda and hoped there was a genetic match. Results: one matched the Uganda chimps' genome. Dr. Andrew sent the reports to the other sanctuaries and found the other match.

Eureka. The smoking gun. We had proved that Vincent's lab had two chimpanzees that had come straight from Africa. As we'd hoped, task force agents and Interpol officers went to Vincent's lab and caught them red-handed lying about their animals' pedigrees. Don phoned me with the news.

"Hey, Julie, guess what? You were right. Vincent is one of the culprits."

"I knew it!" I crowed. "Will he get his wrist slapped, or what?"

"Well, there are procedures, you know." Anne, Norm, and I would hand off our evidence to the experts (praying they wouldn't ask how we got the chimp hairs with the DNA). The Ashland lab, used to receiving anonymous tips and evidence, was willing to front the prosecution of U.S. companies for violating CITES and lying on their animal procurement documents. Interpol would back them up.

Don said it would take a while to actually remove the illegally acquired chimps, but just knowing they would be rescued – and the lab would be monitored indefinitely – gave heart to us all. I told Desta, who was now recuperating at home, and I'm convinced it speeded her recovery.

Next day I was sitting with Nick in the hospital cafeteria gloating over our victory. Suddenly I jumped off my chair as if I'd been electrocuted. A horrible thought had just occurred to me: *What if there had been animals in the pipeline when the receivers were busted?* What happened to them? Were they now stuck in crates in some depot, with no one willing to come forward and claim them? Visions of starving thirsty cramped animals made me cringe.

"What's the matter, Julie?" Nick asked, worried.

Ignoring him, I grabbed my cell phone and called Jeff, my contact at Interpol. He remembered me. I blurted out my fears. Would it be possible to go up the pipeline and save animals that were en route?

"Already done," he said casually. "We always make arrangements for that beforehand."

"Oh, thank god. I nearly had a heart attack. I was afraid that..."

"That we wouldn't follow up? Julie, we've had a high-powered task force going after this guy ever since you gave us his name."

"Oh. Did I ruin your undercover operation, or blow your cover, or whatever you call it?"

Jeff chuckled. "Well, our men weren't exactly pleased to have our prime target leave the country with his two top trackers, I can tell you that. They're loose cannons now, instead of being under our surveillance. Keep that police protection if you can." I had already thought of this. Rensselaer and the two Ugandans were still missing.

"Don't know how long it will last. The local constabulary has plenty of other work to do. Gee, I'm really sorry about interrupting your operation..."

"Well, can't be helped. It's not the first time we've lost our targets and had to find them again." Made sense. This was international crime, after all. Jeff went on, "I just wish people realized how hard we're working on this."

In a rush of gratitude, I said, "Well, I realize it. You guys are geniuses."

"Yeah, I'm an unsung prodigy just waiting to be discovered."

"Really?" I felt relieved and chatty. "You want to get out of the office and into the field?"

"Heck yes. Got the hero genes – Dad's in the air force, a real hot dog. This outfit is kinda tame, actually. Too bad we don't cover kidnappings."

"Gee, maybe Interpol isn't the best place for your talents. What's your last name again, in case I read of your exploits some day?"

"Conroy. I keep hoping Pinkerton's will notice me."

"Jeff, should you be saying all this out loud at work?" I wondered.

"Oh, that's ok. They're pretty good here about personal time, I'll give them that. I'm doing security training on weekends. This job is ok for now, but in another two years I'll be hollering, 'Get me out of here!'"

I laughed in friendly camaraderie and rang off. I explained it all to Nick. There are professionals on the job, I assured him. I relaxed. Any minute now I can retreat from this adventure, flirt with Nick, go back to college sophomores and graduate assistants, and read some student papers with incomprehensible grammar.

In my free time, I tracked down a teacher and learned more ASL signs so I could talk to Kijana. I still wondered about Rensselaer and the two Ugandans. Rensselaer had probably ditched them and gone underground by himself, and they must have made their way home. Meanwhile, when nothing happened day after day, my police protection was withdrawn. They said that what the newspapers had printed about the attackers and my newly high profile would keep the men from trying again. Easy for them to say! There was some reason those guys had flown all this way to capture me. I cudgeled my memory: what had I learned over there that was so threatening to them? Only one thing, and they couldn't even be sure I knew that: Rensselaer's identity.

Minnie was getting ready to leave the hospital. The social worker had found a place with the right level of care. Nick's eyebrows rose when he heard which one – apparently it was the most expensive nursing home in the area. "How can you afford that place, Minnie, you little urchin?" he asked. She answered him without hesitation.

"The settlement from my house," she said with undisguised pride. We clamored for an explanation. "I was cheated on some home repairs, and when the plumbing broke and water leaked all over my oriental carpets, I sued."

"When was this?" Nick asked, thinking no doubt it was a twenty-year-old story.

"Last year." Hm. She'd still been sharp enough to wrestle a shady contractor to the ground.

"So, did you replace the orientals?"

"I did not. I never liked those Isfahans anyway." We laughed together.

Then I said, "So how much were they worth?"

"Oh, about $30,000." There was a respectful silence.

"Each."

No wonder she could afford Arlington Court.

"That young man from the consumer affairs department said it was perfectly acceptable to keep the money instead of replacing the carpets." Remembering the times I had pocketed the payout from being hit in fender benders rather than fix my twelve-year-old car, I thought that made sense. Minnie added, "I put it in hedge funds. They've done very well."

There was something extra smug about her smirk. I took the bait.

"Hedge funds? I thought those were pretty risky."

"Well, they used to be." She was making me fish for every morsel. "That nice young man from the consumer affairs department came to see me after my construction lawsuit. He wanted to catch some shady stock dealers." I remembered how the disgraced Lincoln Savings had sent limousines to the homes of old people who were too feeble to come to the bank.

They'd sent their slickest sharpers to pry life savings out of octogenarians.

"Soooo, you called up the local brokers and announced you had a chunk of change to invest? You posed as an innocent?" Nick said with a teasing grin.

For answer, Minnie changed her expression. The alert, searching gaze was gone, and she looked like an innocuous sweet little old lady.

"Well, hello," she said in a quavering voice. "Do come in. Would you like some tea?" Nick and I collapsed in guffaws. "I do hope you'll be able to advise me where I should place my savings."

"Oh, stop," I begged. "I'm going to wet my pants."

Still in her little old lady character, Minnie gave me a syrupy sweet "you poor dear" gaze of sympathy. "Well, miss, the bathroom is just down the hall, past my guest bedroom. We'll wait until you come back." She transferred her vacuous gaze to Nick. "May I show you my Hummel china collection?"

Then instantly Minnie was back, looking at each of us in turn with a pert smile of satisfaction. We were still gasping for air.

"Oh, I feel sorry for those guys," Nick finally said admiringly. "I bet you had 'em trussed up like turkeys for the prosecution. Did you wear a wire?"

"I didn't have to. The agents were in the other room. As soon as the house call with the con artists was arranged, they came and set it all up. They were listening from the other room. And taping it."

This gave me an idea. Old people are famously targets for con artists. Minnie's acting talents were being wasted. I should link her up with the local gendarmes to set and spring traps for con men. And I could be in on the sting, too – I could analyze the facial expressions and vocal tones. I would find a way to put it into my university workload. This could be a great teaching project as well as satisfying personal justice. Research protocols began dancing in my head. Let's see; Minnie already knew "that nice young man in the consumer affairs department." Then there was the campus security chief – he might know someone we should investigate… Wait. Stop jumping to a new project every minute. Wrap up this case first.

I retraced my steps. What did I know about Rensselaer? Was he any more than a washed-up expat scrounging a living any way he could? It occurred to me to find out who was the greatest user of Rensselaer's research. Maybe there was a connection. I called in a favor, telephoned Jiang Li, and asked her to go to the Science Citation Index to find out how often Rensselaer's research on cancer was cited by the same person. I wanted to know who was Rensselaer's biggest customer. I could have done this legwork myself, but it was more fun visiting Desta and spending time with Nick.

The next day Jiang Li called. "Wow, that was fast," I said. "Read me the list. Ok, ok, got that one. Yes, I expected Vincent to be one of them. Do you know who else leads that field?" My summer vacation project had rippled out, involving widening circles of people. Jiang Li offered to call some of her medical friends and find out the buzz words and top people in the cancer field. Boy, I was going to have to throw a party for everyone who had helped me in this little adventure. For one aching moment I wished Matt were here. I continued to Jiang Li, "Yes, once you get those names, look up their articles and see if they cited Rensselaer, and how often. Oh, you *would*? That's even better. I didn't have the nerve to ask." She volunteered to go the extra mile and determine how important each citation was to the gist of the paper. That would help.

~~✺~~

One day in the hospital lunchroom, Nick confided in me. "I'm looking around for another job," he said quietly.

"Oh, no! You're not leaving, are you? What for?" I was surprised at the intensity of my dismay. Nick had become a valued source, not only for news about Desta, but for those subterranean vibes I hadn't felt in a while.

"No, another job, as in 'additional job,' " he clarified. "I'll still be here." He elaborated. "My son is really good at gymnastics. Really good. He lives with his mother," Nick added. "I want to get him the best coaches. Do you know how much it costs to train an elite athlete? Lessons, road trips, equipment, uniforms… it never ends. That's ok by me. Anyway, they pay me well enough here but not enough to really set him up." The pride of happy fatherhood was in his face. "Then there will be college in three or four years."

We talked about his son for a while. Nick attended all his competitions and exhibitions, remembering when the little guy had been in elementary school and loved to jump from one chair to the other in the living room without touching the floor. The boy would go to the back yard and set up odd contraptions from old bits of furniture and junk from the garage, then make up his own leaps and moves. When the divorce came and Nick moved out, Nick signed him up for proper gymnastics classes and went with him every week.

"I tried some of those moves," Nick told me with a laugh. "Good way to ache for two days. But his old man did help in a way. I could teach him the different muscle groups and how the body is made, how far you can twist the spinal column, stuff like that. I gave him my old anatomy books. I really think it's helped him."

"I'd love to see him compete," I blurted out. "Will you let me know when his next competition is?" I was aghast at what I'd said. Now I've done it. Suppose he's not as interested as I am? Going to a child's event is an unofficial relationship landmark. Time to backpedal fast. "And about another job for you – I'll keep my ears open." I pasted a businesslike smile on my face and made an excuse to leave. I hoped I wasn't blushing. When I got to my office, I called Jiang Li to ask about the SCI clue. She answered promptly. "First of all, your paper on Rensselaer wasn't cited that much. Sorry, pal."

"Never mind. It narrows the field of suspects. Who did cite it?"

"Well, some university president in an ethics article he wrote for an administrative journal. A blogger complaining about the corruption of science by money and using this as an example."

"Oh," I sighed. "Well, it was a long shot. It doesn't mean my article isn't a link, though – just that whoever read it didn't publish anything about it."

"Do you want me to keep my notes, just in case?" Jiang Li asked.

"Oh, yes thank you," I replied and rang off.

That link didn't pan out, but we had other leads. There was our hairy star witness. Kijana had recognized a real boat, having seen one in a photo. If I showed him a photo of possible suspects, would he be able to pick out the black man who had shot Desta? or the white man who had kicked him? I smiled at the thought. A lineup run by a chimpanzee. Just think of the impact on law enforcement if we could really get animals to communicate. Cold cases could be solved. Animal witnesses could be debriefed. Kato the dog, for one. I made a mental note to find out if animals had ever given useful clues in forensic settings before. I already knew about insects – you can tell how long a body dumped in the woods has been dead by determining which bugs were munching on it. Grisly evidence, but solid. Leslie told me all about it.

Arlington Court was a sprawling one-story brick building that 35 old people called home. That is, when they called anything anything. A lot of them were withdrawn and hardly talked at all; others were clingy. Some were not frail yet but they moved here willingly, knowing they would some day need help. I admired their courage and foresight. I'd be in denial until you dragged me to the rest home. A few were still vigorous, taking yoga lessons and pounding the piano in the living room, playing songs from my mother's youth: The White Cliffs of Dover, I'll Be Seeing You, the Tennessee Waltz.

Of course the staff arranged the usual activities – music, drawing, bus trips to the mall – and even some unusual ones, like having the old people grow vegetables and flowers in waist-high raised beds behind the home. I guess there's something soothing about seeing new life, even if it's only a tomato plant. One of the nurses told me that the residents who planted and dug in the garden were happier than those who didn't.

The hospital social worker pulled some strings and got Minnie accepted here ahead of some others on the waiting list. The move was for the best, but it meant a final break from her independent life. A hard step. Minnie relapsed to a querulous grumbly attitude, so my visits were short at first.

I didn't tell Nick much about my adventure; I didn't want him to associate me with danger and drama. I'd had enough of that with Matt. Besides, there was something soothing about his normal daily life. Work, his son, helping people, his favorite hobby of amateur beer making – all this was very far from cruelty and greed and the death of animals.

Nick showed me the magazine article that gave him the idea to brew beer. The author, a journalist writing about the archeologists who were reconstructing ancient beer-making techniques, had brewed up a batch of what he called "stone age beer." After a week of letting it steep, he gingerly tasted it. "I cannot tell a lie," the journalist reported with chagrin. "It was unspeakable. To call it swill would be an insult to bad alcohol everywhere."

"Gee," I said, making a face. "I hope yours is better than that!"

"Of course it is. He didn't do it right. I'll let you try some one day."

This was slightly encouraging. I still wasn't sure if Nick felt the same erotic buzz I did. I went with him to watch one of his son's gymnastics competitions, a date that ended politely at his front door. As his son bounded boisterously inside carrying his gym bag and the little box which held his latest medal, the phone rang. I said tentatively, "Nick, I really liked coming tonight. Kyle is really a marvel. You've taught him well." Nick was smiling, whether at me or his son's success I couldn't tell. Just then Kyle hollered,

"Dad! Mom's on the phone!"

With a wry face, Nick said, "Sorry, I should go." His smile said, "See you soon."

And he did. One night I stayed at the hospital visiting Desta until practically lights out. Just as I was getting ready to go, he came in the room and asked if I liked dancing. If I would just wait an extra half hour till his shift was over, he would show me a splendid little club. I didn't take much persuading. When we arrived at the club and got to the dance floor, I was pleasantly surprised at his sinuous grace, a joyous physical presence, as if music set him free. He didn't push up against me to filch a cheap thrill, though he was clearly glad I was there. His pleasure was in sheer movement. No wonder he was so responsive to his son's athleticism. But pretty soon I wasn't thinking about his parenting skills... Before the night was over, we agreed to do this again.

Bonnie, Arlington Court's receptionist, had promised to call me if a nursing job became available there. One evening I came home to find a message on my answering machine. "Hi, Julie, this is Bonnie. Nancy Miyamoto just decided to retire, so we have a job opening up in about a month. Does your friend know respiratory care? Let me know. Maybe I can get him an interview before we post the opening."

Oh, man, this would be great. Minnie and Nick under the same roof again. Should I phone him at work? Telling him in person would be fun, but it would take so long to drive over there. The news was too good to keep to myself for an entire half hour. I dithered. I called the hospital. The extension at his unit was busy. Good. Now I *have* to drive there. Just grab a jacket – no, this one looks better – and jump in the car. See, this will be good, he can work at Arlington Court and keep an eye on Minnie as well – uh oh, she'll tell him all about our anti-smuggling adventure and he'll want to stick his nose in and be like Matt and take risks or else he'll stick his nose in and tell me *not* to take risks, he'll be the me in this relationship – wait, it's not a relationship, he's just someone I know, anyone would drive across town to tell an acquaintance about a job opening, anyone would drive round and round the streets looking for a place to park and then hustle in through the emergency entrance to tell him about it *right now*.

I got lost in the huge building, cursed the architects, and immediately panicked. Soon I would actually be facing him. My errand was not urgent. He was at work. Maybe he was helping someone change a bandage. Would he really want to see me? Maybe I was only imagining he was interested. Maybe he just needed someone to keep him company dancing and at his son's gymnastics competition.

To stall for time, I paused in front of a bulletin board and read the flyers. One offered a class on how to test your own blood sugar. Another announced a class on breathing. I can do that, I thought. I'm doing it right now. Oh. It says *deep* breathing. Good idea. Again. One more. Gee, they're right. Your heart rate does slow down.

Well, I'm here to give him a job lead. I'd almost forgotten. I asked the next person I saw, "Can you tell me where to find Nicholas Jenkins?"

"He was here a minute ago," she began.

"Julie! What are you doing here?" Nick's voice seemed so loud. Where did he come from? He was smiling. Gee, he's cute. "C'mon, let's go to the break room," he said and led me along. I relaxed marginally as we walked. Hospital architects are so smart – they create a special room for workers to rest and talk and meet their girlfriends – oops. Stop that. I'm forty years old.

"Speak up, girl. How's Minnie? Have a seat. Want some coffee? Oh, I forgot, you don't drink hospital coffee. Well, just for that, some of my special stash." He went to a locker and got out a small square cooler. Stealthily, with wide eyes and careful movement, he pulled out a jar full of dark amber liquid and poured me some.

"Do you like it?" He looked at me anxiously. "It's a new formula. Did you know ancient Egyptians drank beer? The archeologists have found bits in the bottom of old pots and published the ingredients based on the DNA they found there." I didn't understand a word because I was sitting there with a silly grin on my face. "I'm trying to replicate it. You take brown rice, and grapes, and honey, and something called hawthorn fruit. Don't worry, this isn't alcoholic – it hasn't fermented yet. I wouldn't bring that to work. This is just the preliminary, the pilot study, you would say."

Nick was animated, drawing in the air with his hands as he described all the measuring, guessing, stirring, and pouring that had taken place in his basement. Thank goodness he had so much to say. I felt a gush of gratitude. What a guy. My face was one big smile. I understood about half of what he was saying. Gradually I tuned in.

"So then you pour it off and chill it for three days – I'm not boring you, am I? Say something. Speak or I'll finish telling you about the brewing process. I'll bend your ear until you scream for mercy."

Please bend my ear. Fondle it, tickle it… I promise not to scream.

People were coming in. Lockers were opened and closed, the refrigerator was peered into and emptied of mysterious parcels. People left.

Nick was speaking. "And then his coach said to him, right in front of the whole team…"

Suddenly I noticed the time. "Oh my god, we've been here an hour. You'll get in trouble. They won't fire you, will they? Tell them it's my fault. Tell them…"

Nick shook his head. "Relax. My shift is over. I was just signing out when you arrived."

Oh. Suddenly everything changed. I got nervous again. He wasn't at work now, apt to be called away at any second. This wasn't a stolen moment. It was a legitimate moment, in fact a legitimate hour. Someone will have to decide how long to keep talking and what to do then. Put off the moment of decision. Keep talking. Speak up, girl.

"May I have some more swill – I mean, your experiment?"

"You like it?" He was elated. "Want to see how I make it? Oh, you're probably busy. Classes in the morning and all..."

More gratitude. He's nervous about me now! Could he be buzzed, too? Control that grin. Maybe there's nothing to be nervous about. Maybe this won't be awkward. "Yes, I'd love to. No early classes." So we packed up his precious glop, put on our jackets, and arranged a caravan. I followed him in my car. Cars are wonderful. And city planners – they put up traffic lights, street signs, arrows painted on the pavement to show you the right lane – everything you need to find your way to a special man's house. Aren't human beings brilliant?

After we got to his house, I covered my nervousness and started right out telling him about the job opening at Arlington Court. He seemed interested, but pretty soon we weren't thinking about work, at all. He turned on some music, something slow and smoky I'd never heard before. He looked at me with a subtle question in his eyes. I met his gaze and held it. Stood up, stretched, swayed a little. He came closer, matched my swaying rhythm, reached out to me. I filled up with a new feeling from head to toe. My mind became quiet and then very, very happy.

～っc～

As the weeks wore on and Desta grew stronger, Nick often went with me to take Scalawag for a run.

One day when he was at work, I decided to take Gambado too, and packed her and her backpack-style cat carrier in the car with me and Scalawag.

Point Isabel was crowded with dog lovers, as usual. The parking lot was almost full, but I found a spot far away from the trailhead and pulled in. Scalawag, recognizing the place, was already excited. I caught Gambado from the back seat and persuaded her to get into the carrier so I could strap it on, with her in front. Once we were assembled, I got out and opened the passenger door so Scalawag could bound out. Since Gambado hadn't been here before, I kept Scalawag on his leash. There are only so many things I should try to manage at once, especially since I was spending so much time these days thinking about Nick and wondering whether this was a relationship or a fling.

Gambado stopped her car-protest yowling and looked around in sheer surprise. Vast expanses of field, huger than my fenced back yard, stretched into the distance, past the expanse of water, to the city by the bay. The carrier held her close to my chest so I could stroke her with my free hand. Somewhat reassured, she looked around like a kindergartner checking out the holiday decorations. Every few minutes as we walked along the path she would crane her neck upward, look at me, and give a little meow. I told her I was proud of her.

The bay was still. For once, the wind wasn't whistling up a chill as it often does down by the water. Scalawag looked longingly at the other dogs, who were off leash and galloping joyfully after frisbees and tennis balls. I kept at least twenty yards from everyone so Gambado would feel safe and enjoy her first outing. We reached the end of the park and stood by the water, where I paused to enjoy the views of San Francisco and the Golden Gate Bridge. Today the pointy top of the Transamerica Pyramid had impaled a passing cloud. Workers on the top floor would be having a foggy day, while workers a few floors below could look down and see the sun shining on the water. Suddenly Gambado growled. There's no other word for it. It's the low-pitched threatening sound cats make when they see another cat in their territory. "What is it, sweetie?" I asked, puzzled. There were no cats here.

"Kule. Kule sasa."

I froze. It meant, "There she is." I spun around. Two tall slender black men were approaching. They had just started stepping apart from each other – preparing to surround me. I glanced wildly around. We were at the edge of the water. The other dog people were half a field away, laughing and running and throwing balls. I dug my feet into the ground and faced the men. Gambado yowled. Scalawag picked up my fear and began to growl too. Uh oh. These guys had guns. But wait, Rensselaer wanted me *alive*. So if I could just hold them off long enough…

"What do you want?" croaked out of my throat. I knew what they wanted, but I had to make my voice say something, make a sound. "Scalawag!" I screamed. "Get them! Get them!" He had never been trained to attack, but he picked up my fear and their menace, and snarled and ramped at the end of his leash. The men kept coming. "Help!" I screamed, "Help!" I couldn't afford to look at the dog people but I prayed one of them was listening. I let go the leash. Scalawag held his ground, baring his teeth and snarling.

"Nenda zako," I said as menacingly as I could. "Go away." The men came closer. I said, "Mimi rafiji fika hapa!" I hoped this meant, "My friends are coming." But the Ugandans had undoubtedly followed me for half a mile from the parking lot. They knew I had no friends here; no human ones. If only Scalawag could hold them off long enough – I scrabbled in the cat carrier's pockets with my left hand while clutching Gambado in my right. Thank goodness I had indiscriminately dumped my entire purse in there before leaving home. Yes, there it was.

One of the men grabbed at me, pulling the carrier askew. Gambado got one paw out and snarled and hissed. He reached again. She scratched his hand smartly. Finally I found the mace. Covering Gambado's face, I shut my eyes tight and sprayed toward the man in swinging arcs. Please don't let Scalawag get maced, I prayed as I held down the spray button and waved the hissing weapon back and forth. Scalawag kept barking. A voice screamed and the man's pawing hands fell away. From the ground he shouted something in Swahili. The other man – where was the other man?

The barking ceased. Scalawag buried his teeth in the second man's leg and was worrying it. Good old pal. I caught my breath. The first man was writhing on the ground covering his eyes. He would be out for fifteen minutes. I measured my steps. Approached the second man. Held my breath. Covered Gambado's face again and maced him.

"Down!" I shouted to Scalawag. "Here!" Bless the dog, he came. I maced the man again.

We were safe. For now. Scalawag jumped up on me and softly barked. "Good dog," I said gratefully, and pushed him aside quickly so I could keep my eye on the men. Gambado meowed and tried to jump out of the carrier. "No, no sweetie, stay there," I tried to calm her.

All this took thirty seconds.

Slowly I became aware of sounds, voices, the rhythm of running feet.

"Hey, lady, you ok?" shouted a man. He was running toward us. I stared at him. "Call police," I croaked. Thank god, he had a cell phone. "Stay with me," I whispered. He stayed. Shakily I handed him the mace after three other people ran up. Dogs were now trotting all around. "Stay away! Keep the dogs away!" he told them. "There's mace in the air!" The people formed a circle around us and the attackers, who were gasping and moaning on the ground. The people collected their dogs and sorted them out and re-formed the circle. Two more people pulled out their cell phones and excitedly starting talking into them. Thank god for human curiosity and rubbernecking. The first man stood over my attackers, ready to mace them again. Nobody approached me to hold my hand.

I stood there panting, feeling like a circus exhibit. Finally a woman came over and silently handed me her water bottle. Gratefully, I took a long drink as her little dog bounced around our feet, wanting attention. Scalawag gazed regally down at its maneuvers, then back at me. Slowly my heart rate returned to normal and the story began forming in my head, pictures and movements and terror turning into words to tell people. Sirens again. Black and white cars squealed to a halt. Police officers jumped out. I patted Gambado and picked up Scalawag's leash. I loved them so much.

An hour later I was explaining myself to the police again. Different city, different police station, same attackers. But this time, they were under arrest.

"Call Officer Halloran in San Francisco," I said. "He knows all about these guys already. I need to go. My cat and dog are still in the car."

"Just a few more questions," one officer said soothingly.

"Can I call my boyfriend now?" I asked shamelessly, promoting Nick by proclamation. The police officers didn't know any better. I lied. So sue me.

~♪ XV ♫~

I got another fifteen minutes of fame, but fortunately the buzz died down sooner this time. Frank Halloran smoothed the way for me and asked if I wanted police protection again. "&*@#, yes!" I said, but relented after a few days and called it off, since the perps were in jail and I was sure Rensselaer was long gone.

Four weeks after the shooting, and one week after the two men were captured, Desta was able to go to work a few hours a day. The first thing she did was talk to Kijana. He was excited to see her again and pant-hooted loudly.

"**Desta hurt**," she signed. "**No chase**." She showed him her bandages; he fingered them gingerly. He had been in a lab and knew what bandages were for.

Meanwhile, a guy from the zoo's publicity department was setting up the videotape equipment so we could ask Kijana about the shooting again. We scheduled a time when Glenn was in town doing a fundraiser and hoped this time Kijana would stay focused. We certainly wanted to capture this for posterity... and for the district attorney. Not admissible, of course, but we'd heard she was interested.

We knew that taping wouldn't faze Kijana. Chimps are taped all the time in Tucson, where Kijana had lived for almost two years, so he just ignored the preparations. After signing for ten minutes about routine things, Glenn asked him about the shooting.

He signed, "**Desta hurt**." Kijana looked at him expectantly. Glenn added, saying aloud for the videotape, "**Kijana see?**"

"**Car ride**," Kijana signed back. "**Desta big house**."

Even though I expected it, I gasped. Here was an animal, another life form, describing to me something in the past that I had seen myself. Kijana was telling of his visit to the grassy yard behind the hospital. Well, now I would get to find out how you signal "**before**" to a chimp. Glenn approached it in a roundabout way, starting before the incident.

"**Desta here, Kijana here. Desta play with Kijana. Desta happy**," Glenn signed.

"**Happy**," signed Kijana.

"**Then man hurt Desta**." Uh oh. He was leading the witness. Well, this could never be used in court anyway.

Desta signed, "**Who hurt me?**" and spoke the words aloud.

"**Man hurt Desta**," Kijana signed. Maybe Kijana's next answer would be what we were hoping for, but this little interchange would not convince the skeptics. All the words had already been put into the conversation by the humans. They would say he was just copying. But for our own curiosity, we wanted to know about this incident and the chimp lovers in the room wanted to know what he knew, on general principles.

"**What kind of man?**" she asked next.

"**Black**," Kijana signed. We collectively took in a breath.

"**Black drink hurt Desta?**" Desta signed. Clever. She knew Kijana loved coke and was hardly ever allowed to have it.

"**Black man**," signed Kijana. "**Black man hurt Desta**."

We let out our breath. Baby in my drink.

"**Not white man?**"

"**White man toilet stink noisy**," signed Kijana and began rocking angrily from side to side. We couldn't help laughing. Kijana was disgusted with the loud obnoxious bully who had kicked him. We were so proud of him.

"**How did man hurt Desta?**" We held our breath again. How would he say "gun"? He had never seen one, or even a picture of one.

"**Push Desta**," Kijana signed.

"That's right!" Desta exclaimed. "He pushed me against the lockers first."

"**How did man hurt Desta?**" Glenn repeated.

"**Noisy stick**," Kijana signed.

Noisy stick. Good name for a gun. After a few more questions and responses, the taping ended and we took turns hugging and tickling him. Hopeless contamination of testimony. I wondered if we could get mug shots of the Ugandans and show them to him.

But now I was even more worried about Kijana. For the tenth time I asked myself, did the attackers remember he had seen them? Did they know that he could recognize individuals and communicate to humans? If so, a zoo or sanctuary was not enough protection. On my next visit to Arlington Court, I told Minnie about the canned hunts – wild animals were put in a pen and shot by bozos who paid a fee and didn't even have to hunt them. I concluded dismally, "What hath Ernest Hemingway wrought?"

"You're overestimating those bozos," Minnie said sardonically.

I frowned quizzically. She went on grimly, "What makes you think they can *read?*"

Desta went back to work almost full time and we devised a totally illegal game. I brought treats (such as kiwi fruits) and showed them to Kijana through the mesh. Then I went to the side gate and handed them to Desta. Soon I would see the interior hatch at the back of the enclosure open and the treats would appear. Of course, I only brought things he was allowed to have and we did this when no other staff members or visitors were present. I was now a smuggler! Soon Kijana realized I was Bringer of Treats and hastened straight to the hatch as soon as he saw me. The other chimps caught on and started waiting at the hatch to grab his loot. Just like care packages at summer camp, I sighed, and brought larger servings so he could share. I wondered how long we could keep this up before we were caught.

This was a good opportunity to see if Kijana would try to sign to the other chimps. Part of the purpose of transferring Kijana from Tucson to San Francisco, after all, was to try this very experiment. Would he try to teach them to sign? Silvana had taught her babies to sign. I could imagine Kijana testily conveying, **"Hey – that's mine! Find your own Bringer of Treats!"**

Desta and I watched eagerly. At first, Kijana was frustrated when the other chimps didn't respond to his signs for **"mine."** He fell back on the natural chimp vocabulary of vocalizations and body language. Desta watched nervously, hoping his signing skills wouldn't fade. No problem. He continued signing to Desta and me, while using regular chimp signals with his fellows. Eventually, I suspected, they would learn what the sign **"mine"** meant.

Over the ensuing weeks, Desta told me all about current signing research. After thirty years, the tide is finally turning. At conferences the Madisons don't get rude skepticism but rather questions about how long it takes for a chimp to learn its first hundred words, whether chimps ever make up their own signs, and whether there are dialects.

Then one day in the Chicago zoo, a female gorilla rescued a little boy who had fallen into the concrete gorilla enclosure. The gorilla (Binti Jua by name) picked up the unconscious toddler, carried him to the nighthouse gate, handed him to the keepers, and nonchalantly went back to her afternoon.

It was amusing to watch the skeptics try to explain that away.

On the whole, I'm glad that science is such a demanding religion We make offerings of facts and theories, submitting to the humbling rituals of cross-checking our work and being scrutinized by rivals. I willingly slog through the trials, replications, debates, and revisions. But I didn't read the scholarly papers on primate communication. It was a luxury to have something to look at freshly, to be a regular citizen who acknowledged the commonsense, visible evidence. Kijana described the assailants. Binti Jua saved the little boy.

The semester was moving along. My star student finished his dissertation and we scheduled his oral defense. Some progress had been made on our anti-smuggling project. After slowing the trade in birds, I had linked Norm and Anne with the people at NIH and Fish and Wildlife Service; gotten Ezekiel to gather some information; helped Interpol to tackle the smugglers in Africa; and started a probe into suspected medical labs. On the other hand, I'd drawn danger to Desta and Kijana, and Rensselaer was still on the loose. Besides, there were other smuggling operations going on. There were too many ways animals could be converted to money or pride.

After videotaping the questioning of Kijana, Glenn went back to Tucson, where Carolyn had been minding the store during his latest fundraising trip.

He promised to keep in touch and left us his private cell phone number. Anne, Desta, Norm, Leslie, and I stayed on the case. I did most of it while the others worked (Norm and Leslie), continued recuperating (Desta), or took care of their children (Anne). As long as Rensselaer was still at large, I had to be careful, though. How long would I be looking over my shoulder?

More than I ever had before, I started spending time with people I trusted. Today it would be Minnie. Oh yes, and Nick. Seeing him often was easy, now that I was a regular at Minnie's residence.

"Hi, Scalawag!" called Bonnie, Arlington Court's receptionist. "Come over here, you rascal." Scalawag padded behind the counter and stood by her chair so she could ruffle his fur. Bonnie smiled and said to me, "They're in the day room, Julie," so we went there. About a dozen residents were watching tv or looking at magazines; one was waving out the window at the oldsters who were gardening in the back yard. As soon as Scalawag and I went through the door, little movements rippled around the room – a straightening up, a turning around of wheelchairs. Scalawag marched up to each resident and stood quietly to have his head and neck stroked.

Some residents ordered him to sit or shake hands. I'd never taught him those things, so it was a comedy of errors at first. They would reach out their hands hoping for a pawshake, and he would lick their fingers. They would pull their hands away, and he would circle the hand with his nose. The day he finally lifted his paw on command there was much delight and laughter. I seemed to see in my mind's eye the much-loved dogs, now long dead, of each wheelchair-bound senior.

I'd started bringing Scalawag when Minnie moved here, to ease her transition. She loved to have him beside her as she walked the halls with her cane. So many other residents kept leaning over to pat him that my visits grew longer to accommodate them all. Finally Scalawag was an expected part of my routine. Animal-assisted therapy had existed in other places for years, but Arlington Court hadn't installed an official program yet.

In the art room, half a dozen residents were making presents for their grand-children or great-grandchildren, a touching reversal of those early years when little hands made crayon drawings their parents stuck to the refrigerator. They stopped what they were doing when Scalawag and I sauntered in, and greeted him happily. I knew Nick was nearby when I heard his booming voice down the hall saying in a mock scold, "All right, who's been pillow fighting in here?"

I finally joined the San Francisco Zoo so Desta wouldn't have to keep ushering me in whenever I visited Kijana. He was glad to see me now, I was sure; very few of the zoo visitors tried sign language with him, as I always did. Something puzzled me, though. Each time I arrived, he made a few signs I couldn't understand, but he only made them once at the beginning of each visit, so I didn't have time to learn them. Finally I asked Desta, "Why does he keep doing that?"

She laughed and replied, "Oh, didn't you know? That's his name for you. He's telling himself you've arrived." Gee, I've been christened by an ape. I asked, "How does he sign my name? Surely there's no ASL sign for 'Julie.'"

"No, he names people by some trait or event he remembers."

"Well, what's mine?"

"**Hug lady**," she replied with a grin. I laughed.

"Cute. But why does it mean *me*?"

"Oh, we were talking about the – the – shooting," she gulped. "And he told me you were up in the tunnels with him hiding from the black men."

I was touched. Kijana remembered our frightened stay in the overhead tunnels, hugging and rocking. I told Nick about my new name, and he said, "I approve. Now, how do you make those signs?" He made pretend signs in the air and his hands ended up on me. He said solemnly that he expected me to live up to my new name. His son picked up on this sobriquet and started calling me Hug Lady, too.

Just don't let this get around the faculty lounge.

One day we got a break. The San Francisco police took the shooting seriously, of course, and didn't give up even as time passed. The ballistics experts couldn't match the bullet to a known gun but the detectives tracked down a family that had been arriving during the mass exodus from the zoo grounds. All four of them had seen two black men and a white man push other people aside rudely and jump into a van, which they could describe. The parents remembered the incident because they were trying to teach their young children manners and pointed out the rude men's behavior as what not to do.

The police also appealed to anyone who had been there that day to send them their photographs. Since some doting parents snap pictures of their darlings on every possible occasion, this appeal actually turned up some images that had been taken in the parking lot. With digital enhancement, investigators found the van and, wonder of wonders, could even read its license place. I'll never criticize camera nuts again.

After some old-fashioned police procedural work, the van was located outside a warehouse in South San Francisco. They staked it out. Frank Halloran told me that within a day, the man who had rented it was arrested on probable cause. Rensselaer behind bars! This time I was happy to see the story on the eleven o'clock news and next day's newspapers. A heavy weight of background fear lifted. Of course, I would eventually be called to testify and relive the terrifying events, and so would Desta, but for now the worst was over.

Meanwhile, our animal rights allies confirmed the lab in the photograph was NIRS. This lab and its breeding facility were still certified, but my contacts said that was completely undeserved and that the experimenters and administrators there were horribly abusive.

NIRS was where Vincent got his research animals; the legal ones, anyway. It occurred to me that just because he had fired Rensselaer for fudging his data, Vincent was not necessarily innocent. I had discovered one thing through the Science Citation Index: as time went on, his publications were being cited less and less often by other experts. Then I looked up his early papers, the ones that in any new scientist's career always build on the work of the scholars who have gone before. Sure enough, back in the 1970s his reference lists were always sparse, his claims just a bit grander than they should have been for a young man.

This was a red flag. In my field, it is drilled into us that we are only adding our little brick to the great wall of knowledge and that it is unrealistic, not to mention poor taste, to claim more. Perhaps in medicine the rewards are so great… the multi-million-dollar research contract, the gleaming Nobel black-tie ceremony fueling one's fantasies… that perspective is lost. Anyway, I suspected Vincent had the same grandiosity as his lieutenant; he just disguised it more skillfully. I made a few phone calls and snooped about his character. He was described as a driven man, hard on his graduate students and research assistants, minimizing their contributions, grudging in his praise of others, and slow to acknowledge error. No wonder Sonya was embittered.

I bet he wanted a Nobel.

This is just the kind of thing that goes on in the seamy underside of science: raw ambition. In my "follow the money" strategy, I'd forgotten that for some people, influence and recognition are a hundred times more intoxicating. Vincent's studies were no longer producing results that were considered cutting edge, because whole new avenues of research were opening up. Real scientists take this with resignation, knowing that ruling out dead ends is just as important as making an original discovery. But narcissists can't stand it when their findings aren't special. That was Vincent. He was slowly being relegated to the backwaters. His star was dimming.

Vincent fired Rensselaer not from pure motives but because he was afraid of being dragged down with him. Privately, in the tradition of honor among thieves, he had thrown Rensselaer a lifeline: I'll pay you to go to Africa and get me a steady supply of research subjects.

For Rensselaer, this was a humiliating descent. From being the shining boy wonder with every hope of a glittering career, he had become an outcast from the community whose admiration he craved. After the initial shock, his friends drifted away, his savings dwindled, and finally he had to sell his house. Vincent's shady smuggling money was all that kept him from the welfare line.

Well, that was my reconstruction of it, anyway.

In his new role as a wildlife smuggler, Rensselaer became the bully I had heard about, a hunter so nasty that he drove his own trackers from the field and took the reckless step, which almost became a fatal one, of trying to intimidate me.

I explained all this to my hardy crew one night at Norm and Leslie's. They were dubious at first, so I reminded them that there are big payoffs for scientific dishonesty – you could make a fortune in grant money to develop things in military technology, pharmaceuticals, even crime prevention. If your research doesn't go as fast as you promised, shine up the few facts you like and hide the rest, maybe even cook the books completely. The worst scientific dishonesty occurs when drug companies suppress research they don't like. This is legal. They make researchers sign a contract saying that the company funds and owns the results, so it can publish them… *or not*. Norm and Leslie were disgusted.

We didn't get to shut down Vincent's lab, but from now on he would be watched more closely. Conditions in his labs would be monitored. His supply of chimps would be strictly supervised. With such crumbs we had to be satisfied. We gave ourselves one day to celebrate, and then began strategizing again.

We met at Anne's home one night. She sent the kids to their rooms. Every once in a while we could hear giggles and thumps that sounded suspiciously like kids jumping on their beds. We sat drinking an audacious little Napa wine, quietly happy but mindful of the future.

Norm said, "Well, we got one gang of smugglers out of business, but now what?" Good question. There would always be people looking to corner a market or sell an animal.

"Let's invite Desta to join us," said Leslie. "She's fully recovered now."

"Yeah," Anne exclaimed. "She's probably just waiting for us to ask."

We concluded that the time was right for that, and I mentioned the labs.

"Should we sneak into the labs? Tucker has bowed out after doing one measly raid, so we'll have to recruit another spy."

Anne disagreed with that plan and said we needed to nail the buyers. Continuing our tradition of dreaming up more schemes than we could possibly implement, Norm said he was more interested in the beginning of the trail. He said, "Instead of imprisoning the poachers, let's get more of them flipped, turned to our side. Like Ezekiel and his friends."

I teased him, "You've been reading too many spy novels."

Norm objected. "No, seriously. Most of them are only doing the animal trade to survive. You know that."

This was one tactic, anyway. Carl would know how to flip people – he was always talking about reuniting the fragments, or transforming the shadow, or some such thing. The villagers around Bwindi would have jobs and clothes and school fees. Realistically, Anne pointed out, "But there's not enough money to give them all ranger jobs."

I remembered something Melissa had said about Maurice Gordon, the internet billionaire, wanting to travel. One of my university friends is expert at getting grants, so I bullied him into burrowing into Gordon's billions. It turns out there's a whole sector of the economy called "philanthropy" that consists of huge piles of money. Its guardians just wait around for people to show up and ask for it.

∼ XVI ∽

At Arlington Court, Nick was in his element. He wasn't put off by age and illness, but was as jocular and lively as ever. There was a circle of peace around him, because he didn't look at the residents as depressing omens of things to come. Old age, when he was present, was just another part of life. Even the grossest part of extreme old age – toilet time – was somehow not so demeaning if he was in the room joking with the orderly and making the procedure seem normal.

Nick would exclaim in a hoarse lisp, "Sufferin' succotash!" to get the dejected ones to smile. He would enter a room to change bandages, nudge the resident and say teasingly, "Did you fall off your motorcycle again?" On evening shift when it was time for lights out, he would holler, "Did your parole officer say you could be up this late?"

Carl teased me about how happy I was looking. "So who is this guy? Is he good enough for you? Don't go any further with him until I give my seal of approval."

"Ok," I said with a smile. "You can meet him. Just remember…"

"And if he'll keep you away from those cockamamie adventures, good."

"Hey, no scoffing. Maybe I like adventures."

"Well, take him to Tassajara to meditate. Nice and peaceful. And when does he get to meet your family?"

"Don't go so fast. You're making me nervous," but I smiled as I said it. Our conversation drifted to his sister. Carl had found out the cult's latest leader was charming, charismatic, and good at reading what each person most wanted. He could pick out which follower wanted a little bit of power and make them the equivalent of a corporal, and a hierarchy is born. Carl's sister always like to boss around the few friends she had, so he imagined that her cult leader found the perfect role for her, with just the right number of Indians to be the chief of.

"That all sounds pretty different from the Uganda cult I kept hearing about," I said. "Kony's cult is supposedly based on the Ten Commandments, but it also includes local folk customs. And he captures girls for sex slaves and boys for soldiers."

"Unfortunately that's not unique," Carl said, shaking his head.

"I wonder what it's like for the kids to be dragged into a whole new world," I said speculatively. "Not even counting the abuse, what about all the stuff they're being told?"

To my surprise, Carl laughed. "Kids are in a world that astonishes them every day!" he said. "I still remember how surprised I was in third grade when our teacher told us that nylon stockings are made from coal. Filmy see-through cloth made from scratchy black rock!"

I agreed. "And those are just the oddities we call science. Look at all the crazy things people do and call religion." I wanted good solid social science about beliefs and defenses. "Besides," I went on, "Even if you understand a cult, how do you oppose them without playing right into their hands? Most of them *want* an enemy; they thrive on it, build whole cosmic dramas starring themselves as the misunderstood chosen few."

Idly I wondered which type Kony was, then put it out of my mind as our conversation drifted into other channels. I'd probably never find out anyway.

~ ༄ ~

One day after the fall semester started, I was having lunch with Jiang Li. She mentioned that a friend of hers wanted to talk to me. "He's a television producer," she said, as if that explained everything. "He does documentaries. This is about your new favorite subject. Go ahead, call him," she urged. "Here's his number." Well, I'm as curious as the next person. I bit.

"We're doing a series on international crime," he said when I reached him. "You were involved in the zoo shooting and there's an African connection. It fits right in. We want to film the entire narrative – you know, chimps in the wild, poachers turned rangers, all the links you were finding out before the attack."

"I get it. You'll interview me here, and blend it with stock footage of wild chimpanzees, that kind of thing?"

"Oh, no, this is a documentary. Not news. Probably won't be shown until next fall. No, we're going to recreate the whole back story. Few shots of you in your office, some at Bwindi, then…"

"Bwindi? You're going to Uganda?"

"That's where it happened, Uganda, right? You'll be shown talking to the ranger who used to be a poacher, visiting the island, etc. Then some scenes at the San Francisco Zoo. The filming schedule won't go in that order, of course."

I couldn't believe it. I said, "Gee, are you guys made of money? Do you know how much an airplane ticket to Uganda costs?"

"No and yes. Interested?"

"Yes," I said hastily, before this disembodied ticket-bearing genie vanished. "When do we leave?" Wow – keeping the smuggling problem in the news AND a free ticket to Africa. I was as happy as a hummer owner with a personal oil well.

Next time my star student came in to prepare for his oral defense, I gave him something he'd always wanted, a teaching opportunity.

"I need to be out of town next week," I said, "You've always wanted to sound off – well, here's your chance." I had only two classes that term, each meeting twice a week, so he couldn't get into too much trouble. He was smart and passionate, and my other students wouldn't be cheated by my absence (I told myself guiltily). With a few instructions about logistics, I gave him my lecture notes, knowing he would add his own little gems.

After bidding Nick a fond, physical, and attention-getting farewell at the airport, I flew to Uganda with

Jiang Li's friend and his crew of two technicians. On the long flight, I told them more about what had happened on the previous trip. Caught one of the technicians fibbing and had a chance to show off my expertise. I made a smooth transition so he wouldn't be embarrassed, and turned it into an opportunity to give an enthusiastic description of a few facial muscles and micro-expressions.

"This could be useful in your work," I said. "You have opportunities most people don't – you get to tape your subjects talking in closeup interviews. You could play the tapes at slow speed to catch micro-expressions."

"How is that useful?" asked the producer. "We couldn't very well include them."

"No, but you could view them yourselves after filming and decide whether you believe what your interviewees said. Wouldn't that help you write your scripts, or voiceovers, or whatever you call them?" That did arouse their curiosity, so we discussed the possibilities in a friendly fashion throughout the long flight.

In Uganda, we first went to the chimp sanctuary on Ngamba Island. The producer wanted to get footage of them, to show some happy endings. Then we went to Chambura Gorge. I'd warned them that it was less likely we'd actually see chimps there, but we were lucky and the cameraman got some decent shots. I showed them a few tracking tricks. They were impressed.

"Wait until you meet Ezekiel," I said. "I'm a total amateur. If you want to see tracking, follow Ezekiel." They asked about his name, and I said that lots of people in Uganda had names from the Bible, relic of English colonialism and the Christian churches still operating here. There were still missionaries all over the place.

Sure enough, Ezekiel wowed them on the trail, finding golden monkeys, Ruwenzori turacos, and L'Hoest's monkeys. We even went out in twilight. The laser pointers Anne had brought on our previous trip helped Ezekiel show us nocturnal animals. The film crew got excited about all the vivid creatures large and small that they were filming, and I began to fantasize about recruiting them to the cause.

Then it was time to film the scenes about poaching. Even though Rensselaer was now in jail, there were other smuggling rings and Ezekiel was nervous about being identified, so they filmed him from the side against bright sunlight and used a voice-altering gadget. He laughed to hear his disguised voice when they played it back. His children dragged me into their house and showed me where they had placed the photographs of themselves that Anne had sent. The film crew responded to the crowds of giggling children by taking pictures of everyone in the village. They had brought along a small printer, so every family got its pictures the next day.

The crew finished filming in five days. After flying 12,000 miles to a country and people I had grown to love, I was not about to waste all that transit time, so I stayed a few extra days in Bwindi. I waved goodbye as the producer and his doughty crew clambered aboard the open-top van, and told them to keep their cameras rolling.

"You'll be driving right past the elephant crossing! You'll love it! And the lake where the hippos hang out!" I yelled. "Keep your cameras rolling!" I waved and went back to my tent, reveling in my free trip to the wild.

Next day I awoke wondering if I could get into another gorilla trek on such short notice. Not quite getting my hopes up, I left my tent, walked half a mile to the trailhead, and approached the ticket office. The usual small cluster of people with hats and cameras was surging and chattering eagerly, clearly today's lucky few. One was arguing with the leader. She was saying, "I'll wear a mask! I'll stay far back, I promise! I won't touch anything." Oh, I get it. She had come down with a cold, probably on the long flight from London, and was being bumped from the trek. I felt sorry for her but glad the guides were holding firm and protecting the gorillas from human germs that are truly dangerous to them.

Luckily, I had cash on me. I stepped forward, said to the leader, "Ningependa twende?" (which I hoped meant "May I go?"), and wordlessly extended my handful of cash to the upset woman. She paused. "But I came all this way..." Her voice trailed off. The other group members were sympathetic but kept their eyes on their own gear, not wanting to catch her bad luck. I held out my hand. At least she would get her money back. She sighed, shook her head, and took my money. Then she had a thought. "Take my camera with you! Get some pictures! Please," she repeated with a pleading face. How could I say no? She showed me how her camera worked. Reminding myself that I was grateful for camera nuts now, I shouldered it.

Another gorilla trek! Anne would be so envious. I decided to spend the three-hour trek looking for interesting bugs to tell Leslie about. The group assembled and we started down the trail. I looked back. My unwilling benefactor sadly watched us go.

This time, I saw things I hadn't noticed before. The gorillas have individual temperaments. One youngster (perhaps six months old) was shy and clung to its mother, but another the same size frolicked about, climbing up saplings, throwing around pieces of a discarded bird's nest, and exploring the clearing like a hyperactive pre-schooler. A female juvenile was trying to play with the shy youngster and made whimpering sounds when the mother kept pushing her away.

Every once in a while, I dutifully pointed the camera and pushed buttons, aided by some friendly advice from fellow trekkers. One of them suggested that I pose for a picture in the unlucky woman's camera, so that she would have a nice memory of the person who took her pictures for her. Personally, I thought she would hate my guts and never want to see my mug again, but I sighed and politely stared into the camera while the photo was snapped. They grinned and promised to deliver her camera.

Next day, I visited the village, bought a drink at the little café and greeted some old acquaintances. They remembered me, though of course they knew nothing of the role I had played in the downfall of the angry loud white hunter.

～♪℃～

Two days later, it was time to leave Bwindi. I packed my gear, double-checked my passport and airplane ticket, and handed Abel the driver another pile of clothes. I had planned a three-day layover in Paris on the way back, which I regretted now, since it would keep me away from Nick. Two vans were leaving. One carried the driver and five Japanese tourists who had taken yesterday's trek. They waved merrily as they pulled away. In the second van I rode with Abel, the sixth Japanese tourist, and everyone's luggage, which took an extra twenty minutes to load. Since the other passenger spoke no English, we contented ourselves with polite nods and smiles while we waited for the luggage to be piled in. I gave him an energy bar and he smiled and bowed.

Finally Abel drove us away from Bwindi, talking boisterously, expertly wheeling the jeep around the potholes that pocked the road. The Japanese man was showing me his fancy new GPS device when we reached the elephant crossing and slowed to a halt. This was their usual time of day to cross from the lake to the forest. Dozens of the huge creatures moved ponderously across the road in pairs or small groups; it seemed like a river of pachyderms. Young ones broke into a trot now and then to catch up with their mothers. One big bull that brought up the rear of the parade eyed us suspiciously, but eventually let us pass and followed the stragglers across the road. Abel was just starting up the motor when I heard him gasp. I followed his gaze. On the other side of the elephant path, facing us on the other side of the road, was an open jeep. Three men were in it. They were pointing guns at us.

Time stopped. Abel and I sat frozen. Could this be happening? I looked at Abel. He was staring and breathing rapidly. I'd never seen him frightened before. I guessed that meant I should be frightened, too. The jeep drove slowly toward us, the men swiveling the guns to keep them aimed at our hearts. One man jumped out and strode toward us. "You come," he said to me.

What is this? Robbery? Ransom? I'd spent most of my cash on gorilla treks but maybe I had enough left to buy them off. I was slowly reaching for my money belt when the man frowned and gestured for me to get out of the van. A man in the jeep shouted something. I got out and stood on the ground, leaving my stuff in the van. The man grabbed my elbow and half-dragged me toward the jeep. Slow motion. Every step was taking me away from my familiar life. Would this be like that long-ago killing of tourists? Would I ever see Abel again, or Nick?

I told myself: Don't think – watch.

One man in the jeep kept his gun pointed at Abel to keep him from interfering. He shouted something to the third man, who jumped out of their jeep and marched toward us. I held my breath, but he passed me, grabbed the Japanese man, and pushed him toward the jeep. Another man dragged Abel out of the van and got into the driver's seat.

Abel hadn't even turned off the engine.

I looked at the Ugandan man nearest me. In horror, I realized he was not a man; he was a boy, a teenager with smooth chin and big hands on bony wrists. This must be somebody's idea of a prank, I thought, and relaxed fractionally. Then a sickening thought came. Oh no, it couldn't be, not here. We're over a hundred miles from the danger zone. The religious fanatics we'd heard about capture *Ugandans*. What would they want with me? or with a Japanese tourist?

We were pushed roughly into the jeep's back seat. I still had the GPS unit in my hand and shoved it into my pocket. The jeep started with a jerk, made a violent 180-degree turn and headed back the way it had come. One of the abductors drove our van behind us. I made one last beseeching look at Abel, who was standing in the middle of the road. His face was a mask I couldn't read. After a quarter mile we turned off onto a side track, jouncing along at a slower speed. Should I jump out? Would Abel be following on foot? The man next to me kept his gun pointed at me. I stopped looking at him, since a fixed stare is a threat signal in anyone's facial language, and tried to remember each part of the road.

Useless. The ride was too long and the turns too irregular. I gave up and looked around the jeep. It was dusty, rusted, and bare. It broke down once. I didn't try to escape; that would be a provocation and I would easily be recaptured quickly in country that they knew and I didn't.

The engine started again.

Who were they?

Hours passed. We bumped over roads, tracks, potholes. The Japanese tourist, a middle-aged man, said nothing. Villagers scattered as we drove through. This was very different from the excited welcome the tour vans always received. It was almost as if they were afraid of this jeep, of these men... Who among their own people did they fear so much that they'd leave their goats and chickens, grab their children, and run inside?

A grinding fear took me over. The sun had been at our backs when we started and was now on our left, hovering over the treetops. We were going north. Toward Kony's country.

Another hour passed. The jeep slowed and stopped. The man – boy, really – on my left roughly grabbed me by the arm and hustled me out of the jeep. I didn't resist.

This wasn't exactly a village, more like a camp. There were three or four buildings and some tents. It was early evening.

Several people looked at me as they walked past, showing me a mix of curiosity, enmity, and respect.

Others seemed oblivious or absorbed in their own tasks and thoughts. Their eyes were glazed.

I was taken to a man of some authority. I could tell because he had better clothes, sat while others stood, and maintained a little space around him. My captors spoke to him rapidly, no doubt telling how and where they got me and that Abel had been let go. I suddenly had a sick thought – had Abel known about this in advance, colluded with them?

No one got close to me. The personal space they were allowing me hinted that they didn't see me as usual war booty to be robbed, or worse. Why would that be? I could catch only a few words in Swahili. The higher-up man frowned and made a "take her away" gesture. He looked irritated, not murderous, so I apparently wasn't in immediate danger. The one who had captured me led me to a small building. Inside were two young Ugandan girls sitting on the floor. They jumped up in fear. The man said something to them, pushed me in, and shut the door.

The girls remained standing. As my heart slowed, I looked at them. One appeared to be about ten years old, the other about thirteen. The older one pointed to a corner, where I could see a rough cot and blankets. "U hali gani?" I asked. (How are you?) Slowly my small Swahili vocabulary returned. "Jina langu ni Julie." No reply. I didn't ask anything that could be construed as trying to escape, such as, "Where are we?" The younger one was trembling. She's afraid of me, I thought. Have they told her scary things about white people? Uganda has plenty of white citizens, but mostly in cities – Entebbe, Kampala – and these two waifs probably came from this north country where tourists don't go.

I sat on the cot to make myself shorter. I didn't know why I was here or what to do, but I could do one thing that was in front of me: soothe frightened girls. I sat still and gestured for them to sit down. Later I thought they saved my sanity, giving me someone else to worry about. If I'd been locked up alone, I would have been overwhelmed by fear.

I looked around the room. Glanced at the girls. Asked safe questions. Asked their names. They didn't reply. Gathered they were supposed to look after me. That suggested advance planning. How long had this been prepared? A bad sign – the cult meant to keep me awhile. It was also a good sign – they meant to keep me alive awhile. I looked out the window at the comings and goings of the camp's residents. Strict gender segregation. Yep, fundamentalists all right.

An hour went by. I began to notice sounds – ancient vehicles coughing to life or creaking to a halt, male voices barking commands. I watched the bugs and geckoes in the room. The girls watched me. Finally, I couldn't wait any longer. I said, "Iko wapi choo?" (Where's the toilet?) No reply. It dawned on me that they don't speak Swahili. The language of northern Uganda is Acholi and boasts three quarters of a million speakers. In frustration, I pantomimed my need. The older girl gave an Aha! face and led me outside to a rickety shed and back again.

Slowly night fell. The door opened and a plate of food was handed in. By the small candle I couldn't tell what was on the plate and tentatively ate a little. The girls sat in the corner. There was no food for them. I stifled the impulse to share mine, from a vague instinct to give no signals, defy no expectations, provoke no punishment, discard no privilege that might mean something later.

Full dark. Outside, animals gave nightfall calls as they bedded down.

Why was I here? Simple robbery would have been committed hours ago at the elephant crossing. Kidnapping me probably meant ransom. Then I remembered the short article (two column inches) a shopkeeper had shown me in the tiny local paper (circulation 300) saying "American Professor Returns to Bwindi." Someone at Uganda Wildlife Education Centre, where I had taken the documentary crew, may have mentioned my return to someone, who mentioned it to someone... Could I have value as a bargaining chip? Has Kony mixed me up with someone else, a diplomat or someone important? Maybe he wants someone to give them legitimacy, a mouthpiece.

I gave up trying to figure it out and started to think about getting away. What was Abel doing right now? Would he tell anyone, and if so, who? Ezekiel, I hoped. Maybe Ezekiel still had the envelope Anne had sent the family photographs in a few weeks ago. Actually, she had been sending him supplies for years. Good – he would have her address even if he didn't have that recent envelope. But if Abel was an accomplice of the kidnappers and didn't tell, Ezekiel would assume I was on the plane flying home.

Who else was there? The disappointed gorilla trek lady – the one with the cold – would have a recent picture of me in her camera that could be used to alert people. But she might be in the bush somewhere, out of touch for days, or on the way to Kenya or the Ngorongoro Crater in Tanzania. Even if she was still in country, she might not hear about my predicament. The kidnapping of a visitor is not exactly something the tourist bureau wants to broadcast.

For hours my mind spiraled on the possibilities. I sat on the cot, leaning against the wall, until finally I fell asleep.

⸺ XVII ⸺

I awoke with a start, stiff all over. In my sleep I had curled up on my side. A tattered blanket covered me. I looked up and saw a moldy ceiling and walls with peeling plaster. I was lying on a rickety cot, covered by a thin dirty blanket. Sounds came from outside: footsteps, a bullying voice, a whimper. I was a captive in a decayed old European-style house in the middle of the rainforest.

I looked around. The room was bare, dusty, and already hot. The younger girl was asleep on the floor, twitching. She woke up crying. I tried to convey sympathy with my expression, but she glared and looked the other way.

The older girl came in. Her eyes were alert and met mine. She was smart, watching everything around her attentively. Over the next few days she often guessed what I wanted. She brought me some food, an unidentifiable goulash plopped on a rough wooden plate, and I ate hungrily. She was gone when I was finished eating, so I put the plate on the floor. I surveyed my resources, which consisted of the clothes I was standing in. Out of habit, I patted my Coat of Many Pockets and discovered the Japanese man's GPS. There hadn't been time for me to learn how to operate it, but I could make out a series of digits – a long row of even numbers and a letter or two. I located the power button and turned off the little gizmo. Looked around the room for a place to hide it. No furniture except the cot, no built-in drawers. Suddenly I remembered where Kijana and I had hidden on that ghastly day in the night house – above eye level. I glanced up and saw that there were rotted places between wall and ceiling.

Silence. Hurriedly, before anyone could come in, I stood on the cot and groped carefully around the holes. No critters bit me. I gingerly poked until I was sure the hole was deep enough, then stuffed the GPS into it. A little rearranging of wood crumbs disguised the spot. I softly stepped down to the floor and found to my relief that the hole was not visible from below. I didn't know what would come of this plan, but just knowing I had a tool on my side gave me a small measure of confidence.

Outside there were muffled sounds. Many voices were singing without enthusiasm – was it some kind of religious service or military anthem? I nervously cracked open the door and looked out. No one was in sight. I wondered if I should tiptoe out for a look-see while they were all occupied. I stood there craning my neck to see as much as I could of the camp grounds. I called it a camp because I could see only the two buildings and a few tents, though by the sound of things there were dozens of people around, maybe a hundred. If this was indeed Kony's outfit, I was not in the main headquarters but an outpost. I decided to stay put. I was still alive and didn't want to risk changing that fact.

Slowly the day passed. I studied the room. It was about ten feet by twelve, with wooden shutters that could close out the daylight. The building seemed over a century old and was a residence at one time, probably the home of a long-departed missionary. Those resolute Christians from Britain had fanned out all over Africa. As I knew, there were still missionaries here, some from sects that hadn't even been invented when Stanley went in search of Livingstone. And now the most macabre fanatics of all had taken over the site.

Night fell again. I kept my mind busy by speculating on their purpose for bringing me here. Maybe they were quarreling over what to do with me. I kept waiting for something to happen. My fears rose and subsided in waves, depending on the vagaries of my imagination. I wondered where they had put the Japanese man and how he was faring. I nicknamed him Mr. Moto.

I was tended, or perhaps spied on, by the young girls Kony's army had captured. Several more came and went over the next two days; mostly the first two I had met. Some of them were hardened, like orphans who had been shunted to too many foster homes, but some were still shocked and crying. I tried to guess which of the hardened ones might have given up hope of escape and become tools of their captors. This defense mechanism of the conquered is called by various names: identifying with the oppressor, Uncle Tom, the male identifier, the Stockholm syndrome. Not to mention that the indoctrinated boys carried guns. I had to be careful.

In case my captivity would be a protracted affair, I needed a plan. Dredging up my knowledge of cults, I thought of one. At first, I would convey polite skepticism, not wanting to look suspiciously eager. Then I would insert some reluctant religiosity – "I always wanted to be with a special group, but am I worthy?" Oh, here's a good one: "How can I be a good Christian when I don't have a husband to obey?" This thought almost made me retch, but I knew the surest way to ingratiate yourself with any type of fundamentalist is to endorse female submission. They all live in fear of a wrathful god, so the men desperately try to create a class lower than themselves, inventing beliefs and myths to justify it. With someone else to kick around, they can temporarily feel like the wrathful deity, not the cowering mortal. Why any woman in a free society goes along with this, I can't imagine.

On the second morning they let me out into the compound. In the open area, I could see what I supposed were indoctrination classes, people sitting in circles on the ground being lectured by urgent emphatic men wearing army uniforms. Probably they wanted me to see their numbers and fear their power. I sat in the shade of the house I had been held in, unblinking when I saw soldiers slap the youngsters.

Sitting there in the shade, I unobtrusively looked for my fellow captive. He must be around here somewhere. I hoped they weren't abusing him and tried to think of ways to communicate with him. If he used the same outhouse, I could leave a signal, but how? I didn't speak or write Japanese.

Nothing else happened and finally I was pushed back into my room. "My room" – the very notion was unnerving. Well, I was weaponless, but not defenseless. Using my professional skills, I could read Kony and his lieutenants, searching for some slight advantage. My first order of business was to hide my feelings about warlike fundamentalists and child abusers. Disgust and contempt are two of the half dozen basic emotions that show on the face, readable in any culture. It wouldn't be wise to show them here. Or fear. To mask my reactions, I watched the people whenever I could, noticing patterns, detecting the power hierarchies, and seeing who was in control.

On the third day, peeking out of my window, I saw one of the child soldiers, almost a teenager, and wondered if he was one of the gang that had captured me. He looked fierce enough, and roughly bullied the younger ones. It was a wretched sight to see a boy morphing into a monster.

When I wasn't busy observing, I tried to remember if I had left a money trail. I had paid for this week's gorilla trek in cash. The first trek so many weeks ago had been arranged by Anne, so the travel agency wouldn't have records on me. Does anyone in Uganda know who I am? Aha – Dr. Andrew at the wildlife center. He could email Anne. Let Ezekiel remember our link to Dr. Andrew, I prayed. We had told him about the Ngamba Island sanctuary. The film crew might have mentioned it. I hoped.

And when would anyone miss me at home? My note to Terry asking her to feed Scalawag and

Gambado had been vague; she wouldn't miss me for a while. At the university I had told my star student I would be gone for ten days, missing just one week of school. I racked my brain, trying to remember what I had told him. Did I set up an appointment with him for the Monday morning? Thinking so hard made my brain hurt. I did what the yoga flyer at the hospital said and took some deep breaths.

"I'll be gone ten days," I had said as I handed him my lecture notes for the coming week. "Just leave the papers you collect from the seminar students in my faculty mailbox."

"I don't have the key," he said.

"Oh, that's right. Ok, I'll meet you here at ten o'clock Monday morning. You can give me the papers then."

Good, I had that nailed down. He would miss me Monday morning. How long would he wait before notifying someone? At this stage in my career, I had a roomy faculty office that I didn't have to share, so there was no intimate colleague who knew all my comings and goings, who would immediately raise the alarm. Fortunately, this was my brightest student and we had often talked about his future career in academia. He wouldn't be intimidated by the faculty and would start knocking on doors and asking questions.

Had I told him where I was going?

"Oh, taking off for a week!" he had said. "Lucky you! Is it that security conference in Atlanta?"

"No, no, I would have arranged that long in advance. No, I'm going overseas. Got to keep my passport from getting lonely." Stupid banter. Had I said, "I'm going to Africa"? "to Uganda"? I was pretty sure I hadn't.

I hoped that someone at the university would remember the zoo incident. After it became clear that I was unharmed and all the villains were captured, everyone ribbed me about my brief moment of glory. That was several months ago, but surely one of them would put the pieces together. I told myself, Look, they're smart people. They'll think of Uganda immediately. Someone will go online, look up last summer's newspaper articles about the shooting, get Anne's name, track her down at the Oakland Zoo. They may not be detectives, but they are scholars. They know how to find information.

Now that I had imagined a sensible script in which someone knew what hemisphere and what country I was in, I felt a little better. Surely it would happen that way. There would be anxious friendly people arranging phone calls and search parties. Outside the university, Anne would hear of it first, and she would call Norm, and he knew people everywhere. Gary and Randy, oh good grief. They would shake their heads and say what an idiot, we told her to let us handle it and now she's overseas, outside our jurisdiction.

Jurisdiction. International task force. Interpol.

Interpol would look for me.

No they wouldn't. I remembered my phone friend Jeff saying they don't do kidnap cases. Wildly

I hoped Interpol would make an exception and get their wheels turning and helicopters flying before someone found out it wasn't international animal smugglers who had me, but home-grown religious fanatics.

I remembered my last conversation with Jeff. He had said,

"Yeah, I'm an unsung prodigy just waiting to be discovered."

"Really?" I said. "You want to get out of the office and into the field?"

"Oh, I'm a rescuer, all right. Got the hero genes – Dad's in the air force, a real hot dog. This outfit is kinda tame, actually. Too bad we don't do kidnappings."

"Gee, maybe Interpol isn't the best place for your talents. What's your last name again, in case I read of your exploits some day?" Oh, that was rich, reading about *him* in the paper. He had replied,

"Conway. I keep hoping Pinkerton's will notice me."

Maybe he would follow this up on his own time, earning his detecting wings. Though I knew this last wild hope was unlikely, I was relieved that my memory was working so well. A remark of Samuel Johnson's came to mind: "The realization that one is to be hanged in the morning concentrates the mind wonderfully."

~ ༄ ~

With so much time on my hands, I started imagining how the people I had seen got to this ragtag cult city. The first wave would have been idealists or friends of the leader; then some came fleeing from hunger; and later the captured children who grew up in the cult and became its soldiers. How could they help what they were?

A loud uproar from outside interrupted my thoughts. Squealing brakes, shouts, many footsteps. Cautiously I looked out the window. A new bunch of kids was being dragged into the camp, about a dozen of them. Some were crying, some struggling, some slack with terror. Teenage thugs, well indoctrinated by now, beat and yelled at them. Any sympathy I had for this gang vanished and my terror returned. I closed the shutters, but sounds seeped in, telling me what was happening to the kids. Stop! I told myself. Turn your mind to surviving. Use your logic.

But it's hard to think when you're frightened. The mind can't hold onto things or make sensible connections. I fiddled around with little things in the room, looked for interesting spiders, inspected my nails, paced, re-tied my shoelaces, all the while wondering *why*. Why had they kidnapped me and brought me here?

They certainly don't want me to join them. If, for some bizarre unknowable reason, they wanted to convert me to their ways, they would have started already, with isolation, mind-numbing lectures, endless hours of unpaid labor, every event interpreted in light of cult dogma. At least that's how they do it in America, where they don't actually kill you. Here I was isolated from everyone I knew, but they let me interact with the two girls. Far from being lectured to or threatened, sometimes I was bored. I was allowed food and toilet.

So, why? Maybe some overeager lieutenant out on duty on the perimeter had just seized me as a lucky prize, without orders or a plan. Maybe they had never taken a foreign hostage before and didn't know what to do with me. When they got me here, they'd turfed someone out of this room and given it to me, to keep me until – until what?

To use me as a bargaining chip, they have to show the world I'm alive. Well, they hadn't sat me down in front of a camera with today's newspaper. That's the usual way. But I doubted this gang had a newspaper, let alone video equipment. There was no electricity anywhere. Last night was dark except for fires and candles. Only the guns and vehicles were modern.

So if they were trying to use me that way, they'd have to bring in an outsider. I wondered if the International Red Cross does hostage videos. Not the kind of service they'd list on their home page… How odd that would feel, to be in a room with the video crew, face to face with someone who was free to go; to be able to speak and shake hands, and then be left behind, still a prisoner.

A sick, sinking feeling spread through my body. I might be here a long time.

Will I ever see Gambado again? She'll be purring in Terry's lap now. Will she miss me if I never come back? Will Terry understand her signals, when she wants her chin rubbed and when she wants her canned food? I hoped Terry would take Scalawag out for walks.

And what is Nick doing right now? He'll finish his shift at 3 o'clock, maybe take his son to gymnastics practice, go home and brew some oddball beer. That brought a smile. If I ever get out of here, I thought, I'll drink every damn potion he ever concocts.

After a few hours I became restless. I long ago exhausted the attractions the room had to offer. Carefully I opened the door, leaving it ajar in case I had to rush back in. One step, two steps. Along the little hall were two other closed doors. At the end, another door led outside. The floor creaked. A musty odor pervaded the little house. I could practically inhale the vibrations left by the Christian missionaries from a century ago. They would be aghast to know that their cottage had been turned into headquarters for people they would consider infidels – a den of vipers, they would have said. Egad, new thought. Watch out for snakes.

I tiptoed back to my room, shut the door, and looked out the window. I began to give nicknames to people I could see. A thin muscular man I dubbed Whipcord. The nervous lieutenant who lashed out at everyone when he was caught out in a mistake (I could tell he was lying) became Quivering Blamer. Among the women were Watches-the-ground, Scarlett, and Scurry. A few very young children ran around playing. One thing struck me. There were no old people.

By the fourth morning, I knew where I was the moment I awoke. This is the day I should have departed from Paris for home. It was oddly comforting, as the hours slowly passed, to think what would be happening so far away. Now the plane is taking off. Now it is over Greenland. Now it is arriving in San Francisco. I tried to remember if Nick was supposed to be there waiting for me. Think, think. What had happened between us on the day I left?

We had taken Scalawag to the dog park at Point Isabel. Scalawag loves Nick because he can throw the frisbee farther than I can, and for longer sessions. "We should go," I said finally when Scalawag sat panting in front of us. "Terry will be taking me to the BART station in an hour." Luckily, the BART train runs all the way to the airport.

"Is she picking you up, too?" Nick asked. "I mean, when you get back?"

"I haven't thought that far ahead," I answered. "I suppose so. I'll ask her in the car."

"What time is your plane?" He had that look.

"Really?" I said excitedly. "You'd pick me up at BART?"

"If you're really good, I might even come all the way to the airport." I looked up and gave him a roguish smile. Running my fingers down his arm I asked, "What do I have to do, to be considered good?"

"Oh, a little of this," he showed me, "and some of this, and one of these." We were in public, but dog people are tolerant.

"Oh heck," I said at last, "I'll give you my whole itinerary." I dug it out of my pocket. "See, by tomorrow morning I'll be in Paris, then by Thursday evening I'll be in Entebbe. Then on Friday…"

He fell quiet. "Are you really so eager to get away from Berkeley?" he asked. This didn't sound like a neutral question. Now, I thought. Say it now. I hesitated. The moment passed.

"Oh, I loved Uganda when I was there before. You would love it. Do you have a passport?" But he had pulled back. He was not at heart a traveler, and I could almost hear his mind clicking. A distance settled between us.

Now I wasn't sure if his offer to pick me up still stood. To cover my confusion, I called for Scalawag. Grabbing the frisbee from Nick's hand, I threw it clumsily. It veered toward the road. Scalawag pursued it, galloping recklessly right into traffic. I watched in paralyzed horror. A gray sedan swerved and missed him by inches. I looked my fright at Nick and gave Scalawag an extra long hug when he trotted back to us, frisbee dangling. Nick put his arm around me and we walked back to the parking lot. Insanely, I said, "Sure you don't want to come with me?"

"No," he said, "But I'll pick you up at the airport."

"It's only ten days," I replied and we smiled.

~ ❧ ~

Look innocent. Make quick tiny glances, collecting observations to review later. Peek out the window no more than once an hour. First time look to the left, second time to the right. Compile a panorama without seeming to scout the terrain for escape routes. Draw a map of the camp with a finger on the dirt of the floor of my room, then rub it out. Watch where the women with buckets go to get water. One of them always came back later than the others. Probably she got sent to the farthest water source. Must be lowest in rank. Did that make her the most likely ally, or the least?

These amateur reconnaissance efforts didn't mean I honestly expected to bolt into the jungle some moment when no one was looking. These people know I can't go through miles of rainforest to safety; I don't even know in which direction safety lies. The advantage is that they don't bother to lock me up. I just reconnoitered because I had to do something with my mind. Besides, in an ultimate emergency (visions of Jonestown), flight would be my last chance.

One day on my way to the toilet, I saw Mr. Moto heading away from the outhouse, eyes downcast. He heard my gasp and looked up. We froze. In case we were being seen by someone, I made a little hand-writing gesture and tilted my head toward the outhouse. He nodded briefly and went his way.

How could I follow up that spontaneous communication? Shutting the door, I looked around for a place to hide messages. Ah, back behind the hole in the ground was a gap between the wall boards. I returned to my room and pawed through my Coat of Many Pockets. Pen but no paper. Just as well – white paper would stand out too much in that shack. Didn't want to think what would happen to us if we were found plotting. What about something common, something seen around here every day... aha, a leaf. Next time outside I would casually pick up a leaf.

The days wore on. This limbo was inexplicable. Keeping me here for no reason made no sense. Aren't they going to drag me in front of the leader to receive a harangue or a threat? Kony speaks English, as do his top Acholi lieutenants, according to the newspapers. Swahili, too, apparently; some of them are tri-lingual, like the Swiss. That's a good thing, as my Swahili is pretty basic and my Acholi nonexistent. When I wasn't trying to divine their plans, I looked around. Saw a scuttling brown cat-sized animal with a posse of little ones waddling along behind. Mongoose.

By the second week, I had come to a few conclusions. They were holding me for some purpose. I could almost certainly not get to safety by myself. There were disaffected people here, maybe even factions, who might be allies if I could read them right. The cult had some contact with the outside world – occasional departures and returns of vehicles followed by a flurry of agitation and activity.

I can't do it myself. These people are not my friends. Ergo, I'll need outsiders.

This brilliant deduction, which any sane captive realizes in about two seconds, slowed down my mind to a useful pace. But I refused to be passive and hope blindly for the cavalry to arrive. To continue my reasoning: Some people, Nick and my travel agent, would know where I was the day before my flight to Paris. Other people, citizens of this country, know about Kony and his LRA and hate it. So, get people A in touch with people B.

How? I could think of only one way: entice my captors with money. Ransom money. Even outlaws living off the land need cash to buy weapons and ammunition, and to pay off a few corrupt officials. How many guns could Kony get for my price?

Then there's the small matter of where the money would come from. Who would offer money to rescue me? Besides family, of course. Don't think about them. Mom will be hysterical inside, but put on a stoic front. My brother will try to be strong and will hide the facts from Vanessa. I smiled. If Vanessa finds out from someone at school, she'll be sure to start taking notes and interviewing people.

Who with power would want to rescue me? Would my university make any efforts? Some famous alums had connections in diplomatic circles. Then there's the State Department, which tends to retrieve hapless Americans abroad (while cursing their stupidity under its breath), but only if the situation fits with current policies and priorities.

Well, do I fit? Let's see. I'm a respected professor at a top university. I recently helped a large government agency improve its methods for capturing smugglers. Fortunately, that little favor is completely irrelevant to the politics of this situa…

O my god. I stopped breathing. IS it irrelevant? Could Kony have picked me for a reason? I'd presumed I was just a random hostage, a blundering visitor who strayed too far from my herd.

Suddenly everything looked different.

Smuggling kingpins are armed and ruthless. Kony is armed, ruthless, and probably insane.

Here I am between them. Suppose for a minute that they're in communication. That would suggest that – Another clamor outside. I peered out, trying to remain unseen. They were drilling the new boys, lining them up under a tree. A tall beefy man barked instructions and cuffed any boy who moved too slowly for his liking.

Some of the boys were too small to carry the rifles that had been thrust into their hands.

Closing the shutters, I dragged my mind back to my train of thought. Maybe I'm not between two groups. Maybe they're the *same* group, Kony in league with the smugglers. I thought about this. They have one thing in common – they don't have enough simple humanity in them to fill a thimble. But from all I'd heard, even in spite of his crimes, Kony really believed his personal hodgepodge of Christian and native ideas. Surely such a fanatic would never collaborate with unbelievers, for any reason.

There was one other possibility. One group was using the other.

Which was the user, and which was the used?

I couldn't believe Kony is the equal of kingpins. Terrifying as he is, he controls a small part of a small country by kidnapping children, forcing them to kill their parents, getting them inside a membrane of brainwashing and coercion, and assimilating them like food inside a monster. A long-lived monster, but not a clever one.

International animal smuggling gangs had to be organized and astute: collectively they set up networks, travel across borders, identify and bribe baggage handlers and customs officers, speak different languages or enlist people who do, know enough zoology to capture the desired species, find willing buyers, and launder money. All this required more sophistication than any lunatic dictator.

I didn't know which I feared more.

The international smuggling mafia probably killed people like swatting flies, in clean professional hits. When my cult captors met resistance, they cut off hands and lips.

I decided to lie low for a while.

Remembering my meditations on the 5,000-year-old Ice Man and his tribe, I thought: *Use what's around you. Watch the kids.* These adults were already numb, communicating little with their faces or bodies, and I quickly learned that in order to read a situation, I should look first at the semi-broken children. They were still learning who were the cruelest captors, and their fear showed on their faces. I made a mental note of the men to avoid.

One day, the older girl came in with a bruise on her face. She kept her eyes down as she put a plate of food on the floor. I gestured for her to sit down on the cot, touched her face gently, and let her see the sympathy in my eyes. She trembled at first but in a few minutes she was weeping in my arms. Silently I rocked her. In the U.S. she would be in seventh grade. Like Vanessa.

When her tears slowed, I set to work. "I'm Julie," I said, pointing to myself. "Julie." After a pause, she repeated it. And you? I gestured. She replied with sounds I couldn't parse. I tried to mimic what I'd heard, drawing a tiny smile from her. Say it again, I gestured, and she did. I finally gathered she was saying Fekolina. I repeated this until she nodded. "Julie," she said again. Pact made.

Fekolina brought me food again. I accepted it and ate some and then tried a little test. I gave her a tiny glance when handing her my half-full plate. She held my gaze a fraction of a second. I nudged my edge of the plate toward her and gestured "eat." Her face showed fear. Aha – she wouldn't be permitted to take the food away and eat it elsewhere. Leaving the plate in her hand, I went and stood by the door, showing her I would prevent anyone else from coming in. She stood frozen a moment, then squatted on the floor and ate quickly. She nodded shyly as she left. After that, I gave the girls as much food as seemed sensible. Not knowing their word for "secret," I put my finger on my lips. They nodded.

Over next days, we tried to pluck some humanity from our situation. We shared food, made faces at each other, imitated some of the guards. Fekolina whispered to the younger girl, whose name was Filda, and I acquired another protégée.

I found a leaf. Since I didn't know Japanese, the only message I could send Mr. Moto was a crude map of the camp with an X indicating my room. On my next trip to the outhouse, I stuffed it into the gap, wondering how long it might take for Mr. Moto to find it.

But nothing could distract me for long from my nightmare scenario. Maybe Kony was going to sell me to the smugglers. This train of thought led to uncomfortable speculations, such as: Why would the smuggling mafia want me? Not to escort me politely to the airport, that's for sure. They must have noticed the disappearance of Rensselaer. They'd pay money for me for only one reason: to eliminate me, probably after squeezing me for information, in ways I didn't want to think about. *Not* a clean professional hit. I shuddered. They would want to find out how many other people know what I know. Bechard, the San Francisco furrier, knew who I was.

This little camp began to feel safer than the unknown tentacles of the smuggling web. For some reason, I remembered the network of tunnels at the zoo where Kijana and I had hidden. Tunnels, webs, and networks, visible and invisible.

I have an invisible link to Nick. Do thoughts travel over unseen highways? Nick, if you can hear me: I know there's no promise between us. Don't forget me. I should have said something before I left, but I was afraid. That fear seemed pretty small now. Silently I willed my words to fly to him.

I hoped that instead of dealing with smugglers, Kony would go for ransom from my people. Ransom. Such a nicer word than price.

Money is always a good tool, but maybe Kony was aiming for release of some of his men. IF the Ugandan army captured any of them. I tried to remember what I'd overheard about the government's forays against Kony... but judging from Kony's atrocities and his track record of refilling his battalions by brutalizing children, he wasn't particularly loyal or merciful even to his own. If they got captured, he would shrug, or decide that meant that their god had rejected them or they didn't have the right stuff. He would let them languish.

All in all, I didn't think it was a prisoner swap.

That night, waiting for sleep to come, I wondered how religion got this vile. I was brought up in a plain vanilla Protestant church so undogmatic you could hardly tell there was anything to believe. My church was the golden rule, some damn good hymns, Christmas pageants, and the place for weddings and funerals. Love your neighbor as yourself. How do simple good intentions like these become tools for greed and madmen?

~ ɔ ç ~

On the fourteenth afternoon I was fetched. No knock, of course, just a man striding in and giving orders. By now I had perfected my strategy: go along with whatever they said – enthusiastically. I put on my best "thank you for having me" face and followed him as he marched purposefully to a larger building. People we passed looked at me furtively from behind their own impassive masks.

It was a small room. "Stand there," ordered the man who had summoned me. A more important man was seated behind a rickety table. I stood, looking around with an admiring expression on my face. A yellowed scroll of the 10 commandments was pinned on the wall, with Thou Shalt Not printed in the largest letters. I seized on that. "How wonderful that you have this posted," I said. "So many places don't. Isn't that shocking?" He seemed watchful and, judging by the levator palpebrae muscles above his eyes, a bit surprised. "Did you know that in my country some schools don't have them posted?"

"You are professor," he said.

"Yes, but I'm only allowed to teach science. It's very frustrating. Sad," I added, in case they didn't know the word "frustrating." I hoped I wasn't overdoing this. Quick, in case they call my bluff: what are all 10 commandments? Trying not to peek at the scroll on the wall, I recited to myself: Don't lie, steal, bear false witness, kill, have other gods, covet, um um adultery, um um honor thy parents, um, oh, forget it.

"You are in newspapers." So that's why they chose me. The little article in the local paper ("American Professor Returns to Bwindi") had reached him. He went on.

"You are famous. People listen to you." I was right. They wanted me to be a voice and face to give a message to the world. But famous? If I admit to this, I'm an uppity female. If I downplay it, I'm of less value to them.

"Yes, some people do," I hedged.

"Important people." Oh, he really did have me confused with someone. Well, *work with what is at hand.* "Yes," I lied.

"Speak to them. Tell them we will wait no longer."

My plan was to play along unless they demanded that I do something immoral. So I said, "But do they deserve to hear The Message? Shouldn't it be kept for the elect?"

"We don't ask they join us. Just leave us be. We have enough for the Kingdom. They should just leave the Kingdom alone. Take back their warriors."

I see. Truce. I was torn. Truce meant Kony could keep operating, kidnapping, terrorizing.

Outside the window, I saw a monkey clambering among the treetops.

"Here," said the man in charge, and held out a cell phone. So they do have one sign of modern technology. "Here," he repeated, more loudly. Oh, they meant *now.* I wasn't ready. I'd been hoping I could stall until later, tomorrow… Visions of having my hand cut off drained all my courage. I shakily accepted the cell phone and did as they said. I heard a mumbling and knew that there was someone on the other end of the line. "I am the guest of Mr. Kony," I began. "I have been impressed by his determination.

He wishes to convey that his patience is at an end. You are to tell the army to retreat from – "I looked at the man, who remained expressionless " – from their front lines."

The man watched me narrowly and took back the cell phone when I was done. He waved me away and the underling took me back to my room, where I sat shaking for a long time. Even though I had guessed that this was their purpose, I found the whole transaction incredible. Did they really think that a few words from a stranger would make a difference in their war with the government? Was this the opening gambit for some other development? Was Kony's insanity reaching a climax? I didn't want to be around to find out.

I couldn't stop ruminating about it, though, trying to figure out the angles. I had hours every day to kill. Maybe using me to appeal to their opponents mean they were desperate – *down to last* – seeking a truce to save themselves. Or it could mean the opposite, that they were overconfident, audaciously trying to dictate terms to a head of state.

In either case, I needed to get ready. I remembered that prisoner of war during Vietnam – what was his name? Fenton, no, Denton. When his captors paraded him in front of the cameras and forced him to make an anti-American speech, he blinked "torture" in Morse code so our guys would know he was not a willing turncoat.

Another night fell; another morning arrived. In public, I kept praising everything in sight and pretending to be excited about their religion. I needed to strike a balance between being a fearless person they would respect enough to keep alive, and being sufficiently agreeable that they wouldn't kill me for being an ugly American. Solution: I pretended I didn't even perceive the coercion, as if every command was just what I wanted to do, yet remaining quietly deferential so they would feel in charge. I wonder how many captives over the centuries have tried this. It works, at least for a while, but at what point did one slide into actual surrender?

Keep hold of your wits, I told myself, and just play the two roles simultaneously. I've taught dozens of students to do that. Even if you catch someone in a lie, I'd told them, don't show disgust or triumph or curiosity. Just ask the next question. Let them hang themselves in the rope you dole out with a neutral look on your face. I'd learned how to do this well.

My life hadn't depended on it before.

Maybe I should try to bargain with them, negotiate, offer money. Remembering the atrocities these fanatics perpetrated, I was afraid to make a move. If they kept me much longer, I would praise Kony, pretend to weep with joy at being given a skirt to replace my increasingly grungy zip-off expedition trousers. Plead to be reassured which day it was so I could observe the Sabbath properly.

The day after I reached this conclusion, I told the lieutenant, "You knew I was at Bwindi with a television crew? Television," I repeated. "Television is better. Get more people to believe, understand.

Maybe the president will heed Mr. Kony at last." If only I remembered the name of Uganda's president, I could have pretended I'd already met him and knew how to twist his arm.

"It's unfortunate – sad – that we don't have a video camera here," I went on, hoping they would remember the van full of visitors' luggage that they had commandeered when they captured me and Mr. Moto.

Finally they bit. The next day Mr. Moto appeared from wherever they had been keeping him, looking apprehensive, small videocamera in hand. The man who was always sent to summon me pushed him into position to film me. He looked weary and nervous but, like me, eager to please the captors. We exchanged glances. I faced the camera. After the usual fiddling with the device, Mr. Moto signaled me to begin. I swallowed hard and began.

"I am Julie Heidebrecht. I am with a detachment of the Lord's Resistance Army," I began, for all the world as if I were an embedded correspondent. I tried not to show fear. Well, my students would be able to read my micro-expressions if this amateur video ever made its way to the outside world. To make certain my real message got through, I also used sign language. Luckily, the cultists never bothered to tie me up. "**Help. Send big bird**." That's the only way I could think of to signal "helicopter." I made the signs ever so slowly while speaking enthusiastically, and prayed that someone back home would be clever enough to play the tape at high speed and read my signs.

What I actually said was, "Mr. Kony is an important leader. His many followers worship him. The world would do well to take note of his directives." And more of the same sickening stuff.

The man in charge dismissed me. Mr. Moto was let go to deliver his film clip. I suppose they drove him south a long way, to within a quarter mile of a road, and pushed him out of the jeep. Time went by. I hoped that he got the film to someone who would know what to do with it, like contact the Navy SEALS.

Meanwhile, I kept refining my strategy. What is the most frustrating thing to a religious fanatic? It depends which type they are. Some of them love to have enemies – it creates their whole heroic drama and lets them justify setbacks and failures. Other cult leaders are baffled by the world's indifference or opposition and desperately need to latch onto some explanation to reduce the dissonance. I must find out which Kony was. If he loved having enemies, I would flatter his craving to be unique. If he was baffled by the opposition, I would give him a palatable explanation, avoiding obvious ploys like "they're jealous" or "they're infidels."

I hoped my Interpol friend Jeff would remember our conversation, especially how it ended: Get me out of here!

Time passed. By now Mr. Moto and his thirty-second video clip of my plea would be in Kampala. By now someone had seen it, shown it to someone else. Maybe it had reached the U.S., where someone had played it at high speed and read my signed message. It was odd, being so out of touch with the world, not knowing what happened next, instead of having global news instantly at my fingertips. I prayed my U.S. film crew would see this footage and remember I never voluntarily sit still this long. They'd had to cross-cut their shots because I fidget so much.

⌒ つ ℭ ⌒

To pass the time, I thought about incomprehensible student writing. I even remembered one gem. "The words bleed into the tenor of the text as my eyes gaze across them, and at any moment, like a whirlpool, invite or seduce the reader into a vertical descent through some passage realized through in its unpacking." I was sure Koko the signing gorilla could do better than that. She at least invented phrases that made sense: she signed "**finger bracelet**" for ring; and, on seeing a mask for the first time, signed "**eye hat**."

Finally one day another dusty ramshackle jeep bounced over rutted tracks into camp, rudely discharging its passengers before wheeling around and tearing off down the track. Two men got out and marched purposefully toward an end of the camp I had not visited. I hoped they had come in response to the video clip. But another day went by and nothing happened.

There must be some reason the outside world keeps sending emissaries to this place. Surely the smugglers could get animals in neighboring countries. There are plenty of primates there – golden monkeys, red-tailed mangabeys, owl-faced monkeys… Aha! There must be a truly rare species, found here in this corner of Uganda and nowhere else on earth. The outsiders want access for capturing them. Maybe they even have an actual buyer already in place, someone like those super-rich art hoarders who send out an order for a Matisse or a Vermeer, and then lock the resulting stolen painting in their underground gallery, where they exult and admire it in selfish secret.

I recalled something a Ugandan guide said when, by great good fortune, we had actually spotted a famously elusive primate: "Look at that little aye-aye," the guide had said fondly as we stared happily. "The only thing rarer is the black-tailed guenon."

That's it. Rich guy orders a black-tailed guenon, and Kony holds the keys to the kingdom. This is why Kony clings so tenaciously to this corner of Uganda, even as the army closes in. The visitors were rich guy's minions checking on the guenon order.

It all fit together. I felt a great sense of relief. I had a map. I knew who was pulling whose strings. Everything I noticed in the next few days confirmed this hunch, or at least "was consistent with" it, as the forensic professionals like to say. I'd located the levers of power. Now to operate them.

Suddenly, as if encouraged by my reading of the strings of power, a plan arrived fully formed. The GPS unit I'd found so long ago – was it only three weeks? Before hiding it, I had scanned the numbers displayed on the little screen. I tried to coax them up from the unconscious – tried, that is, by being calm and not forcing it. Sure enough (good old mental back burner), some numbers came up. But I didn't know if they were accurate.

Later that day when no one was around, I climbed up on the cot and retrieved the GPS, praying that the batteries still had power. Switched it on. The screen was faint but I could read the numbers and letters. Impressed these on my memory. Hid the GPS again.

Thought about Nick. The smooth skin right where his neck joined his shoulders, his warm breath on my back at night, his enfolding arms. If only he could wrap around me and make this nightmare go away. I pretended he was sending me messages on the invisible highway and melted into them.

~ 𝄞 ~

I was summoned.

"They have not given us what we demand," said the man in charge ominously. His facial muscles said he was suppressing something. He's worried, I thought. He's fearing Kony's displeasure and pouring his fear onto me. I wondered what happened to Kony's lieutenants who didn't fulfill orders.

"But they haven't seen a proper interview," I said. "Look," I pointed out the window, "There are people who haven't seen the camp. That little camera couldn't show your life here, and your determination. And maybe the Japanese man – the man you sent – has not been found. If only my television crew were still here," I lamented, "They have real cameras." I pretended to be resigned, sighed and privately hoped the seed would sprout. Next day the man in charge summoned me again. He looked at me with a suspicious expression, but it was clear someone had overruled him.

"He says yes, television, but not your people." Fine, it would be faster to get local ones anyway. I hoped a sane Uganda tv crew would have the nerve to come here.

"Please tell Mr. Kony that I will be humbly honored to enlighten the world through the wonder of moving pictures." Again a cell phone was thrust into my hands. This time there was no one on the line. I understood that I was to make the connection. This was not easy, as there was nothing so mundane as a telephone book here and I didn't know how this country's operator system worked. It felt weird. I would be talking to the outside world, where receptionists answer the phone and take messages and go to lunch. I hoped it wouldn't be too much like American outside world, where companies hide behind voicemail labyrinths and phone calls dead end in nameless coils of digital recordings.

After some struggle, I was finally connected to the BBC's branch in Kampala. Now to persuade the receptionist I wasn't a crank.

"Hello. This is Julie Heidebrecht," I said, and paused.

"It is? The one that's missing?" she said in an incredulous tone. Good, she had heard my name on the news.

"Yes, I'm at the LRA camp." Keenly aware I was being closely listened to by the lieutenant, I spoke slowly. "I would like to speak to your news bureau." This was one sharp receptionist. She transferred me without another question. To the next voice, I went through my lines again. My mouth was dry. "Would you like to cover this story? The LRA is prepared to offer a truce to the government. Mr. Kony wants to make his case himself on camera." I could just imagine the scramble at the other end of the line.

"Yes, yes, we will come," said the voice and I handed over the cell phone so the lieutenant could give instructions.

The next day the television crew arrived. It came in a huge helicopter, thank goodness, not one of those dragonfly-sized traffic report midgets. It set down in a clearing. Cultists with guns drawn surrounded it. A pause as the rotor blades slowed and stopped. Finally a man got hesitantly out. From my room I looked out anxiously. I was summoned with more alacrity than usual and prodded toward the clearing. As I'd hoped, the tv crew members had finished setting up their gear and were waiting for me. I was shoved toward them into a chair.

I faced the camera. Placing my hand on my heart, I said, "This is Julie Heidebrecht. I'm in Uganda."

I shifted in my chair and went on. "I've been told to ask for two million pounds sterling. They'll tell you how to deliver it." Wriggling around uncomfortably, I said, "They are serious. Please help. Ask Aunt Panthea for the money." Rubbing my forehead, I said, "They're treating me well." I squinted at the man on my right, who kept gesticulating at me. "Oh yes. Tell the army not to interfere." This went on for a long time. Finally my captors were satisfied. They huddled together, talking rapidly.

I slid off the rickety chair, hoping that someone out in the world would decode my silent message. While I was speaking into the microphone and appearing to fidget, I was also conveying with my hands, ever so slowly, the GPS coordinates **2 46 0 N, 32 18 20 E**. There is no Aunt Panthea, but there is Panthea Morrill of the speech pathology department at Berkeley, who taught me how to use sign language.

I looked around to see where I was supposed to go now. In the bustle, my immediate guard was nowhere to be seen. The cameramen were getting ready for Kony to speak. I could tell from a distance that Kony was approaching. The crowd surged closer, men were shouting, and finally I saw him. He was a man of middle height with a stone-faced countenance, striding purposefully with his massive entourage. People in the crowd stepped back to let them pass. Someone didn't move fast enough. Kony snarled and lashed out, and the culprit shrank back in fear. Kony sat down and imperiously signed to the tv crew to begin filming his demands.

He settled into the chair and spoke to the camera, slowly at first, then more and more loudly and rapidly. This was surely the biggest event that had ever taken place here, ever. The strongest male residents of this miserable camp took advantage of a lapse of discipline to crowd around their leader and the camera, while new recruits and all the women stood back.

Incredibly, I had gotten lost in the shuffle.

From thirty yards away I watched. My professional curiosity took over and for a few moments I felt no fear, only an intense desire to read this man. I needed to know what kind of cult leader he was – the kind who thrives on enemies, or the kind who hopes to win them over. He looked proud and arrogant as he spoke (no surprise), but in a moment I spotted something puzzling in his expression. I was trying to decipher it when someone jostled me. Wakened from my trance, I looked around. People everywhere. To my right, the helicopter was parked on a little rise in the clearing. One person sat in it, unmoving.

There was only one person that could be.

Use what's around you. An impossible hope sprang up. A helicopter and a pilot, due to leave in a few minutes as soon as the tv crew climbed aboard. No one was keeping track of me. Could I seize this moment, not wait for the cavalry to get my GPS message, engineer my own escape?

Hardly breathing, I sidled away in the opposite direction, then circled back around the crowd, inching closer to the helicopter, trying to be inconspicuous. I hoped the pilot was not a buttoned-down obedient apparatchik who never exceeded orders, but an old-fashioned independent cuss with a romantic barnstormer streak.

Suddenly I saw Fekolina. Oh, no. How could I leave the girls behind? But there was no time to scoop them up and explain. Fekolina caught my eye. That decided it. "Come quick," I gestured and made my face show an expression she had gotten used to: Trust me. She dived under the crowd and disappeared. A moment later she appeared at my side with Filda in tow. Taking their hands, I tugged them along with me, dodging and weaving.

Kony was still ranting, his voice rising. It sounded rehearsed, as if he were repeating a well-worn diatribe before getting down to business. That was fine with me. Please let him keep rambling until we get to the helicopter, I prayed.

The pilot was still seated. I looked at him and said, "Thank you for coming to get us." He looked at me speculatively. I held his gaze. I had to convince him quietly and fast.

I said, "They're not watching. They don't have anti-aircraft weapons. Quick."

He looked at the African girls holding my hands. He was an African, too. I hugged them close to me and together we looked at him. The crowd behind us was still milling and babbling. Silently the pilot – may his tribe increase – gestured for us to get in. I thanked him with a nod while we climbed aboard and found seats far in the back.

Crouching as I buckled the girls into their seats, I held their gaze as fiercely as I ever have in my life. Widening my eyes and smiling, I conveyed, "This will be good. Quiet." I fastened my seat belt and sat nervously, hoping the girls wouldn't wiggle or call out to anyone in the crowd.

It took forever for the tv crew to return. I sat as still as I had when Kijana and I were hiding from the gunmen, every cell in my body on alert. I remembered old superstitions and thought of some new ones. If I don't move a muscle, we'll escape. If I don't look out the window, no one will see me. If I think good thoughts… It was probably less than fifteen minutes, but I think my brain circuits were permanently altered.

The cameramen arrived and climbed in, chattering to each other and busily securing their equipment before taking their seats behind the pilot. Another day, another photo shoot.

Heart beating rapidly, I prayed the pilot would take off before we were missed by the guards or noticed by the tv crew. After an endless pause, he moved some controls and we lifted into the air. I stared straight ahead, not wanting to tempt fate by looking out the window at the crowd that was falling away below. They were an army, they had guns, and they were commanded by a madman. Just now the madman was busy accepting the sycophantic praise of his entourage. He didn't look up.

The girls sat absolutely still. I made reassuring gestures. Minutes passed. We were flying over the camp's perimeter, leaving the camp behind. I breathed again. Filda and Fekolina began to look around, fiddle with the seat belts I'd fastened around them, whisper to each other. I looked at them fondly. I was shaking and I'd been a captive for less than a month. What horrors had they been through? For how many months? Are their parents living? How do we find them? Will they take them back, or be afraid of them? If the parents don't take them back, they're too young to be on their own. Thus I occupied myself and never saw the land moving below us as we flew.

The camera people finished their debriefing, looked behind them, and realized that their interviewee had stowed away – with two Acholi girls as well. After their initial amazement, they peppered me with questions. Frankly, I was too weak to think of explanations and begged them to wait. Wait at least until the gabble effect kicks in and I need to talk, I thought to myself. The helicopter landed at Entebbe airport. It was odd to see a place I had been to three times already, a normal place with cars and planes and windows and people on sidewalks.

The next thirty hours were a whirlwind. I talked to the tv crew, took a long shower, put on some clothes they found for me, and handed Fekolina and Filda to some kindly people who promised to take care of them. I hugged them goodbye and told the nice people I would stay in touch and send money. I was debriefed by the government and assorted other officials. Finally I was allowed to leave.

I had created my own rescue. Good thing, too, people told me later. Even if my GPS message had been read and a rescue operation mounted, the American embassy would probably have dragged it out, hedged in by rules of diplomacy and the routines of tactical hostage negotiations. I learned later that frenzied maneuvering had gone on between my American television crew (who had, as I'd hoped, heard about my dilemma from Dr. Andrew at UWEC), the medical charity Doctors without Borders, which had a project nearby, the Japanese embassy, and the Ugandan army. But in the end it was Interpol that requisitioned the helicopter. I was ultimately saved by that casual conversation with Jeff Conway, a man I never met.

As my plane to Paris left Entebbe, I realized something. During this whole saga, I hadn't once thought of Matt.

⤳ XVIII ⤶

Nick met me at the San Francisco airport. It wasn't until I saw him that I realized how drained I was, how weak with exhaustion and relief. I collapsed in his arms and wept. He held me, stroked my hair, murmured things I needed to hear. Somehow he guided me to a chair and we sat wrapped around each other as I blurted out bits of the last four weeks.

At length I stopped gabbling and looked at him, soaking up the pleasure of seeing his attentive, smiling face.

"I thought about you," I said. Such inadequate words.

"I know."

I punched him lightly. "Did not. Are you a psychic or something?"

"Desta told me. She said you had a nickname for me."

I blushed. I'd totally forgotten that. His name in sign language was "**Hot**." "Yeah, well, I guess so."

"She showed it to me." Oh, great. So much for my self-control, my suave management of this relationship. Well, that had disappeared in the last ten minutes anyway.

"I couldn't believe you signed it right in front of the fanatics," he said admiringly.

"I did?" I was amazed.

"Sure, right after you signed '**bird, big**.'"

That had been at the end of the first clip, the one taken by Mr. Moto. I must have been signing to myself, just the way chimps do. I felt weak from amazement. Now it was Nick's turn to be surprised.

"You mean you didn't do it on purpose?"

"I signed '**hot?**' " I repeated. He laughed and hugged me again.

"What on earth did the translators think?" I wondered.

"No worry. They thought you were saying it was hot in Uganda. Bring big bird, and it was hot." I was embarrassed. Nick picked up on it and said softly, "Never mind. Just sign it to me every day and I'll be satisfied."

A rush of happiness. Looked at each other. I signed "**happy**." He made an unintelligible gesture imitating a sign, ending with his arms around me. After a long precious moment he whispered, "Next time, take me with you."

I jumped back in alarm. "*Next* time? There's not going to be a next time. I'm not going nowhere. Staying bundled up at home for the next three months. You're invited – no, assigned to keep me company. At home." I slumped back into his arms. "Ok, maybe I'll go out for classes."

"Yes, and your classes will have a waiting list a mile long. You're famous now, you know. You may have to clone yourself."

"No, thanks. I prefer to do it the old-fashioned way." He laughed, relieved that I had revived enough to muster up a flirt.

"Well, brace yourself," he said. "It'll be more than that." I was puzzled. "You could have another fifteen minutes of fame, if you want it. The television people are drooling."

I looked around. "Television people? Well, where are they? How did you keep them away?"

"I kept mum about when you were expected. I could have been a Supreme Court nominee for all the straight answers they got out of me."

"And my mom? You told her I was ok, didn't you?" I was suddenly anxious. I had resolutely kept Mom and Jimmy and his wife and Vanessa out of my thoughts those weeks in the camp. Now concern flooded back. And Carl and Terry... Terry would be so worried.

"Don't worry, don't worry," he calmed me. "Remember, I'm a professional soother and manager of scary news." That's right. I had seen him juggling doctors and lab tests and nervous relatives.

"But they know I'm safe, right?"

"Sweetheart, you've already talked to them on the phone, remember?" I'd forgotten. The American embassy in Uganda had arranged phone calls soon after the helicopter landed in Entebbe. An official was waiting and scooped me up. He was surprised that I insisted on bringing the girls with me, but he gallantly gave in and took charge of them.

The Ugandan government had debriefed me in a short but intense session, and then kindly let me go when I promised to write up my experiences and confer with cult experts at home to send them a more thorough report on what I had observed about Kony and his army. The embassy got me an emergency passport. My original one is probably still floating around somewhere in Africa.

As soon as the dust settles, I would get in touch with the aid workers who had taken charge of Fekolina and Filda. Maybe I can arrange for them to get Kriegsgefangenerschadigungsgesetz. Compensation for prisoners of war.

But all that was for later. Right now I was basking in the pleasant glow of my hot man. We snuggled as comfortably as two people can on airport chairs. Suddenly I thought of something.

"Say, so how did you manage to meet me all by yourself? Where is everyone? Not that I want anyone but you here this minute," I added hastily.

"I bullied your friends and family and said I had first dibs and if they wanted to know why, I would have to get your permission. I pretended they were patients, you see, and jollied them into doing what I wanted. They're expecting a call as soon as... as soon as you're in the mood. They really love you, you know," he said gently. I teared up again. After a moment, he said, "See, that's why it was so smart of you to catch a plane that was arriving at 3 am. Did you do that on purpose?" We talked for a while about my last day and a half of freedom. Finally we stretched, stood up, and sauntered slowly arm in arm to the parking garage.

A furry shape was sitting in the car. Nick had brought Scalawag! When he saw me approaching, he bounced around inside, barking eagerly. I opened the door and he almost jumped out. Grinning as if my face would break, I shooed him back in so I could climb in to get a proper canine face-licking knee-pawing welcome. I buried my face in his fur and sobbed. I was alive, and safe, and hugging my dog.

As he drove, Nick told me what it had been like for my friends and family after the news came out that I was being held as the "guest" of the religious fanatics. They were terrified. Some of them remembered the massacre at Jonestown. It turns out I really hadn't known everything about Kony after all. My friends had time to hear the news reports of his decades of atrocities; my university friends went online and read things that nearly made me faint when they told me. Thank god I hadn't known all this. I would have been paralyzed.

"Your mom was fantastic. So brave. She said, 'Julie will take care of herself.' Say, I didn't know you climbed up on the roof to watch for Santa Claus when you were six." I blushed. How much else had he learned about me from my proud and voluble mother? "I asked her if she was ok and she said she was staying at your brother's house." I could envision this, Jimmy and Mom vying to be the strongest caregiver, Jimmy's wife free to voice all the fears. Nick added, "Vanessa says to call. She's going to write a report about you." I laughed and cried in relief.

"Let's go to Florida and see them."

"Ok," he said cheerfully, and brought me home.

Home. My friendly old faithful Maybeck house. Seeing my smile as he parked the car, Nick let me gaze at it for a few minutes. Then we went in.

～♪℃～

Later, after we called Mom and spent an hour on the phone, Nick went to work. The hospital had been generous with giving him personal time off during the last month, but he really needed to show his face there. Terry came home and greeted me with a huge hug. Strangely, she seemed anxious, almost regressed. Then she began to cry. It was hard to recognize the savvy young woman who volleyed word games with me. To calm her, I said, "How was Gambado? Did Scalawag drive you crazy demanding walks?"

"Oh, I didn't take him walking. Nick did all that."

"Nick did? All what?"

"You know, feeding them, brushing Gambado, taking Scalawag for walks. Oh, you should have seen him." She smiled at the memory. "He talked to them for hours."

"Hours? Here?"

"Well, yeah. He practically camped out." She smiled, her tears drying.

"Really?" I didn't know whether to feel flattered or invaded. But then, she'd probably needed him for her own moral support.

"He was so angry the day you were supposed to be back. He showed up here and asked where you were. I said I thought you had her. We looked around. Hope you don't mind. There were no suitcases and your car was still in the garage. He called the airline and found you weren't even on the flight." Terry shook her head at the memory.

"You hadn't changed your reservations so we knew something was wrong. Oh, Julie, I was so scared!" Tears again. "We thought maybe you'd fallen into a river and been eaten by piranhas." I couldn't suppress a smile. Piranhas are in South America. "So Nick started staying here. I gave him a key. I hope that was ok." She looked at me anxiously. "Yes, yes, that was fine," I said.

"He had to go to work sometimes, of course, but mostly he was here. Oh, except when he was going to the embassy and stuff."

I smiled all over my insides. Nick had been on the case! He had dropped everything to watch over me, be close to me in every way he could. Maybe thoughts do travel on invisible airwaves.

"And once it got in the newspapers, he talked to the reporters. He's really good at setting limits, did you know that?" I didn't, actually.

"One time this reporter kept banging on the door right when your mom was on the phone. She must have really needed to talk to him that day, because Nick really bit that reporter's head off."

"Nick talked to my mom?" I already knew he had, but I was hungry to visualize this scene from Terry's vantage point.

"Oh, yeah! They were on the phone every day. He let me listen sometimes. Your mom kept saying who are you and he said a friend and after two weeks she said you sound like more than a friend to me and he said well yes and finally one day he said, 'Mrs Heidebrecht, I hope to spend the rest of my life with

Julie.'" Terry made an Oops face and put her hand over her mouth. "Oh, he made me promise not to say that. Don't tell him I told."

Wow, how do you conceal a discovery like that? I did my best but I couldn't stop smiling. A week later he threw me a homecoming party. Terry helped him put together a private event – Norm and Leslie came, and Desta, Carl, and Anne with her husband. Glenn and Carolyn sent video greetings. Minnie had demanded to come, threatening to start a riot in the nursing home if she wasn't invited. At the party, she pretended to scold me in her crotchety way but then shed a tear and hugged me with surprising strength. "No more overseas detecting," she said in a voice that was trying to be dictatorial.

My department gave me a party, too. Jiang Li, the chair, the whole research division, the clinicians – they all came. Hallie came too, from the biology department, the one who got me into the Oily Man case. Even the colleague who passed that lousy dissertation showed up, and I was even glad to see her. My closest pals had made a video of one person giving a message in sign language and another making outrageously silly translations full of department in-jokes. Finally, when my sides were aching from laughter, they brought out dessert: Pistachio ice cream, made with liquid nitrogen.

~✦~

The trials began. The two men who had attacked Desta and tried to kidnap me were lucky – there wasn't enough evidence to indict them, but they were deported. Rensselaer was nailed on two points: I could identify him by his voice, and the van used in the attack had been rented in his name. My testimony about voice and facial characteristics of deception helped, as the prosecution played their videotaped interview with him (after they read him his rights, of course). I walked the jury through the signals that indicate deception. They listened attentively and convicted him of conspiracy and resisting arrest, and sentenced him to a year in jail. Not enough, in my opinion, but at least his career as a smuggler of wild animals was over. No one would ever hire him again, even those cold-hearted folks who profited from the ugly trade.

The medical labs denied any involvement, of course, and made virtuous pronouncements about their ethics. Their attorney pounced on the chain of custody of the hairs that I had gotten from Tucker and tried to cast doubt on the reliability of the evidence. I was afraid the case would be dismissed, but to the relief of our whole team, the judge instructed the labs to hand over some hairs from the named chimps as evidence, giving the labs enough rope to hang themselves. New hairs were collected (under scrutiny, of course), and proved that they came from chimps who had come from Africa. The judge slapped the lab directors with fines and strict supervision for the foreseeable future. They would have to provide DNA regularly to prove that they were not using smuggled chimps. Melissa was thrilled that the culprits were not zoo people. Glenn and Carolyn happily welcomed the two African chimps to their sanctuary.

Then the lab researchers and administrators began the finger-pointing, each department blaming the other. I taped their court testimony to show my students as examples of lying under oath. The case made headlines. Two people went to jail for perjury; not for tormenting animals, sad to say. Norm, Anne, and I watched the television news with feelings of righteous vindication. This was much more fun than waiting to see if my face would be plastered on the screen right after the shooting in the zoo.

In Uganda, Interpol was working to shut down Kony's part of the wildlife smuggling trade. I was right that he was using animals to get money for his army. No one was sorry about the fate of the obnoxious American, but malnourished people would continue to look at wild animals hungrily. I started sending money to the Jane Goodall Institute, which has a fantastic program for providing livelihoods in the region. It wouldn't be enough, but it was a start. Maybe I would even take another anti-smuggling case again some day.

~ ɔ c ~

So much had changed since I got that phone call from Tony Tilbertson. I had been to Tucson, Washington DC, and Uganda. I had learned to speak sign language to chimps, risked my life, and made new friends. Their lives had changed, too. Anne was doing conservation full time and Norm and Leslie had some more funding contacts. Glenn and Carolyn had new links with people who were fighting animal smuggling. Minnie, realizing she could help catch crooks, got a wicked thrill from joining a police sting operation and snaring people who preyed on old folks. I had moved from protecting English grammar to protecting living creatures. I had found Nick.

"Come on, Scalawag," I said one day, and almost made the sign for "**car**." "It's our day for Minnie." Scalawag lashed his tail and bounced around eagerly. "Bye, Terry," I called. "We'll be back in a few hours."

After arriving at Arlington Court, I let Scalawag off his leash. By now he knew better than to gallop down hallways when we were at the nursing home, so he padded quietly by my side as we greeted everyone. He wandered off when I paused to greet one of the staff. "Scalawag, you rascal!" I heard Nick exclaim delightedly. "Where's your luscious human?" I could hear the friendly pats and thumps that big dogs love. Nick came around the corner, holding Scalawag by the collar and stroking his head with his other hand. "Come back to the station when you're done visiting everyone. Guess who's learned some new signs this week?"

Nick had been introducing signs to the residents ever since he read an article about baby sign language. Babies and preverbal toddlers can make meaningful gestures long before they acquire language, signs for "**up**," "**down**," "**hurt**," "**more**," and so on. The researchers discovered which signs babies could make and which ones they needed most. The parents were thrilled.

So Nick began introducing signs at the nursing home. Minnie didn't need them, of course, and probably never would, but her new roommate was feeble and hardly spoke at all. Minnie was disgusted at this and thought Alma had given up too soon. "Hi, Alma," Nick would say loudly. "Do you want something to **eat**?" and he made the sign "**eat**." After a few weeks of repetition, Alma signed "**eat**" late one afternoon. Nick was ecstatic and ran out to the nurses' station to get some candy to reward her before she forgot about it. He bragged about her to the other residents. Of course, he had to give the sign for "**eat**" when telling them the story, so before long a few of them were doing it, too.

After this victory, Nick got them to signal "**ready**." Some of the other nurses got curious and wanted to learn how to make the signs. The most useful words were more, help, hurt, when, eat, drink, light, nap, again, toilet, sorry, and thanks. This improved life at the home – the feebler residents didn't feel so isolated and the staff didn't have to do so much guessing. After we had gotten permission to bring trained therapy animals for visits every week, two new words were added: **cat** and **dog**.

The End

⎯⁀) Author's Note (‿⎯

The Lie-Catcher in the Primate House is a work of fiction, based on actual events: the smuggling of endangered species, the kidnappings and atrocities of a violent religious cult, and the use of scientific expertise to detect deception. I began writing this book in 2004, a few years after a trip to Uganda alerted me to the many dangers facing our nearest primate cousins and other wild animals. Since then, many animal species are ever more threatened with extinction, but thanks to the efforts of devoted conservationists, populations of some species, including mountain gorillas, have actually increased.

The scene in the zoo primate house's overhead tunnels sprang from a real-life behind-the-scenes visit to the gorillas' inside quarters at the Woodland Park Zoo in Seattle. My Uganda traveling companions and I had gone there to learn more about the animals we would be seeing on our trip. As I gazed upward at the tunnels, the possibility of hiding there from danger occurred to me. The idea for the heroine's profession came from a set of stories on human deceptiveness in the *American Psychological Association Monitor* (July/August, 2004), and a closeup magazine photograph of a monkey inspired the plot sequence leading to the identification of the unscrupulous medical laboratory. The magazine article about stone aged beer quoted on page 256 is by Larry Gallagher ("Stone Aged Beer", *Discover*, November 2005, pages 54-58).

If you would like to help the animals and people who have been impacted by the real dangers this book portrays, you can make a donation to these organizations:

Uganda Wildlife Education Centre (www.uwec.ug)

Jane Goodall Institute (www.janegoodall.org)

War Child International (www.warchild.org)

SaveNature.Org (www.savenature.org) does not work in Uganda, but helps preserve rainforest and coral reefs, and the rare animals and plants that live there, in seven other countries around the world. Donations to SaveNature.Org are welcome.

You can help endangered species in other ways:
- Don't buy exotic pets – your local shelter has plenty of cats and dogs needing good homes.
- Don't buy products made from animal body parts (fur, feathers, ivory, tortoiseshell, etc.).
- Visit your local zoo and contribute to its conservation projects.

Thank you for caring enough to help save endangered species.